WHERE ALICE BELONGS

The Impact of War on a Family

JO HOWARD

Contents

PART ONE 1941-1945

War may sometimes be a necessary evil.

But no matter how necessary, it is always an evil.

Never a good.

We will not learn to live together in peace

by killing each other's children.

—Jimmy Carter

39th President U.S.A. 1977-81

Chapter 1

8th March 1941

Saturday, eighth of March 1941 was when the nightmares began. Helena had arranged to meet Freddie and go to the West End, have some fun. She sat in her bedroom and wondered how she was going to get out of the house without her mother and stepfather stopping her. There had been another row. She never had any fun because Mother always took Edgar's side. She hated him.

With her shoes in her hand, Helena crept down the back stairs into the boot room. She listened; Cook had not heard her and anyway, wouldn't tell Mother. The back door opened easily and she let herself out. She smothered giggles as she walked along the side of the house down to Queens Road then on to Hendon Central Underground station. She struggled to see her watch by light from the moon and wondered if there would be another bombing raid, it was bright enough. She'd better hurry; Freddie would think she'd stood him up. She pulled her coat tighter; it was March, but spring hadn't arrived yet. The chilly breeze made her shiver, but with excitement rather than cold.

Freddie was waiting for her, grabbed her hand and together they run to catch the Tube train. She was looking forward to dancing with tough men, muscular, sure of themselves, ready for battle. At Piccadilly Circus and were swept along by the crowd; the West End was full of young people who wanted to live recklessly. The blackout added an air of desperation. Helena hugged Freddie; they were going to have fun.

'We're meeting inside; come on we'll have to push our way through this lot.'

'Give us a kiss.'

Helena turned; a tall soldier grabbed her. 'Take pity on a poor man, off to fight the enemy.'

She giggled and flung her arms round his neck. 'You can have more than a kiss if you like; I'll give you a hug too.'

Freddie gripped her arm, dragged her away. 'You need to be careful.'

'Don't be such a stick in the mud.'

Freddie hustled her down the stairs into the Café de Paris. The music throbbed and after walking through the blackout, the light from chandeliers made her blink. People were dancing to Ken 'Snakehips' Johnson and his band; his face was like polished ebony; she was mesmerised, he was the sexiest man she'd ever seen. She moved towards the dance floor, but Freddie held her back.

'We're meeting at the bar.'

'Let's have a dance first.'

'You know I can't dance.'

Helena pulled a face and grabbed the arm of a soldier standing nearby. 'Come on; let's show them how to do it.' She caught a glimpse of Freddie's back as he headed for the bar; she didn't care.

The band had launched into 'Oh, Johnny, Oh, Johnny' when the bombs fell. Flashes of light before darkness, a rush of scalding air and falling plaster knocked her backwards. The creaks and groans as the roof caved in. When she cried out for help, she could hear nothing, only ringing in her ears. She struggled to breathe, buried her face in the soldier's jacket; clung to him. She felt herself falling and landed on people lying on the ground. The soldier fell on top of her, his head lolled against hers, she tried to push him away, but her hands touched splintered bone and blood; he must be badly hurt, dead?

Her dress was torn so it hung open, it felt wet and sticky. She struggled from under the soldier's body and managed to stagger to her feet. Her chest ached: her lungs were on fire: her head hurt and felt something running down her face. She groped her way over and around the dead and dying; fell against a wall and picked her way hand over hand towards what she hoped was the way out.

After the initial silence, wails and cries of the wounded made her cover her ears. Survivors called out for those they'd lost. What had happened to Freddie and the rest of them; would they come looking for her? Where they all dead? She leaned against the wall, what did it matter? Nothing mattered much.

She slumped to the floor; she hadn't the strength to move. Someone would find her; she'd just stay here in the dark and wait.

Shouting, and being shaken by rough hands jolted her into consciousness.

'This one's alive,' someone shouted, 'come on love, let's get you out of here.'

'Where's Freddie?

'Can you walk?'

'I think so.'

A policeman dragged her to her feet. 'Best to keep your eyes shut until I get you out.'

She slumped against him; he lifted her over his shoulder and carried her up the stairs and into the street. The policeman handed her over to an orderly and rushed away. By the light of torches, she could see she was drenched in blood, was it the soldier's or hers. She felt tears track their way through the grit and plaster dust coating her face, a sob caught her throat; the world had gone mad.

She heard the ringing of bells and someone bundled her into an ambulance with blood stains on its stretchers and walls. The driver crammed more and more people inside and raced off towards St. Bartholomew's Hospital. They were unloaded and herded into the hospital. Helena watched as the ambulance hurried away. Someone grabbed her arm and dragged her inside. The sound of another wave of bombers coming over left her shaking.

An elderly doctor examined her. 'We'll have to keep you in overnight; you have concussion and a nasty wound on your forehead. Nurse will stitch it then take you up to the ward. You may have to sleep on a trolley.'

She was given a bed where she lay still and listened. The drone of planes and the boom of bombs continued; perhaps Hitler was determined to get her. Her heart was racing, she had to get away, but where to? Hitler was bound to know this was a hospital; it would be his next target. Exhaustion dragged her into sleep.

'How do you feel; how's the headache?'

She was jolted awake. 'I want to go home.'

It was the same doctor she'd seen the previous night.

'If we let you go, you must get someone to collect you; ring from sister's office. Get plenty of rest; if the headache returns, go to your doctor.'

Helena nodded, as he moved to his next patient; when did he get a decent night's sleep?

Sister's office was empty; she waited a few minutes then came out.

'My mother is on her way,' she told Sister who was walking towards her.

When no-one was looking, she left.

The streets were littered with glass, rubble and burnt-out vehicles. As she approached Blackfriars Station, she saw a double decker on its side. How many had died, how many families would wait for someone who would never return? Clutching at the hospital gown a nurse had given her, she headed for the river. A walk along the Embankment would help to clear her thoughts; she could find her way home from there.

She had no money for a ticket. People looked away as they hurried past; they probably thought she'd escaped from an asylum. She felt a jacket being draped across her shoulders, turned and sobbed as a stranger held her in his arms.

'Shouldn't you be in hospital?'

'I want to go home.'

When they left Hendon Central station, he put an arm round her shoulders; she leaned against him, her legs too shaky to walk. He stopped.

'How far is it?'

'I don't know exactly, not far, but... I don't know what my mother will say; I didn't tell her where I was going.'

'She'll be so relieved to see you, she probably won't ask.'

'You don't know my mother.'

'Shall I thumb a lift or shall we walk?'

'The fresh air will do me good.'

They walked past parkland with trees and clumps of daffodils; she brushed away tears of relief, she was still alive.

Mary opened the door; she usually left that to the maid.

'I've brought her back, just about in one piece.' Robert smiled.

'Come in.' Mary stepped back, 'we had no idea where you were, Helena.'

'I couldn't let you know, Mother, they kept me in overnight.'

'I had to help this maiden in distress, but I won't take up any more of your time.'

Robert paused, 'Would you mind if took your address, I would like to keep in touch with Helena, see how she is. My unit's going abroad soon and a letter from home is always welcome.'

Mary nodded, 'You've been very kind; thank you for all you've done.

After that, Helena stopped going into town. She felt guilty about the soldier who'd saved her life, but sacrificed his own. Did he have a family, did they find out what happened to him? She found it impossible to get out of bed some days, swamped by despair. She did nothing yet fatigue dogged her both day and night and yet she couldn't sleep. When she managed a few hours, nightmares intervened. Night after night she was back there, dancing a dance of death. The deafening booms, the smell of blood and cordite never left her. She didn't hear from Freddie; he must have died too. Life would never be the same.

Slowly the darkness lifted; perhaps she'd been affected by the dreadful weather, as well as shock. She'd longed for sunlight to lift her spirits, but dull, wet, and cold days merged into each other. Was God punishing mankind?

She had returned from her Swiss finishing school with no idea of what to do; then the war started. Now there was talk of young women being called up to replace men who were sent to the front; perhaps she'd work in a factory, many young girls did, but what could she do? She wanted to preserve life, not destroy it; perhaps a letter to her saviour would help.

Dear Robert,

I am beginning to feel better and I've made enquiries about training to be a nurse.

What do you think?

We're doing well here although the bombings continue. Luckily, we are too far to the north of London to have to cope with much.

I know you can't tell me where you are, but I hope you're safe and will be home soon.

Your dear friend
Helena XX

She went to collect the post each morning, but the only letter she received was from St. George's Hospital, Marble Arch. She was to start her training at the beginning of May. A week later his letter arrived.

My dear Helena,

What a wonderful nurse you will make, I'll be so proud of you.

It is hot and sandy here, but we are all in good spirits. I don't ever want to make another sand castle.

Rumours have hinted we will get some leave very soon, fingers crossed.

Thank you for your letter; you'll never know how much it means.

I'm looking forward to seeing you.

Yours always Robert.

Chapter 2

1st June 1941

Mary watched Edgar and wondered what he was thinking. She so seldom saw him now. During the day he worked at the Foreign Office and each evening retired to his library; his fascination with Russian History and the rise of communism took up most of his spare time. As his manuscript progressed, he and Mary discussed the work which she proofread for him. Other than that, he left her to her own devices. She wondered if he thought of her as a literary assistant rather than a much-loved wife.

'Helena will be starting her training soon.'

Edgar put the paper down. 'Do you think she'll stick at it?'

'Why wouldn't she?'

Edgar stared at her, 'I know I have no first-hand experience of child rearing, but your daughter's personality doesn't seem suited to nursing. Have you ever wondered if she's inherited her father's tendencies?'

Mary felt her face flush and looked away; Gilbert, the father of her children, so brilliant, but so flawed.

'Edgar, please don't say that, I can't bear it.'

'Consider her mood swings, her unreliability, how the hell is she going to cope with sick people?'

'Darling please, don't you remember what happened to her at the Café de Paris.'

'Exactly, what was she doing, going to the centre of town during a bombing raid?'

'But the raid didn't start until after she got there; she wouldn't have known…'

Edgar folded his paper, 'There are times, Mary, when I wonder if your ability to overlook Helena's behaviour is because she reminds you of Gilbert.'

Mary looked away; Helena always managed to create tension one way or another and it was getting worse. Thankfully she'd start her training soon and stay in the nurses' home. It would make life more comfortable for everyone.

'What about this young man?'

'Robert?'

'Does he have any idea what he's letting himself in for.'

'He seems kind, though not really our sort. He's coming home on leave; Helena is expecting a visit.'

'You might have warned me.'

'I didn't want to bother you when you are so busy. I thought you'd be pleased someone was taking an interest in my wayward daughter.'

Edgar raised his eyebrows, folded his paper and stood up as Helena rushed in.

'Robert is on his way, he's walking down the street now. Do you think he'd like dinner with us; he's probably been living on bully beef.'

Mary watched Edgar; his expression said it all.

'I'm sure this young man will have made plans for you both, dear.'

'But you've not met him, not properly; I want you to like him.'

'But…'

'You never want my friends here.' Helena turned and flounced out.

Edgar left before Mary could reply; the sound of the library door banging shut reverberated, made her head hurt.

Mary wondered if Edgar was right. Mental instability, it was something she'd never discussed with anyone, but she could still picture Gilbert's body hanging from the garage rafters, all those years ago when Frances, Helena and Matthew were tiny. Edgar had been there to relieve her of widowhood and seemed willing to accept her children. She long ago realised it was no more than accept; there had never been any emotional involvement on his part. Maybe it was a blessing for the rich; they could leave their children to be cared for by a nanny.

She jumped when the doorbell rang and Helena's feet pounded downstairs and across the hall.

'It's Robert,' she shouted, 'Mother, Robert's here.' She dragged him into the sitting room. 'Look who's here.'

Mary studied him, this extremely handsome, bronzed soldier smiled and immediately it was clear why Helena was smitten, why she'd spent all her spare time writing to a man she scarcely knew.

'Glad to see you again, Robert, army life suits you. Will you be home

13   13

for long?'

'I've got four days.'

'Oh, no, that's not fair.'

'It's more than many get; things are warming up. My dad's been ill, pneumonia; he was gassed in the first lot. His lungs were damaged; so I've got compassionate leave really.'

'Then don't let us keep you, make the most of the time you have together.'

Mary watched them from the window as they ran, hand in hand, down the road towards the station; it had been like that with Gilbert once, but Edgar had never been inclined to show his feelings. Perhaps it would have been different if they had had a child together. Had their childless state made him feel he was less of a man? She often wondered if writing was his cherished family, not her and her children.

She went to the kitchen to see what Cook had managed to find for dinner. Rationing made menu planning a nightmare. Bill, the gardener, had been given permission to grow vegetables and soft fruits in a plot beside the house which helped as Cook had the devil's own job to find anything fresh in the shops.

'My brother's been out on Parliament Hill Fields, Madam. He set some traps and look what he got.' Cook held up two wild rabbits. 'He borrowed his mate's bike to bring them over; shall I do a casserole? I've got some dried peas and pearl barley and Bill has some potatoes in store.'

'That sounds excellent, do thank your brother for me.'

Mary wandered back to the sitting room. She couldn't rest, felt anxious all the time. Frances was in Birmingham helping to run the Longbridge factory which now made munitions and military equipment. Mary hadn't heard from her recently and Birmingham was being flattened by the Luftwaffe; if only she could drive up to see her first born, but petrol rationing made it impossible. At least she could be contacted, by phone, in an emergency, but was anxiety an emergency?

Matthew was a submariner and she knew he was somewhere in the North Atlantic and that was all. She stared out of the window; the day had been dull, with heavy cloud. It was bound to get dark early. Would there be another raid tonight? German forces were getting ever nearer, Norway and Denmark were occupied and still the Nazis advanced. How would she cope if anything happened to Matthew; it was the not knowing that made life so hard. If only she could talk to Edgar about her fears.

She turned on the radio. The news had been so bad recently, she wondered why she bothered; they were all damned one way or another. Crete had fallen and troops were being evacuated by the navy; perhaps

14

Matthew was safer in the North Atlantic. She went to their library and Edgar looked up as he replaced the telephone receiver.

'I hope I haven't disturbed you, dear.'

'I was just discussing things with my researcher. You have to keep these young women on their toes. Accuracy is all, but it doesn't seem to matter much now.'

'Don't give up, do what you can while you have her; once she's called up, you'll have to rely on me.'

She smiled and rested her hand on Edgar's shoulder. 'Perhaps a small whisky and water will help; by the way, Cook has a surprise for you.'

Edgar nodded, 'Thank you, dear, but I must get on.'

Chapter 3

June 1941

Robert and Helena arrived at the block of council maisonettes breathless and laughing. Helena was nervous; she had not expected to be introduced to Robert's parents so soon. Did it mean he was serious about her?

'We won't stay long, Dad's still very weak, but I know they want to meet you.'

'Why, to check up, see I'm suitable?'

Robert laughed as he opened the front door. 'Mum, Dad, I brought Helena, she's ready for inspection.'

Helena tried to hide her surprise at how small their home was. Robert's father was in a makeshift bed in one corner while a large dining table took up the middle of the room. Two bulky armchairs were either side of the fireplace where a fire roared, despite the warm weather. She didn't know people lived in such cramped conditions and amazingly, there home was above a horse meat shop. It hadn't occurred to her before that she had such a privileged life, public school, servants; none of it made her happy.

Robert's mother was tiny and looked even more delicate than her bedridden husband.

'Would you like a cup of tea?'

'Don't go to any trouble, Mum, we won't stay long, you both need to rest.'

'Would you like me to put the kettle on, Mrs Warren?'

'No, no, I'll do it.'

Helena realised she was being watched; Mr Warren was smiling at her, he looked kind.

'I'm very pleased to meet you, Helena.' He held out his hand, she took it and relaxed.

'What time will you be back tonight, son?' Gladys stood in the kitchen doorway.

'I'm not sure, you get your meal sorted just in case we're late.'

'But I've saved my coupons and made a stew. There won't be much meat, but it'll be tasty, the way you like it.'

Robert gathered his mother into his arms. 'You spoil me, don't you? Don't worry we'll be fine, perhaps we can have it tomorrow. I'll take Helena home this evening, can't have her wandering the streets. If I'm late, don't worry.'

Helena noticed Gladys Warren at the front door, waving as they walked away. It was Robert she was waving to.

'What would you like to do?'

'You're the one on leave, you should decide.'

'We could go into town if you like.'

'No, I don't think so, not after the Café de Paris.'

'One of my mates told me about that, he was on leave when it happened.'

'I was there.'

Robert stopped, 'Christ, of course you were; not many people got out in one piece. How could I forget? It was how we met.' He turned hugged her, stroked her back. 'It's all been so bloody, it's scrambled my brain.'

She kissed his cheek and held him tight. 'I know what, let's go for a walk, it's a lovely day and it's better to be in the open.'

'What about Battersea Park?'

'As long as we get back before dark; there've been raids nearly every night this month.'

'Right, a walk to work up an appetite, then let's see if we can find somewhere to eat, if not, we'll go back to Mum and Dad's. I knew she'd make something, rationing or no rationing. After that we'll go to the cinema, we can canoodle in the dark.'

'I wouldn't feel comfortable eating food meant for your Mum and Dad, that's not fair.'

'Let her do it, she loves making a fuss.'

Helena wondered if Gladys wanted to make a fuss of Robert's girlfriend or just Robert.

Once seated in a small cafe, Robert put his arm round her. He leaned forward, 'Please may I have a kiss?'

His lips were soft and sent tingles up and down her spine; she gasped and pulled away. It was madness, he'd be going away soon and might

17

never return; all she'd have left would be the memory of his lips on hers.

He took her hand, 'Shall we do something really crazy?'

'What?'

'Let's get married; I'll get a special licence.'

Helena sat back. 'But we don't know each other.'

'When I saw you at Blackfriars, I knew.'

'But…'

'I'm going away in three days; I want to know you will be waiting for me to get home. I don't want anyone else to snap you up while I'm out of the country.'

'What will your parents say?'

'What about yours?'

'They think I'm a nuisance.'

'Be my nuisance, please.'

'Are you sure?'

'If I'm going to die in some bloody desert, I want my last thoughts to be of you.'

'I'd better tell my mother; I'll tell her tomorrow; heaven knows what she'll say.'

They strolled home arm in arm and discussed the film they'd seen, 'Citizen Kane'. Such an extraordinary plot, they'd both been too engrossed to canoodle after all. Once on the doorstep, Robert took Helena in his arms. She could feel his heart thumping; was he the man she wanted to marry? She was confused by her feelings, she longed to be loved. She'd never felt loved like this before; why shouldn't she do what she wanted?

'Will you marry me then?' He kissed her again and again; her head spun and she felt desire, she knew not what for, or did she? She put her hands behind his head and drew him close.

'Yes,' she whispered.

'I'll come round tomorrow as soon as I've put in the application for a licence.'

She wandered round the house all morning, couldn't settle. What would she wear? Any idea of a white wedding was absurd; she didn't have anything special and there was talk of clothes going on ration. Would Robert's parents attend, would her mother and Edgar attend; did she want them to?

She'd inspect her wardrobe. The only thing she had, which looked smart, was her school suit, navy blue worsted and her school court shoes; how pathetic. She sighed and picked her prettiest blouse; at least it was special, pure silk. There was a knock at the front door and Helena heard the maid open it.

'It's all right, Joan, it's for me.'

And there he was. She felt giddy with excitement, it wasn't pathetic, it was wonderful and when she was old and grey, she'd tell her grandchildren about when she married their grandfather.

Robert kissed her cheek, 'Does your mother know or will she expect me to speak to your stepfather, get permission?'

'No need, he'll be glad to see the back of me. Mother is in the sitting room, come on.'

Helena took Robert by the hand and dragged him in. 'Robert has something to ask you.'

'Oh?'

Helena watched Robert's face flush and smiled encouragement.

'I want to marry your daughter.'

Mary frowned, 'Don't you think this is rather sudden, Robert.'

'I know, we both know that, but we have been writing to each other for months and I do believe we are well suited and…' He paused, 'I love her.'

'Mother, please, he's got the licence and everything, please, he's going away soon.'

'I'll talk to Edgar. I am not prepared to let you rush into this, and Edgar is your guardian.'

'I'm going to get married tomorrow, Mother; that's final. I want to live my life my way.'

'May I remind you, my dear, you are under age.'

'Then we'll go to Greta Green.'

Helena listened to raised voices and smiled; would Mother get the better of Edgar for once? She couldn't understand why he would object. He'd always made it clear he found her a trial. The clothes for her wedding were laid out, but would the ceremony take place after they had hitch-hiked north or in Chelsea as Robert had planned?

Chapter 4

2nd June 1941

The wedding did take place in St Luke's church, the day before Robert reported for duty. It was a sombre affair and news on the war was bad; Crete had fallen, but the Royal Navy had managed to evacuate thousands of British troops. With so much death and destruction, Helena wasn't sure if undertaking marriage was appropriate, but Robert was determined. Both sets of parents had decided they would not attend.

As they approached the huge church, Robert asked two strangers to act as witnesses. They walked, hand in hand, up the aisle, each step echoed, emphasising the lack of a congregation; Helena shivered. It was over in minutes and no photos were taken. The two strangers went on their way and Helena wondered if the ceremony had actually taken place.

Robert grabbed her hand, 'Come on Mrs Warren, I'm starving.'

'Where are we going?'

'Maison Lyon, Marble Arch.'

Helena had never seen a restaurant like it; it was relaxed and friendly, unlike the posh places she was used to. A small band was playing at the far end of the room, as they walked towards an empty table, the musicians played 'Here Comes the Bride.' It was a wonderful. A waiter hovered while fellow diners congratulated them; she couldn't stop grinning.

The waiter handed them a very small menu. 'As you know, Sir, we have a limited supply of meat, but…' He leaned closer, 'Chef does have some steak, enough for two…'

Helena put her hand on Robert's 'Why is he whispering?'

Robert put his finger to his lips and smiled, 'Does Mrs Warren fancy a little steak?'

Helena nodded, 'Medium rare, please.'

'And Sir?'

'Well done.'

The waiter nodded and scuttled away.

Robert took Helena's hands in his. 'I couldn't afford a hotel for tonight... a friend of mine has offered his place; he'll stay with his girlfriend. You don't mind, do you?'

This was the bit which worried her. She'd often wondered what sex was like, it sounded horrible, but it couldn't be too bad if people kept on doing it. Did women just do it because they wanted babies?

Robert whispered in her ear. 'I love you Mrs Warren.'

Robert's friend let them in to a basement flat in a terraced house off King's Road, Chelsea.

'You're honoured; my girlfriend has put clean sheets on the bed. What time are you reporting back, Rob?'

'Ten, tomorrow morning, at Victoria Station.'

'Well, have fun.'

When the door clicked shut, Robert put his arms round her, led her to the bedroom. She felt her body tense; he was a man of the world while she knew nothing about this part of marriage. Suppose she hated it. Robert undressed her, stroked her hair, kissed her eyelids, held her so tight she could scarcely breathe. She'd never seen a naked man before; all she knew had been taken from the booklet called 'Growing Up' which Mother had left in the library. It all seemed very clinical; no mention of how she should expect to feel. No-one had ever told her anything.

She couldn't stop trembling as Robert unbuttoned her blouse and eased her out of it, stroking her skin, kissing her again and again, her eyelids, her lips her neck her shoulders. She clung to him. He pulled back the counterpane, helped her into bed then stripped off and slid into bed beside her. His breath on her cheek made her skin tingle, she felt herself relax; it was going to be all right.

'You are the most beautiful woman in the world.'

Excitement bubbled in her throat, she gasped as he rolled on top of her; she was his to do with as he chose. Is this what Mother and Edgar did; somehow, she doubted it. Her mind drifted into a strange place where nothing but feelings registered. His weight was crushing her, but she wanted it to, she wanted more. As he entered her, she felt a stab of pain, but didn't care. He grasped her hips and thrust himself further inside her.

She wondered if her flesh would tear yet now, she wasn't feeling pain. She wanted to sing out with joy, her body was on fire then it was all over while she still throbbed with desire. Was this it? Perhaps she would get the hang of it with practice.

'Darling Helena, I didn't hurt you, did I?'

She leaned on one elbow and stared down at him, 'You'd never hurt me.' She stroked his cheek, 'Kiss me again; hold me, I want the memory of this night to last until you come back.'

'I don't want to go.'

They clung together and listened to aircraft overhead and the distant boom of bombs. Slowly they slid apart as their bodies reached out for sleep; he rested his arm across her stomach to keep her close. She listened to the rhythmic sound of each breath he took and feared what lay ahead. Flickering light shone through thin curtains.

She eased herself out of bed, not wanting to disturb him, and went to the window. London was blazing as more bombs fell. This time tomorrow he would be gone and they had discussed nothing. Where would they live? She didn't think Mother and Edgar would let her stay there after the last row. Would Robert's parents take her in? She wasn't there when Robert broke the news of the marriage; she didn't know how they had taken it. She might find herself homeless.

Chapter 5

June 5th 1941

Mary sat in the sitting room, alone; Edgar had gone to a civil service meeting somewhere, she didn't know where. Each member of the family was somewhere else, only she remained in this huge house, alone again. She wondered where Helena and her new husband were. Perhaps this ill-advised wedding should have been stopped; it could have been. Mary sighed; she could imagine the furore Helena would have created had they done so, particularly if the young man didn't come back. So, the necessary forms, giving permission, had been signed.

Mary poured herself a sherry; she must pull herself together, do something. The demand for more women to join the Women's Voluntary Service was increasing day by day; perhaps that was the answer. She had too much time to sit and think. The only problem was what was she prepared to do? As a woman with servants, she had little experience of cooking, she didn't knit and Edgar would never countenance homeless people being brought to the house.

She knew she was a good organiser; if she could organise servants, she could organise ordinary housewives to prepare and deliver refreshments to firefighters and men clearing up after bombing raids or handing out essentials to the homeless. Administration was her forte; she would contact Head Office tomorrow. Would Edgar approve? As a diplomat and a recognised author from the upper classes, he would probably be horrified; so be it.

She had met WVS founder, Lady Reading, at a Foreign Office dinner some years before. There was no point in not using contacts, if she had them. She must find out where the organisation was based. Should she tell Edgar her plan or wait to see if she was taken on? She heard the front door open and smiled; two people could play the game of keeping secrets. The sitting room door opened, but it was Helena who walked in.

'I went to the station with him; I'll probably never see him again.' She slumped in a chair and sobbed.

'Will it ever end? All this destruction all this death; supposing Robert dies, what will I do?'

Mary felt uneasy when others gave way to hysterical outbursts; it was what attracted her to Edgar, he was of like mind and believed emotional incontinence showed weakness of character. Gilbert had been so different; perhaps Edgar was right about Helena's behaviour. She rang for Joan.

'We would like a pot of tea, please.'

'Yes, Ma'am.'

The sobbing continued.

'Helena, your crying is doing no good at all, to you or to Robert. You knew he was going away; it is probably the only thing you did know. When did you meet?'

'March, I'll never forget it, he was so kind.'

'It is now June and how often have you seen him in that time?

'We've written to each other… loads of times; we understand each other.'

'You cannot possibly know that. Yes, he was kind, made sure you got home safely, but being kind is not the be all and end all, knowing the person you wish to marry, much better than you know Robert, is crucial.'

'But supposing he doesn't come back?'

'You will pick up the pieces of your life and start thinking of others; that was what I had to do when your father died.'

'I can't even remember him.'

'I know and that makes me sad for you. He was a kind man and a brilliant designer, but I wasn't enough; he sought comfort elsewhere. I couldn't stand it. He took the selfish way out with no apparent thought for how his untimely death would affect you, your brother and sister; I can't forgive him for that.'

There was a tap at the door and Joan pushed in a laden tea trolley.

'Thank you; that will be all.' Mary poured tea and waited.

'I'm sorry about the row with you and Edgar. I just love Robert so much.'

Mary raised an eyebrow. 'For love to last it is best if it grows slowly.'

'I don't know what will happen, I'm so scared. Can I stay here… after what Edgar said?'

'Where else have you to go?'

'Nowhere.'

'Then take my advice, make yourself useful; take up some voluntary work, it will help you to fill your days. We must all do what we can; I intend to.'

'You are not going to work in a ammunitions factory, are you?'

'Certainly not and neither are you. You have your nurse's training soon.'

Helena picked up her cup. 'I won't be able to keep my mind on things, I'll be too worried.' She paused, 'I think I'll go upstairs.'

Mary hesitated until Helena was out of the room then picked up the telephone.

'I wish to contact the WVS Headquarters, please.'

Her call didn't take long; she was to attend at Queen Anne's Chambers, 41 Tothill Street, Westminster, on the day after tomorrow at 2p.m. sharp. She'd smiled; there had been a military clip to the woman's voice, Mary approved, this would be an adventure. She checked in the very new A–Z she had recently bought for Edgar; she would take the underground to St James' Park and walk from there.

From what she'd heard, the WVS was an egalitarian organisation, no ranks; duchesses worked alongside char ladies. Each volunteer was given a job to suit her capabilities. It would be like going back to school. She felt exhilaration; who could she tell?

Darling Girl

I have to tell someone and I'm here alone. I am going for an interview with the WVS. Can you imagine your mother distributing food and or clothes? I quite fancy driving an ambulance actually. Not a word to Edgar.

Helena has taken leave of her senses and married a man she scarcely knows. He seems a decent enough chap, but she is now in tears because he has gone back to the front. It is in North Africa I believe. I don't think things are going too well there.

She is driving Edgar to distraction.

More important than my doings, how are you? Have the bombing raids calmed down? I do hope so. Please, please keep yourself safe.

Not a word from Matthew, I mention him in my prayers every night. God bless you, dear.

My love always
Mother

Chapter 6

12 July 1941

Helena hadn't heard from Robert for weeks. There were rumours of the 8th army being in Egypt, but who knew for sure? Perhaps she should visit her in-laws; at least Albert had always been welcoming. Although Edgar had agreed to her staying at home, it wasn't what she wanted after all. She would set up a home for when Robert came back, if he ever did. She wiped her eyes; would she ever stop crying.

'Mother I'm going to see Robert's parents.'

'That's very thoughtful of you, dear.'

'I don't know what time I'll be back.'

'I'll tell Cook to do you a tray.'

Helena knocked on the door of the Warren's maisonette; she should have let them know she was coming, but they didn't have a phone. The door opened and Albert smiled at her.

'Come in,' he said, 'you're a sight for sore eyes.'

'I hope you don't mind… are you feeling better now?'

'There's life in the old dog yet. Mother's getting some shopping; she'll be back soon.'

'I've been thinking, I'm starting nurses' training soon, at St George's, Marble Arch. As we live in North London, it would be easier if I found somewhere near here; it'd be a much shorter journey. I'd be lodging in the nurses' home most of the time, but on days off, I could pop in to see you, let Robert know how you are. I wondered if you could help me; is there any property near here which I could rent?'

Albert paused. 'We've got plenty of demolished stuff, but I don't know of anything empty. I could ask around.'

'I've got some money; it's an inheritance from my great aunt. Mother told me I would receive it when I reached twentyfive or got married, whichever came first.'

'How will your Mum and Dad feel if you leave?'

'Mother and stepfather,' Helena pulled a face, 'we don't get on. Anyway, I thought Robert would want to live near you when all this ends so perhaps I should try to set up a home while he's away. It would be something to keep me occupied when I'm not at work and for him to look forward to.'

'You'll have difficulties getting furniture; so many people have been bombed out and lost everything.'

Helena felt tears gathering, but she mustn't cry in front of this nice old man.

'There's Mother now, she might have some ideas.'

Helena leapt to her feet as Gladys carried in shopping bags.

'Let me help you.'

Gladys shook her head. 'I can manage thanks.' She walked through to the kitchen.

'Put the kettle on, Mother then our daughter -in- law has a problem' He winked at Helena.

The sun was shining as Helena strode to the Underground station; it was a beautiful evening. She was amazed to feel so much better now she had done something positive. As a newly married woman, she would be able to pick second-hand furniture from a WVS depot. She'd given Albert her home telephone number and he promised to let her know if anything came up.

Robert wouldn't be home for months; a report had confirmed the Eighth Army was digging in for a winter campaign. It would give her time to find somewhere suitable and make it look nice.

By the time she got home, Edgar had retreated to the library and Mary was listening to the news.

'Mother, now I'm married, I think I should leave home, stand on my own two feet; make somewhere for Robert, for when he comes back.'

'How on earth are you going to do that?'

'Robert's father is going to track down a suitable property I can rent then I'll be near them while Robert's away; they are both very frail. I'll need my money from Great Aunt Florence for furniture and things. I could sort everything out before I start at the hospital.'

Mary put down her newspaper.

'It isn't as simple as that. We have been empowered to use our discretion to ensure you do not fritter away your inheritance.'

'But my husband and I need our own home.'

'I'm aware of that, but buying or renting a property around there is not a good idea. Hitler isn't going to avoid bombing Chelsea just to suit you; you would be safer here.'

'But it's my money and besides I know Edgar can't wait to see the back of me.'

'Don't talk nonsense. Besides what is the point of renting when you will be staying in the nurses' hostel?'

'I'll have days off.'

'Just suppose you find somewhere, spend money on setting up home and it is bombed, as so many have been, you would be frittering away money.'

'At least give me a chance.'

'For heaven's sake get your tray and go to your room; I've no patience with you.'

Helena sprawled on the bed and wondered how much she should tell Robert. It was all so difficult; could Mother really stop her leaving? There was a way round it provided her in-laws agreed. Robert's room was free and when he came back, as they were a married couple, they would share his bedroom. Why couldn't she move in now? It would only be until she started her training.

Perhaps she should abandon nursing, but she needed to support herself. Perhaps she should do war work. There had been an article in the newspaper about King George visiting some place in Merton recently; it was a munitions factory. She'd find out if they had vacancies. It would be one in the eye for Mother.

She took out her writing paper.

Dear Robert,
She put her pen down, so many choices, so many decisions.
I went to see your parents today; they are both looking well and send their love. There have been fewer bombing raids, perhaps Hitler has run out of bombs. Everyone seems more cheerful now we can get a decent night's sleep.
I dream of you every night and pray for your safe return.
God Bless, from your loving wife Helena. XX

She'd wait to see how everything worked out before she told Robert any more.

'I'm going out, Mother.'

'Is that wise?'

'I want to do something useful; I'm going to Camden Underground station. Lots of people stay there overnight because they've been bombed out. Musicians go too and give concerts; I'm going there to sing, cheer them up. I might as well put all that voice training, you made me have, to some use.'

Mary stared at her and sighed.

Albert found a terraced house on Redburn Street, divided into separate units. Part of the property was available for rent. She hurried over to view it. There were two large rooms on the ground floor, and a small kitchen, down some steps, at the back of the house. The bathroom was shared with three other tenants. Helena hated it. She decided it would seem ungrateful if she turned it down. If they had wanted her to live with them, surely, they would have suggested it.

'Mother, Robert's father has found somewhere for us to live.'

'I see; you are determined to go through with this, put your life at risk?'

'Please let me try.'

'Edgar and I have discussed it and decided to make you a small allowance.'

'Why didn't you tell me?'

Mary said nothing.

'Did you think I'd forget?'

'I worry about you.'

'Why don't you come to see it?'

'My dear girl, I think you are taking a big risk. The less I know about it, the easier it will be for both of us.'

I know you think I'm a pain in the neck,' she kissed Mary's cheek, 'thanks for the allowance, I'll use it wisely'

Helena stood, hand on the door knob, 'I'd better call the landlord now, say I want it then pack some clothes and go over. It's furnished so I won't need much.'

'Be careful.'

Helena laughed, 'I'll let you know when I'm coming back.'

Helena arrived at Albert and Gladys breathless and exhausted. She had packed far too much and her arms felt as though they had been wrenched from their sockets.

'I've rented the place you found for me.' She gave them both a hug. 'Now I can be near at hand and help with shopping and stuff.'

'It's a nice evening, Mother, shall we walk over and she if Helena needs anything?'

Gladys nodded and Helena rushed off, 'I'll try to unpack and get it tidy for you.'

She grinned and grabbed her case.

'Why don't you leave it?' Albert asked, 'our son in law will bring it over for you later.'

'Don't worry, I can manage.'

Gladys prowled from room to room 'Have you told Robert yet?'

'No, I want it to be a surprise.'

Gladys frowned and looked at Albert.

He put his arm round Helena. 'You're a good girl and I know you'll do your best.'

'You'll need curtains, can't have people looking in; I'll see what I can spare.'

Helena took Gladys' hands in hers. 'Thank you.'

They didn't stay long. Helena watched as they walked back, arm in arm, to their comfortable home, small, but cosy and full of love. Her mother and Edgar had money and status, but where was happiness?

A month later, Helena realised she was pregnant. As soon as her condition became obvious, she would be obliged to end her nurses' training, before it started. She sat in her Redburn Street home and wept. How could she live on her own now? Where could she go? She hadn't seen Mary or Edgar since she moved in; that left Albert and Gladys. She must write to Robert, ask him what he wanted her to do.

> *Darling girl*
> *What amazing news; I can hardly believe it. Mum and Dad must be thrilled. I don't want you doing too much; our baby is precious. Don't worry about the nursing, get plenty of rest. Where do you want to stay, with your mother or with mine? I'm sure they'd love to have you. Knowing Mum, she'd spoil you to death.*
> *Decide what's best for you.*
> *Things are okay here at the moment, so don't you worry.*
> *Love, my darling, take good care.*
> *Robert*

Could an intelligent man, like Robert, be so blind to his mother's possessiveness? She'd never experienced it, but from what Matthew said about how Mother treated him, it was a pain.

She would have to let her mother and Edgar know about the pregnancy and what about continuing to live in Redburn Street? How would Edgar cope if she went home? She should be feeling excited, happy, but her head ached and she didn't know what to do.

Unexpectedly Mary agreed to Helena staying in Hendon until after she'd had the baby, but she suspected Edgar had objected. There was no need to keep on the rented property, but she still visited Gladys and Albert regularly even though it meant going across London, by Underground train. She felt contented; she was carrying a new life. Gladys was spending her days knitting baby clothes.

Albert had whispered in Helena's ear, 'It keeps her busy, stops her worrying about Robert.'

The pregnancy was uneventful; Helena rested and stayed out of Edgar's way. Joan, their maid, fussed over her and took an active interest in Helena's health and wellbeing, much to Edgar's annoyance. Helena sometimes wondered if he had blood in his veins or water. Robert would never be like that.

There was a bombing raid the night she went into labour; both staff and patients were terrified. She clung to a young nurse and refused to let go, as explosions drowned out her screams. Finally, a thin wail announced her daughter's arrival. She'd longed for a son and suspected Robert would also be disappointed, but at least they were both alive.

When Helena and baby left hospital, Mary collected her and took them both back to Hendon. It would be a temporary arrangement. Albert managed to find a suitable property nearby. This time Mary released the rest of the inheritance money; Helena promised to keep it for emergencies. As soon as she finished breast feeding Alice, she would get work.

Alice was six months old when Albert and Gladys offered to care of their only grandchild and Helena started at a munitions' factory. Mary called every few weeks and left money to help with extra expenditure; the arrangement went well. Alice thrived and Helena revelled in her life as a wife and mother, but wondered how long Albert and Gladys would be strong enough to carry on.

Of course, her main worry was the brief and infrequent letters from Robert. News from the Western Desert gave little comfort; Rommel and his Afrika Korp were blasting their way to Tobruk. Like a plague, the war spread its tentacles and now both America and Britain had declared war on

Japan after they attacked Pearl Harbour. Where would it all end? Helena dared not discuss the news with Albert and Gladys; they must already be sick with worry. It would soon be Christmas and the cellar, they used during a bombing aid, was freezing; Alice shared her mother's bed; they had to be close in case there was a raid.

Every day was a challenge, an effort to cling to survival. Yet after Dunkirk, Helena clung to the belief the Allies would prevail in the end.

Chapter 7

8th May 1944

Helena shifted to a more comfortable position; she should bring more cushions to the cellar. Not only had bombing raids started again, now it was doodlebugs too. They made her afraid to leave the house. She had too often heard their engines and watched as they flew overhead, praying their engines didn't cut out. If that happened, there would be no time to escape; perhaps the war would only end when they were all dead.

Candle light flickered, cast grotesque shadows on the rough cellar walls. She felt like a mole, spending more time underground than in the open air. Somehow it was comforting, she felt safe. Alice shifted in her sleep and Helena stroked her cheek. It had been a miracle both she and her baby girl had survived the bombing raid that night three years ago. Robert had managed two days leave so he saw them both, but he wouldn't recognise his daughter now. She wasn't a baby anymore. Helena closed her eyes as another bomb exploded, near enough to make the house shake.

Alice had got used to all the noise at night and usually slept through it, barely waking when the All Clear sounded and Helena carried her back to bed. She was a good little girl, but would they both live long enough to celebrate the child's next birthday? Would there ever be peace? Would Robert come home? So many questions and she had answers to none of them. After every raid, Helena expected to find nothing but rubble when she opened her front door.

She hadn't heard from Robert for months and didn't know if that was good or bad. He was with the rest of the Eighth Army in North Africa, fighting Rommel at El Alamein. At the time there had been rejoicing, Churchill had said it turned the tide for the Allies. His speech had raised their hopes, 'This is not the beginning of the end; it is the end of the beginning,' he'd said. But that was two years ago and still the war ground them into oblivion.

The candle flickered and died, but there was a pale light seeping in through a crack; dawn was here and they were still alive. She thought back to Robert's last forty-eight hour leave, when the Eighth was on the move up through Italy. Alice was in bed when he arrived unexpectedly one evening.

'Shall I get Alice up? She's longing to see you.'

Robert shook his head, 'I don't want to upset her.'

'She needs to see you.'

'I'll be back this evening, don't wake her; I'll go to Mum and Dad now.'

'You must come back when it's all over, but suppose you don't; it's been so long, she'll have no memories of you.'

He hugged her hard, 'I don't want any of that silly talk. Look at all the work you've done to make a home for us all. Of course, I'm coming back.'

'I've tried so hard to make it nice, but it's a dump.'

'I don't deserve you; no man could have a better wife.'

Once back from his parents, they crept upstairs and stood by Alice's cot, watched her sleeping. Only then did Helena realised Robert was crying. She closed the nursery door quietly and led him by the hand to their bed. So much sorrow, so much loss of friends and colleagues had changed him; he was a stranger, burdened by a sense of guilt. He'd survived when so many didn't. Although they made love, it felt joyless; undertaken as a duty rather than from desire; passion was dead, it was too dangerous to have feelings.

He was away by daylight, before Alice woke. When he stood at the front door, uniformed and ready to leave, she'd given him a front door key, pressed it into his hand.

'It's to guarantee you come back.' But it couldn't guarantee anything.

The country was poised; rumours blossomed, based on hope rather than facts. The weather was warmer and people sensed something momentous was about to happen. Helena prepared breakfast and made herself a sandwich to take to the factory. She went to the bottom of the stairs.

'Come on sweetie-pie, we're going to be late.'

Alice came down clutching her toy rabbit, Benjy. Her tiny baby was growing into a self-assured little girl with dark curly hair and green eyes just like Robert's. There was a knock at the door, too early for the postman. It was a telegram. Helena tore open the brown envelope.

'Missing in Action' the words took her breath away; she was too stunned to cry. Alice tugged at her apron, 'Mummy, Mummy, I'm hungry.'

'Just a minute sweetheart, Mummy needs to think.'

She was next of kin; how would she tell his parents? Alice put her arms round Helena's waist, 'Why are you sad, Mummy, can I kiss it better?'

Helena pulled Alice to her, held her close and felt release as tears flowed.

'Can we go to see Grandpop and Nana?'

'Yes, let's do that.'

Despite the warmer weather, she felt cold all the time. Death was everywhere and still the bombs came. What point was there to this existence? Alice skipped beside her, scuffling last winter's leaves; how could she save her fatherless child from destruction.

Alice ran ahead, clattered along the balcony to her grandparents' home and banged on the door,

'Granddad, Granny, we're here and Mummy's feeling sad.'

Helena fingered the letter in her pocket; should she just hand it to them and say nothing?

Albert stood in the doorway and raised his eyebrows. She nodded and handed him the telegram; she watched as he swayed and leant against the wall. She clasped his hand and sobbed on his shoulder.

'Nana, Mummy and Granddad are having a cuddle; can I have a cuddle with you?'

Gladys gasped and put her hand to her mouth. Albert hugged Helena and hurried through to their sitting room.

'Now then Mother, I'll put the kettle on and get our little girl a biscuit. Would you like that?'

Alice nodded and clung to Helena. 'I'm scared, Mummy.'

'Mum, Dad, it's only me.' Connie Stanley hurried in with shopping. She stopped.

'What's wrong?'

Gladys handed her the letter.

'Oh, Mum. I'm so sorry.'

Alice slid under the large table and hid. She put her hands over her ears and hummed under her breath. Why were they all so sad? It must be Daddy; they were always talking about Daddy. If she stayed very still, no-one would notice and she could go to find him, bring him back, but where was he? Nobody told her. What did he look like; she couldn't remember. Mummy said he saw her when she was very, very small, but then he went away. Perhaps he didn't like her very much. She sucked her thumb and listened.

'Missing means just that; anything could have happened. He could have been separated from the rest of his unit.' Albert picked up his cup and tried to stop his hand shaking. 'He's very resourceful, our lad; he'll find his way back.'

'Listen Dad, I'll get back home and ask John to bring the car round; he's on nights this week, but he won't mind. He can catch up on his sleep later.' She turned to Helena, 'You won't feel like walking home, will you?'

Helena nodded and picked up Alice. 'Uncle John's taking us home in his car, won't that be nice.'

'Will you stop feeling sad?'

Helena hugged her, 'You're a sweet child; everything's going to be fine.'

Helena jumped as the familiar whoosh of a doodlebug overhead; if she could hear it, it would soon be too far away to do them harm. She felt for the poor beggars who didn't hear it; they would never know what hit them. Alice whimpered in her sleep; had she picked up on her mother's terror? What would happen if Robert were dead; how would she manage on her own? Other women had to, but they hadn't lived with servants who, with her mother's instructions, ran the house. Helena wasn't good at budgeting; would Gladys help her, but did she dare ask?

She leaned back, watched shadows, from dwindling candles, dance. How many hours had they spent down there? They had been lucky to have a home with a cellar; she had Albert to thank for that. Helena pulled the blankets tighter; the chilly air made her shiver; she'd be no good for anything at work if she didn't get some sleep. Sounds came and went, she was floating away to safety and warmth with Alice by her side and Robert holding her hand, the Robert she had married not the stranger who just left. She wondered how his parents felt, but dare not ask them.

It was barely light when she was jolted awake. Someone was hammering on the front door. She tucked the blankets round Alice and hurried upstairs.

There was a man standing outside, it couldn't be Robert. She opened the door and there was Matthew, her darling brother.

'A flying visit before I go to Hendon, sorry I'm so early.'

Helena slumped in his arms, 'Robert's missing.'

He held her in his arms, but said nothing.

'I've just got to get on somehow; thank God, at least you've come back in one piece.'

'Mummy, Mummy where are you?'

'We stayed in the cellar last night; I'd better see to her.'

Matthew dumped his kit bag and shut the front door; he was bone weary.

'Look who's here, Alice.'

'You're not my Daddy?'

'No sweetheart, I'm your uncle.'

'Can you find my Daddy for me?'

Matthew held out his arms, 'Come and have a cuddle for now.'

Alice nodded and leaned her head on Matthew's shoulder.

'Come on you two, let's have some breakfast; are you going to help me Alice?' She turned to Matthew. 'I'll take her round to Robert's parents and we can have a talk; I don't know what's going to happen to us.'

It was raining when Helena and Alice set off and Alice insisted on jumping in every puddle. As usual she ran ahead and knocked on the Warren's door.

'Granny, Matthew's here.'

Gladys frowned. 'Who's Matthew?'

Helena smiled, 'My brother, he's in submarines, been having a rough time I believe.'

'Haven't they all; have you heard anything yet… about Robert?'

'No, nothing, do you think I should contact the War Office or something?'

Albert put his hand on Helena's shoulder, 'You know what Mother's like; I think no news is good news. Let's give it a few days, I'm sure we'll hear if there's a development. Don't you feel up to going to the factory today?'

'No, I'm taking a day off; I've got too much to think about.'

Gladys took Alice's coat off. 'You should have come in your pushchair, you're soaked.'

Helena said nothing.

They sat in the kitchen; Helena lit the oven and left the door open for warmth. She watched him; there was a brittle edge to his easy-going nature.

'How long will you be home?'

'Probably three or four days, they're doing some work on the sub.'

'How are things?'

He pulled a face, 'Better now we've got Radar; we can hunt the buggers down.'

'Haven't heard from Mother recently although she does pop over to see we're okay from time to time.; I don't think I'm her favourite child.'

'As I've always told you, Sis, being her golden boy is a pain in the arse.'

Helena laughed, 'You haven't changed despite everything.'

'Tell you what, some of the lads have arranged to go into town tomorrow night, come with me; have a night out.'

'How can I when I don't know if Robert is alive or dead?'

'Will staying here worrying make any difference?'

'Not really, but Gladys will think I'm being frivolous, unfeeling, disloyal…'

'Let me have a chat with her.'

'Can't see her agreeing.'

'Let me try.'

'What charm her like you do every woman? Surely there is some pretty girl you could wine and dine instead of me.'

Matthew shook his head, 'No Sis, I don't want to get fond of someone or let someone get fond of me… not the way things are.'

Helena remembered the Battle of Britain pilot, who'd lived locally; she'd met him once when he visited his parents. He'd been shot down during a raid over France, an only child. Perhaps Matthew was right, so many young men dead before their time.

Chapter 8

November 1944

Helena stared at herself in the bedroom mirror; had she changed? She smoothed her hands over both hips and stomach. With current food shortages, she was unlikely to put on weight. As promised, Matthew had worked his charm on Gladys and Albert who agreed it would do Helena good to have an evening out. They were going to a jazz club in the West End to meet up with Matthew's navy mates while Alice stayed overnight with her grandparents.

Arm in arm, brother and sister strolled down dark, city streets. There was excitement in the air, a wild determination to enjoy the moment before the next bomb fell. As they felt their way down a narrow stairway, her heart pounded; this was like the Café de Paris all over again. She must be mad to come out; there was Alice to think of. She was being selfish and irresponsible and all the other things Gladys would think of her. And what of Robert, where was he?

Couples were gyrating on a small dance floor, clutching at each other with undisguised passion. Helena struggled to breathe; the air was heavy with foreign cigarette smoke and 'Evening in Paris' perfume.

'I want to go home?'

Matthew turned her to face him, 'No, you and I are going to get a bit drunk and cry into our beer and hug each other until it hurts. I may never see you again; you may never see Robert again. Tonight, is our time, follow me.'

They pushed their way through the crowd to an empty table.

'When are your mates meeting us?'

Matthew checked his watch, 'Now, if they remember; drunken sods, they're probably making up for lost time.'

The music stopped and the musicians went to the bar. Helena watched hot, carefree people milling about. They laughed and joked, embraced and moved on to someone else; tonight, they lived, tomorrow they might be dead.

One of the musicians walked to her table and stopped, he grinned at her.

'What's a lovely young lady like you doing on her own?'

'I'm not on my own.'

Matthew was pushing his way back from the bar.

'This is my brother, Matthew Carlton,' she said.

'I'm glad that's who he is.'

Helena blushed.

'Haven't I seen you here before?'

'No, this is my first time; Matt's trying to broaden my education about music.'

'Well, good for him, come down next Thursday we're having a jam session.'

'I can't, Matthew goes back to sea soon; he's on leave.'

'That doesn't matter; I'll pick you up if you like.'

'I can't, I have a little girl; my in-laws are looking after her. Can you imagine what they would think if I said I was going to a jazz club, with a strange man?'

'Bring a girlfriend.'

Helena paused then shook her head.

'Where's hubby?'

'I don't know; he's missing somewhere.'

'Poor sod, sorry to hear it; hope you get some news soon. By the way, I'm Cyril Davies come if you can.'

Helena smiled; she'd been honest. It would be madness to even think of seeing him again.

'Come and trundle round the floor with your kid brother,' Matthew said and grabbed her round the waist. 'Who's been giving you the eye?'

'One of the musicians, Cyril Davies, he was the one on drums.'

'Well watch yourself; I know what these jazz men are like.'

They walked back through deserted streets, thankful for moonlight, less chance of a bombing raid when it was so bright.

'Stay the night, Matt; you can go to see Mother tomorrow. The sofa's very comfortable.'

'You're on. I'd better spend the rest of the time with Mother; you know what she's like.'

From far away they heard the boom of an explosion. Matthew held

Helena in his arms while she sobbed. 'I can't stand it anymore, Matt.'

He stroked her back until she stopped crying. 'Christ, by the sound of it, it must be one of those V2.'

She made tea and toast and they sat in the kitchen. There was little to say even though they both knew they might never see each other again. Afterwards, in bed, she realised it might become the exception rather than the rule for her to share the house with another adult. There might only be Alice left soon.

As expected, she didn't see Matthew again before he reported back. If the newspapers were to be believed, the German U-boats were being blasted into submission. She'd added his name to Robert's in her evening prayers.

She woke with a start; Alice was coughing so hard she'd made herself sick. When Helena picked her up, she burned with fever.

'Come here my darling, let me clean you up.' They lay together in Helena's bed, but sleep was impossible. Next morning, while Alice finally slept, Helena went next door to her neighbour, Betty.

'Could your lad run round to the doctor's surgery, please? Alice's been awake all night and she's boiling hot. I don't dare take her out.'

While she waited for the doctor, she paced the bedroom with Alice in her arms. The cough was worse and though she drank some water, she ate nothing. Helena should have dropped her at her in-laws and clocked in at the depot by now. What should she do? She ran to the telephone box, called the doctor.

'Whooping cough,' the doctor said, 'a lot of it about. Keep her warm, plenty of fluids; she'll eat when she's ready. Fenning's Whooping Cough Powders will help. Can you ask someone to go to the chemist for you? If there's no improvement in the next day or two, call me.'

Helena nodded and hurried next door.

'It's me again, Alice has whooping cough. Would Alfie take a note to my in-laws after he's been to the chemist? I've put their address on the envelope.'

'It'll give me a reason to get him out of bed.'

'Here's money for the Fennings and sixpence for Alfie, please thank him for me.'

She hurried back; Alice was having another coughing fit and had been sick again. Together they sat on the bed and cried.

Albert and Gladys arrived that afternoon.

'We'll have her,' Gladys said, 'she'll be better with us.'

'Why?'

'Well, you need to go to work, don't you?' Albert said.

Helena stared at him and he looked away.

'I can manage you know. I gave Betty's boy sixpence to let you know about Alice and he got the Fenning's powders for me.'

Gladys sniffed, 'I wish I could afford to give sixpences away,'

'Now then, Mother, Helena did what she thought was best.'

'Be that as it may; John says he'll come round when he finishes work and bring Alice round to us.'

Helena sat down. 'Just a minute, shouldn't you have asked me first?'

Albert patted her shoulder, 'Mother's only trying to help.'

John, bloody John, Helena loathed her repulsive brother-in-law. John Stanley with wandering hands and a smarmy smile, how dare Gladys make arrangements without asking her first.

Albert smiled at her, 'We want you round too, Christmas is round the corner; got to keep an eye on you both while Robert's away; it's what he'd want, make sure you both have a good time.'

He turned to leave and Helena knew there was nothing else she could say.

Alice settled in her father's old bed and Helena sang to her until she fell asleep.

'I'll get myself home now,' she said, 'I've got lots of washing to do with Alice being so sick and I want to clean the place up a bit.'

'Let me give you a lift,' John said and rubbed his hands together, 'can't have my lovely sister-in-law wandering the streets at this time of night.'

'Thanks, but I'd rather walk, if you don't mind; fresh air will do me good.'

As she made her way down dark, deserted streets, grey and slippery underfoot she remembered it was Thursday, the day Cyril had told her to meet him. Sod the lot of them, if they didn't think she was capable of caring for her own child, she might as well go out and enjoy herself. She and Robert hadn't meant to start a family so soon. With the war and everything, there'd been no fun, but here she was on her own for the first time in her life, she might be a widow. She'd go to the jazz club; if she sat alone at home, she'd go crazy.

Chapter 9

November 1944

Helena looked round the crowded club; supposing he wasn't there; it was stupid to have come. She felt a tap on her shoulder and turned.

Cyril raised his eyebrows, 'I didn't expect to see you; it's a nice surprise. Would madam let me buy her a drink?'

'Nothing strong, I've got to get myself home.'

'Don't worry about that. Any news of hubby?'

She shook her head. 'My little girl's ill and my mother-in- law insisted she looked after her.'

'That's kind.'

'No it isn't, she just thinks I'm useless. I came because I couldn't face being alone.'

'She's done me a good turn.'

Helena stared at him, 'Don't get ideas.'

'Any man with half an eye would get ideas about you.'

'I can't stay long.'

'You're not going to walk home in the blackout, don't know who you might meet. I'll escort you home later.' He offered her a cigarette.

'I don't smoke.'

'Good God woman, not too much alcohol, doesn't smoke, you must have some vices.'

Helena smiled.

'You know you said your little girl's ill, well, I've got an idea. You both need a break from the bombing.'

'And how do I manage that?'

'I've got friends who live in the country.'

'Do you work this fast with every woman you meet?'

He grinned, 'Only the special ones.'

'So, there have been lots.'

Cyril pulled a face, 'No more than any healthy man, in his prime.'

Helena laughed; this was fun. She could never have had a conversation like this with Robert; he took life seriously.

'They've told me to go down anytime...'

Helena shook her head, 'It's impossible for me to get away without questions being asked. And I'm at a munitions factory during the week and anyway, I hardly know you.'

'Let's take the opportunity to do something about that.'

'I told you not to get any ideas.'

Cyril laughed, 'You can't blame a chap for trying.'

'No, it wouldn't work. I still don't know if Robert's safe; he's the one who matters.'

'What about a weekend then once you know your husband's safe. I'd pick
you up on a Friday night and bring you back Sunday. You don't have to tell anyone... do you?'

'Yes, I'm expected to go for Sunday lunch at my in-laws.'

'Every week?'

Helena nodded.

'They're bound to think it's a good idea for Alice to have some country air, away from the bombing. Make it a Christmas treat, check if the factory closes over the holiday.'

Alice sighed, 'So you've got a car.'

'No, but my mate has; he'll let me borrow it especially if it's only for a weekend.'

'You've got very obliging friends.'

Cyril grinned, 'Not what you know, it's who you know.'

'I'll think about it.'

'Good.'

It was the best evening Helena had had since before the war, and Cyril insisted on taking her home. He put his arm round her waist as they walked; it felt nice. The night was still with a cloudless sky and stars clear and bright, snow on rooftops twinkled. For a moment it was possible to forget the carnage and the fear. When they reached Helena's house, she didn't know what to do. Part of her wanted him to kiss her on the cheek and go, part of her wanted to be kissed passionately and taken to bed. How could she think such a thing; loneliness was making her reckless.

'It's been fun.'

'Yes, but you've got a long walk home.'

'Don't worry; I'll thumb a lift.' He smiled and waved as he walked away.

Helena watched him go; why did she feel guilty, she hadn't done anything wrong. There was a war on, but life couldn't just grind to a halt, could it? Every Sunday lunch was with Albert and Gladys, but it was their grandchild they wanted to see, not her. It would be a week or two before Alice was well enough to go anywhere; she'd have time to decide what was best.

If they went, they'd be staying with friends, but who were they and where did they live? She would have to ask Cyril for details. It wasn't an out and out lie, the people were friends of Cyril's, but if she stayed for a weekend, they would become her friends too. She smiled; it would be lovely to get away, to see fields and trees instead of mounds of rubble.

Helena wiped her hands and went to the front door. It was too early for the postman and still no news of Robert. Cyril stood on the doorstep smartly dressed with a briefcase.

'You shouldn't have come here; the woman over the road never misses a thing.'

'I've written to my friends, Jake and Freda. I suggested we go down in a couple of weeks.'

'Alice is still with my in-laws and might not be well enough to go, don't rush me.'

'It's only a suggestion, I'll understand if you decide not to go; I'll go by myself.'

He pulled a sad face and Helena laughed.

'My in-laws will be expecting me this Sunday, I'll tell them then.'

He put his hand on her shoulder and kissed her forehead.'

Late, on Friday afternoon, two weeks later, Cyril collected Helena and a sleeping Alice; they set off for Bury St. Edmunds. There had been a thaw and they made good time.

Helena was nervous, still in limbo as far as Robert was concerned; she knew in her heart she shouldn't be in a car with this man. She should be at home, waiting for news; Gladys had made that clear.

Cyril drove down a country lane and parked the car outside a cottage. When he sounded the horn, a man came to the door.

'Freda, guess who's here.'

A plump woman in early middle age joined him.

'What a nice surprise, come in. She held out her hand and smiled then stroked Alice's hair, 'You're a little beauty.'

'I think she's ready for bed, she's had her tea and I've put her in her nightie.'

'I've got a special bed for you,' Freda said, 'shall we go to find it?'

'It's so kind of you to have us, she's been ill, you see.'

Freda squeezed Helena's arm, 'It's a joy to have a child in the house. While you get her settled, in bed, I get on with the meal.'

As soon as Alice was asleep, Helena crept downstairs. She could hear the men, in the sitting room, heard her name mentioned so hurried to the kitchen to see if she could help. It would be wrong to eaves drop.

'You should have let us know you were coming.'

'Cyril said he'd written.'

Freda shrugged, 'The post has gone haywire as well as everything else. Fortunately, I've got plenty of vegetables; we'll manage.'

'Perhaps my post has gone haywire too; you see my husband is missing apparently, in action.'

Freda hugged her, 'You poor girl, you must be so worried.'

'I don't know what to think, it's weeks now; can't get any news from anyone.'

'No news is good news.'

'That's exactly what my father-in-law said, but...'

'Hang on to hope.'

After the meal Freda cleared the table.

'Jake and I will wash up, you two go for a stroll before it is dark. You said you wanted some country air, now's your chance.'

'We won't be long, in case Alice stirs.'

They walked down the lane and Cyril put his arm round her. She pulled away and wiped away tears.

'What's the matter? I want you to enjoy yourself, have I upset you?'

'I'm frightened.'

'What, of me?'

'No, of what will happen here and when we get back to London.'

'O.K. what's the worst thing that could happen?'

'If Robert comes back and finds out I've been away with you. He would never believe I hadn't been unfaithful. He could be letting himself into our home right now and I'm not there.'

'Surely you would have been notified, told he was on his way back?'

'I don't know and the woman opposite us has eyes in her backside and she knows Gladys; she'll have seen you drive up in the car. She's bound to tell Gladys who will take delight in passing on the information to Robert.'

'What can this busybody say? How would she know I'm not a friend of Robert's, keeping an eye on his wife? This kind friend took you both to the country for a holiday, what could be nicer?'

'But supposing Alice says something.'

'Your little girl may be very bright, but I don't think she is old enough to understand the implications of you and me sharing a bed and in any case, we're not going to.'

'But…Freda, she said we'd be on the settee in the sitting room.'

'Stop worrying; if necessary, I'll sleep on the floor in the outhouse. Now come on, you're going to enjoy yourself.'

They walked further down the lane, arm in arm.

'We're going to call at the local pub, it's time you relaxed a bit. I know it's tough right now, but what can you do? If Alice sees you're worried, she'll worry too.'

After three glasses of wine, Helena felt very strange indeed. Cyril lifted her to her feet, she swayed and he had to steady her.

'I think it's time to get you home so we can sort out the sleeping arrangements.'

They walked back past a partly demolished hayrick; Helena stopped and grabbed Cyril's hands.

'Look at that, come on let's lie down and look at the stars. My uncle's farm in Shropshire always had hayricks at harvest time; my sister, brother and I used to have such fun.'

She let go of his hand and started to pull herself onto the top of the rick.

'Come on,' she said.

He lay beside her. The fragrant smell of hay added to the scent of wine, on her breath, were unbearably sweet. He kissed her, but she pushed him away.

'No, it's wrong, please don't.'

'You are so beautiful; I can't get you out of my head.'

'No, that's silly; you don't know me, what about Robert, I love Robert.'

She cried quietly as he undid the buttons on her dress and slipped his hand inside to cup her breast. She gasped and turned away, but she couldn't stop him. It was all her own fault; she knew he'd wanted her from the start. What had Matt said about jazz musicians?

He kissed her again and slipped her dress down to reveal creamy white skin that glowed in moonlight. He stroked and kissed her breasts. He was so strong, she couldn't get away; he'd planned it, got her drunk, on purpose. She gasped as he placed her hand on his groin.

'Undo my trousers, sweetheart, I want you so much, Please help me.'

'But…'

47

Cyril smothered her words with his lips. 'Please,' he said.

The moonlight made their bodies shimmer. She fumbled with each button; this was madness. He watched her as she lay back and stared into his eyes, like a rabbit caught in headlights. He carefully pulled a small packet from his pocket and placed her hand under his as he rolled on a condom.

'It'll be okay, you'll be fine.'

He pulled her clothing out of the way and entered her. She sobbed, how could she be so wicked, how could she do this to Robert?

Cyril whispered, 'No-one need ever know.'

Her body was on fire; his breath was coming in gasps. She started to move in rhythm with him, she couldn't help herself. She gave little cries and clung to him. The moon shone on their faces and her lips parted as he kissed her.

Chapter 10

November 1944

Helena returned to London as planned; Cyril dropped her off and helped by carrying a sleeping Alice up to bed. At the front door, he put his arms round her, but she pushed him away.

'I'm sorry if I've upset you, I only wanted to take your mind off things.'

'By giving me something else to worry about?'

He turned and she watched him before closing the door; what on earth would happen next? She would have to take Alice to Albert and Gladys tomorrow or they would worry. She slid to the floor too numb to shed tears.

As Helena expected, Gladys wanted to know every detail of the weekend away and made it sound illicit and unsavoury. Of course, she was right, it had been; she had betrayed Robert and so had also betrayed his parents. Guilt robbed Helena of sleep; worst of all, Albert supported her and tried to deflect the constant questioning.

Two weeks later, Helena heard from Robert.

Darling Helena

I do hope you haven't been worrying. I was injured, slightly – just a nasty knock on the head. I got separated from the rest of the troop, but a lovely family took me in, hid me from the Germans. The Canadian troops were magnificent and took me under their wing as they advanced. Can't tell you anything else, but I've saved the best till last, dear heart; I will be coming home soon.

Knowing you are waiting for me has kept me sane. Give Alice a big hug and lots of kisses. All my love Robert

He was coming home. She sat at the kitchen table and read the letter again; thank God he was safe, but what was she going to do? She could no longer ignore the facts; she had missed her period; she was always so regular. She was imagining things; it must be her guilty conscience. She'd written to Cyril at the jazz club and told him she would never see him again. Once Robert was home and the war was over, they could get on with their lives and, as Cyril had said, on-one would be told what she had done; that was impossible now.

The following Saturday, she took Alice to Hendon. Mary was alone; Edgar was at a conference somewhere. Helena wondered how much time her mother was alone, rattling around her huge house.

'I've heard from Robert; he hopes to be home soon.'

'Good, I'm pleased for you both.' She turned to Alice, 'Are you looking forward to seeing your daddy?'

Alice nodded and leaned against her mother's knee. 'My Daddy has to go to fight bad men. I don't want them to hurt him.'

'Do you say your prayers every night?'

Alice nodded.

'Say an extra special one for your daddy so he stays safe.'

Helena stared at her mother. Was it possible the war had made her a kinder, more understanding woman?

'How's the WVS work going?'

'I've been amazed by the resilience of people who have lost everything. I'm not sure I would manage so well. So much death, so much destruction; it's humbling.' She paused and smiled, 'I've not managed to drive an ambulance yet.'

Helena sensed it was all her mother wanted to say on the subject and wondered what horrors she had seen.

'May we have a walk round the garden before we leave?'

'We can see if there are any vegetables ready for you to take home.'

Mary dropped them off at Hendon Central station and kissed them both.

'Look after yourselves.' She turned and walked back to her car.

Two weeks later Helena heard Robert would be home the following weekend. Now there was no doubt, the morning sickness had started. She was pregnant and he would never forgive her. How could it have happened? Cyril had used a condom. What on earth would she do?

She knew some local women had been unfaithful while their husbands were away; she'd heard the whispers and, if a woman was unlucky, seen the evidence. Sometimes the babies disappeared, probably adopted. Some were taken on, as their own, by men sick of war and death. There was no point in speculating, Helena knew how Robert would react. Gladys would gloat; all her worst predictions come true. Helena put her head in her hands and wept; would she ever stop crying? How could she have been so stupid?

She had received no reply after her letter to Cyril and was relieved. She accepted he'd taken advantage of her; all his talk of love meant nothing, but everything was different now. There would have to be another letter to Cyril; he had the right to know she was carrying his child, didn't he? Although she had no idea what he could do about it. If she wrote a letter today, she could go into town and drop it off and go to the factory late for once.

More difficult than that, she would have to contact her mother, tell her about the baby. To turn up without prior warning was unthinkable. Mother had never taken kindly to anyone disturbing her well-ordered routine, not even her own children, particularly now she was so involved with the WVS. Helena would call from the phone box at the end of the road and invite her to drive over to visit them the following week.

Mary Carlton sighed and glanced at Edgar over the breakfast table.

'I had a phone call from Helena yesterday.'

Edgar looked up, said nothing and quickly returning to the morning paper. Mary watched him for a moment waiting for a response, there was none. She had always felt their silences were companionable, and an important part of their relationship. Recently, however, there had been an unwelcome change to their existence; now Edgar's silences suggested distance. She was frightened by what was happening to them; why did those she loved always leave her?

She would have to see Helena, it was her duty, but she didn't have to involve Edgar. The best plan was to arrange to visit during the day, drive over to Chelsea on Thursday. Mary's reply was written after breakfast, and the maid told to post it immediately.

Helena heard her letter-box rattle and Alice ran to the front-door.

'Letter, Mummy, is Daddy coming home?'

Helena read the letter and sat down before her legs gave way.

'No, sweetheart, it's just a friend who wants to pop round later. It's Cyril, that kind man who took us down to see Jake and Freda. He's going to call in after work; he just wants to see you're better after the whooping cough.'

'I want my Daddy home?'

'He'll be home, sweetie, he'll be here soon.'

'Can we go to Grandpop and Nana's, let's go soon? Stay for tea.'

'We'll arrange it tomorrow.' Helena folded the letter and put it in her pocket. She wondered if she should call Mary, postpone the visit, but she would have left by now.

'Guess what,' she said, 'your grandma is coming to see us today. Won't that be nice?'

Alice screwed up her face and pouted.

'Sweetheart, what's the matter?'

'Don't like Grandma Carlton.'

Helena scooped Alice onto her knee. 'That's not a kind thing to say.'

Alice put her fingers in her mouth; Helena cuddled her; how perceptive children were. Mary Carlton was no-one's idea of a cuddly grandma. How did her mother feel about children in general and her own in particular; Helena had never been sure. Despite being cuddled, Alice started to grizzle.

'Now stop this silly noise, Grandma Carlton loves you; you must be kind.'

Alice's wails grew louder as Helena put her down so she could rush to the bathroom. She knelt on the floor and leaned over the toilet bowl. Once she had stopped being sick, she saw Alice in the doorway, still sucking her fingers. Helena leaned her arms on the toilet bowl and mopped at her face with a towel.

'Mummy's poorly, I'll be a good girl now.' She patted Helena's shoulder and tried to cuddle her. Helena turned and clutched the child to her, stroked the fine dark hair so like her own. Perhaps it was inevitable Cyril should be calling on the same day as her mother, but he wouldn't arrive until later, would he? Perhaps life was mapped out and she would just have to accept whatever happened next.

Chapter 11

November 1944

Cyril paused for a moment before knocking; it was ridiculous to feel so nervous. He looked like, a government official, making a routine call. He heard running feet, the child's no doubt, and then a heavier tread. The door opened and Helena was there, white-faced, tense.

'Hello, you'd better come in. I didn't expect you this early.'

'Grandma Carlton coming… I don't like her very much.'

Alice turned and ran ahead along the hallway.

Cyril raised his eyebrows, 'So I'm to meet your mother, am I?'

'Good God, no, I'm sorry it's worked out like this. I couldn't put her off and I must see her before Robert gets home.'

'He's okay?'

She nodded.

'You'll be okay then.'

'No, I won't be okay, I'm pregnant.'

Cyril gasped 'Christ, how the hell…'

'Come see my new dolly, Cyril, she's got lots of clothes my Nana Warren knitted. She's nicer than my other grandma.'

'Ssssh, Alice, you mustn't say that.'

'What time are you expecting her?'

'In time for lunch, so I suppose it could be any minute.'

'I think I'd better go, but I need to speak to you, you know discuss things properly. Here's my address and telephone number, can you get to a phone?'

'There's a box down the road, I could pop out when she's asleep. Aren't you at the club in the evenings?'

'Not on Tuesdays and Sundays.'

'I'll phone next Sunday.'

'Daddy, Daddy, coming home on Sunday.' Alice jumped up and down.

'No sweetie, not this Sunday.'

'Let Cyril know when.' Alice grinned and danced round the kitchen.

'I must go,' Cyril hurried up the hallway; when he opened the front door a tall, imposing women was walking up the outside steps.

'Excuse me,' Cyril stood to one side, 'I was just leaving.'

'He's Cyril,' Alice turned to Mary, 'he took me and Mummy to the country.'

'Mummy and me,' Mary Carlton said as she stepped into the hallway.

'I'd better be off, I've another client to see, but you know how to contact me if there are any problems.' He hurried away without a backward glance.

'So, which of your problems is that young man going to resolve for you?'

Helena's cheeks flushed and she looked away. 'He's a friend of Matthew's. I think he's just keeping an eye on us… with Robert away…'

'How kind.'

'I've made soup for lunch and we went to the bakers, didn't we, Alice, and I got a loaf, still warm from the oven.'

'Mummy let me carry it home. I didn't drop it did I, Mummy.'

'You know, my dear, there are many people who take great delight in spreading malicious gossip, do you think it wise to be seen in the company of a young man, a very self-assured young man, while your husband is fighting abroad?'

'He was being kind, Mother, Alice was so ill and I hardly slept while I was looking after her; I don't have the benefit of servants. It seemed a good idea to have a break with some friends.'

'His friends or yours?'

'What difference does that make?'

'If this young man is kind enough to take you to see some of your friends and then picks you up to bring you home, that is one thing.'

'Cyril stayed with us didn't he Mummy.'

'If he takes you to see his friends and stays there too, people will talk.'

'Let them.' Helena gave the soup a vicious stir.

Alice stood mute, her fingers in her mouth.

'If you don't stop that child sucking her fingers, her teeth will stick out.'

'She hasn't been well and she's missing Robert.'

'Surely she hardly knows him. Have you heard when he's coming home?'

'Sometime in about ten days, I'm not sure exactly when.'

'Umm, we'd better have lunch, I don't want to be late; Edgar will be expecting me.'

Once at the table, Helena let her soup go cold; soon after, Alice put her spoon down.

'Had enough,' she said.

'Nonsense,' said Mary, 'eat up or you will never be a big, strong girl. After lunch, you will have a nap.'

She spooned soup into Alice's mouth, took her upstairs and put her to bed.

'You will stay here while Mummy and I do some talking.'

Alice pulled a face, but said nothing.

When Mary returned, Helena was at the table. She'd eaten no more and was crying.

'What is the matter; has it anything to do with that young man?'

Helena nodded,'

Mary sighed, 'Does Robert know?'

'Not yet.'

'Do you intend to tell him when he comes home?'

Helena slumped forward and rested her head on her arms.

'What on earth were you thinking of?'

'Have you never made a mistake?'

Mary snorted with exasperation, 'Are you referring to your insistence on

marrying Robert? Heaven knows I tried to stop you doing that, as you well know.'

'I never wanted this to happen, but Robert has changed so much. Even when he comes home, he's distant as though he has no feelings left…I've been so lonely.'

'That is hardly justification for jumping into bed with the first man who catches your eye; and what of that poor child upstairs?'

'I've done my best; it's just the war, tearing us apart, I do love Robert really.'

'How do you think I manage with your step-father; he's not the easiest of men. Marriages have to be worked at.'

Helena raised her eyebrows. 'Really, you couldn't have been much good at that. After all, my father committed suicide, didn't he?'

Mary sat down and stared out of the window. The circumstances of Gilbert's death had been wrapped up in vague hints of mental instability. Such a tragedy, a talented man, she had certainly never discussed the dreadful truth of his suicide with his children or, for that matter, with anyone else. She could only assume one of the servants had said too much.

'That is hardly relevant to the present situation. It seems to me you have two choices, either you forget this whole business and be thankful you are not pregnant or you leave Robert for this other man. That leaves Alice.'

Mary waited while Helena dabbed at her face. 'I'm not going to do anything yet, not until Robert comes home. He's been away so long, in some ways I feel I hardly know him.'

Mary collected her belongings and walked to the door; there was nothing more to say.

Chapter 12

Mary Carlton felt utter despair, mention of Gilbert had opened an old wound. She had never thought it necessary to make allowances for her younger daughter's behaviour; perhaps she should have. Frances, her first born, was stable, successful and had a good relationship with Edgar: Matthew, her beloved son, had his faults, but none she couldn't forgive.

Who did Helena have? Mary wondered if her desire to please Edgar had blinded her to her daughter's needs. If so, now it was too late; Robert would not welcome an interfering mother-in-law. Perhaps, if she'd known her own mother, she would have done a better job. Acknowledgement of such feelings made her uncomfortable. Did Helena feel she wasn't loved enough, Mary hoped not.

If the worst came to the worst, she would give Helena an additional allowance from her own private income; at least she would be protected from financial problems. Helena had always been a romantic and wilful enough to marry on a whim. Would she be able to resolve the problems she had brought on herself? Only time would tell and what about Alice? It was all a mess with no satisfactory solution in the offing.

As Mary drove home, she relished the prospect of a civilised evening with Edgar. For once, in a long time, they would be able to dine early and spend the evening discussing his manuscript. She would see Cook as soon as she got home to arrange the dinner menu. Humming quietly to herself, she left the car on the drive for Bill to put away. The man had been a godsend; too old to be conscripted, he took on, with enthusiasm, every task he was given.

She went straight to see Cook and Susan, the maid; they were having a cup of tea. They both stood, with a clatter of crockery as Mary walked in.

'I've decided on the poached salmon for tonight, Cook, and then will you check with Bill for fresh vegetables. If there aren't any, I'll leave it to you.'

'Yes Ma'am.'

As Mary walked through the hall, she noticed a note on the table. It was a message from Edgar.

Mary,

I shall not be dining with you this evening; I have arranged to meet one of my researchers to discuss changes to the, manuscript.

I will have something at the club.

E.

Mary sighed and wandered into the drawing room. She sat down by the window and looked out at the garden; thanks to Bill, it looked magnificent. She was a fortunate woman; there were so many beautiful things around her, many of them antiques. Everything was well cared for, polished, gleaming. She had all money could buy and yet she felt lonely.

Looking back over her life, she had always been lonely. Now she was criticising Helena, but perhaps they had more in common than she cared to admit. She had never known her mother who died giving birth to her. Shunned by her father who blamed her for his wife's untimely death, Mary had learned, from an early age, to keep her feelings hidden. She had protected herself from hurt until she met Gilbert; how she'd loved him and yet she hadn't been enough.

Was she, in a different way, as impetuous as Helena, remarrying six months after Gilbert died? At the time she'd justified her decision on the grounds it was better to introduce a stepfather as soon as possible. Passion was dangerous; this time it was a marriage of minds, but perhaps what she needed, after all, was a man with passion. Was she enough for Edgar, was he enough for her?

She rang the bell for Joan.

'Yes Ma'am.'

'Cook to cancel the order for dinner; I shall be dining alone. Ask her to make up a tray, something light, for seven o'clock.'

'Yes, Ma'am.'

Mary closed her eyes; she'd been lucky to have a day off from the Information Centre where she was based. Barnes and Chiswick had been heavily bombed and hundreds of families lost everything. Organising the dispersal of furniture was what Mary enjoyed, it was constructive and the people she met were grateful for anything. It was after the raids when her heart ached. Distraught souls came to see if she or her colleagues had any news of missing loved ones.

The first time she took a young mother to the mortuary, to identify her grandmother's body, she had been haunted by the experience. She'd held the young woman in her arms and didn't feel embarrassed by such intimacy with a stranger. For a few moments she had been able to forget her own anxieties.

'I've no-one left now,' the young woman had said, 'who will care for my little boy while I work?'

That had been weeks ago. The last news of the poor woman and her baby was better than Mary had thought possible. People were still being evacuated from London and the pair had been sent off to Devon. Who knew what tragedy she would be dealing with tomorrow?

First Helena and then Edgar, perhaps her feelings of helplessness were caused by exhaustion. Perhaps Edgar was right and she should stop her voluntary work. It was the second time this week he'd absented himself without prior warning. In the past he had relied on her to do research for him; wasn't she good enough anymore? If she didn't work for the WVS, what would she do apart from rattle round the house?

She switched on the news and relaxed to the soothing voice of Alvar Lidell reading the headlines; none of it was good. Now V2s were coming across the Channel, powerful enough to obliterate London, when would it end? She picked at the food Cook had prepared and wondered if she should accept defeat too and have an early night. Getting into an empty bed would not help her anxiety. Finally, she could bear it no longer and went up to their bedroom.

At eleven thirty he still wasn't home. She wondered if he had had an accident, but was unwilling to phone his club; he loathed anything that smacked of prying. She got out of bed to stand by the window; the moon was a sliver of silver on a clear night. She shivered, pulled her dressing gown tighter and watched clouds darken the sky. She listened for the sound of planes, but all was still. At last, she saw the muted lights of a car as it turned into their drive. She was being entirely stupid, behaving like a love-sick maiden instead of an intelligent, mature woman. She hurried back into bed because she didn't want Edgar to think she had been checking up on him.

As he walked upstairs, she grabbed a book from her bedside table.

'I didn't expect you to be awake, dear. I hope I didn't disturb you?'

'Of course not; had a good day?'

'Busy, very busy, sorry I'm late, got into lengthy discussions with this researcher chap.'

59

Mary smiled, 'You look very tired; you're working too hard.'

'Thank you, my dear, you're right, all I want to do now is sleep.'

He undressed and got into bed, turned his back, and within minutes she heard his breathing settle. She wished she found sleep so easily.

Chapter 13

December 1944

Alice ran to the front door; someone was trying to open it. She stopped and stared when the door opened.

'Mummy, there's a soldier here,' she paused, 'are you Daddy?'

'Yes, sweetheart, I am.'

He bent down and held his arms wide; she ran to him, put her cheek against his.

Helena hurried out of the kitchen. Robert stood with Alice in his arms; he walked down the hallway and hugged her then kissed her gently; she could feel his body trembling. She gave a sob and rested her head on his shoulder.

'My darling girl, I've waited so long; I've dreamed of being here with you both.'

They stood together holding Alice between them. 'I can't believe how much she's grown since I last saw her, but she'll never be as beautiful as her mother.'

Alice wriggled and he put her down so she could investigate his kit bag.

'It must have been so hard, coping on your own.'

'The war can't go on for ever, can it?'

He didn't answer, but took Alice's hand, 'Come with me, I've brought you some presents.'

He handed her a package.

She pulled off the wrapping paper, 'Mummy look, it's a silver snake.' She held up the bracelet and then slid it on; it coiled round her arm three times, but fell off as soon as she moved.

'It's beautiful, look at all the carving and your name is written inside,

Alice. Shall we keep it for when you're a bit older? You don't want to lose it.'

Alice clutched it, 'How long will I have to wait?'

Helena and Robert laughed, 'Shall I get a box for you to keep it in?'

'Yes, please Daddy; that would be a good idea.'

'Your Daddy has lots of good ideas.'

Robert smiled and pulled three wooden camels from his rucksack; they were in a line, joined by silver chains.

'There are no buses in the desert, Alice; they have camel trains just like this.' He put the camels on the kitchen table and moved them along in little jumps, Alice clapped her hands.

'Can they have a little house to live in?'

'Couldn't they live in the box with the bracelet?'

'No, Mummy, camels don't live in boxes, do they?'

'Why don't we put them on the mantelpiece, you can take them for a walk each day.'

'Yes,' she turned to Helena, 'Daddy has lots of good ideas.'

Robert pulled out another small packet and handed it to Helena.

'We went to Alexandria, I got you this.' He handed her a golden filigree ring set with a small emerald. 'I hope it fits.'

Helena's eyes filled with tears as she slid the ring onto her finger.

'I've only got four days, but we are going to have a good time,' Robert said. 'You don't mind if we go round to see Mum and Dad later.'

Helena certainly didn't mind, this time, in fact she was pleased. All the attention would all be on Robert and his exploits. She would sit quietly in the corner and hope Gladys didn't notice anything. After Robert's leave, she wouldn't have to visit for a while except to drop-off Alice and pick her up, in the evening, when she finished work. By then she would have decided what she was going to do.

Alice shouted through her grandparents' letterbox. 'Look who's here, my Daddy's home.'

Gladys brushed away tears as she leaned against Robert and stroked his cheek.

'Oh, Son, thank God you're safe.'

Albert took Robert's hand in his; he couldn't speak.

'Daddy's safe 'cos I said my prayers, isn't he Mummy.'

Helena nodded.

'I've been promoted,' Robert said as soon as he walked into the sitting room, 'I'm a corporal now and if I keep my nose clean, I might make sergeant soon.'

Gladys beamed and bustled about making tea and fussing over Alice. Albert put his hand on her arm. 'Sit down Mother, you're making me dizzy.'

This was proper family life; Helena wished she felt more included. She had never felt comfortable with her step-father and now she couldn't be sure she would ever be regarded as a full member of Robert's family either, not if they knew what she'd done.

Together they walked home, little was said and Helena could tell Robert felt as nervous as she did, but for different reasons. For Helena there was the problem of comparison. It was one thing to feel unsatisfied by Robert's love-making when she had had no experience of another man. Things were different now. Cyril had introduced her to a sexual experience unlike anything she had ever known; she blamed him for that. He was an older man who knew what he was doing; it was not fair to make comparisons. What she'd done was wrong.

It wasn't just the baby; it was that she and Robert would be denied the chance to grow together after the war. Always in her mind there would be the memory of that night with Cyril. How could one night undermine and ridicule the intimacy she shared with the man she really loved for she did love Robert didn't she?

Once home, with Alice settled in her bed, Helena hurriedly undressed and put on an all-enveloping nightdress.

Robert smiled at her. 'You look like a little girl in that.'

He slipped into bed, in his pyjamas. 'My God, I've missed you.' He turned to kiss her and held her tight.

'It's been awful, all the bombing, we were lucky not to be hit.'

'Please God we're over the worst; I want you and Alice to be safe.' He smiled, 'We may even give her a brother or a sister one day.'

'She'd love having someone to play with.'

He stroked her hair then let his hand slide down her neck. He fumbled with the fastening on her nightdress then slipped his hand inside. Helena shivered; it was just what Cyril had done.

'I've waited so long, my darling.'

Helena kissed him hard on the lips and held him close. He tugged at her nightdress, pulled it up until it was bunched around her waist. He stroked her thighs while she lay still receiving his kisses, his hot breath on her cheek; she tried to push her anxiety away, willed her body to relax. She wanted to enjoy her reunion with this man who had gone through so much. She wanted to give him pleasure, but felt nothing. Perhaps it was because she was pregnant; perhaps it was how nature protected the unborn child. Could intercourse do damage? She knew so little about such things.

He undid the drawstring of his pyjamas and rolled on top of her. His body was hot with desire, it frightened her; she prayed he would not sense her lack of response.

'It's been so long, Robert.' She sobbed, put her cheek against his, pulled him closer.

In that moment, she knew what she must do. The child she was carrying should have been his, would have been his if it hadn't been for Cyril. It was his fault; he'd taken advantage of her. He'd got her drunk when he knew she wasn't used to alcohol. It was Robert who really loved her; he wanted to protect her and her children, their children. She would give him a son this time; if the baby seemed a bit early no-one need suspect anything.

Thank goodness she had not been able to phone Cyril; she wouldn't do that now. He would soon forget her; she must get rid of his address and phone number. She lay for a while listening to Robert gently snoring, she rolled over so she could cuddle his back. She wouldn't say anything to her mother yet. It was a relief to know that the subject need never be raised again by either of them. As long as she did not bring scandal to the family name or upset Edgar, Mother would go along with whatever she decided to do, no matter how much she disapproved.

It was unlikely Robert would be home again, for Christmas so he suggested they all celebrated early; it would be a surprise for Alice.

'Come on, darling child,' Robert said, 'we are going to see Grandpop and Nana this afternoon.'

Alice jumped up and down and ran to get her coat. Helena smiled, visits to the Warren's were usually tricky, but thankfully less daunting when she had Robert with her. Gladys always made Robert and Alice the centre of attention.

Connie, and her husband, John, were already there. He made a point of kissing Helena whenever they met. Was that why Connie did not attempt to be friends with her?

Gladys put her arms round Alice, 'You're going to have a surprise soon; Aunt Connie is going to give you a brand-new baby cousin.'

'Better late than never,' John said, 'we can't let you two have all the fun.' He slapped Robert on the shoulder.

'Great news, congratulations,' Robert said. 'I like a bit of competition,'

Alice leaned against her granddad's knee. 'Do you think I could have a baby of my own to play with?'

'Why not, once your Daddy is home for good. Which would you prefer, a brother or sister?'

Alice paused to think… 'Do you think I could have one of each?'

Albert roared with laughter. Helena, my girl, you're going to have your work cut out; this young lady reckons she should have a brother and a sister… at the same time.'

Alice clung to Albert's leg. 'One would do if that's best.'

Albert hoisted her onto his knee and kissed her. 'I'm sure Mummy and Daddy will do all they can.'

'Mummy says Daddy has to go away again soon,' Alice whispered.

'I know sweetheart,' he stroked her hair.

'Mummy was poorly while Daddy was away, but she'd better now.'

'I'm pleased to hear it. We can't have Mummy being poorly, so you've got to look after her.'

'Now come along ladies,' Gladys said, 'we can go to the kitchen and get tea ready while the men talk about things.'

'What things, Nana?'

'Never you mind,' Gladys said, 'you come along too, give us some help.'

'Monty did his stuff, son.'

'Yes, I don't like him, but he's a bloody good commanding officer.'

'How much longer will it go on?' John asked.

Robert shrugged. 'At least that bastard, Hitler, isn't having it all his own way.'

'Connie was scared silly the other day, one of those 'doodle-bugs' came over, she saw it. Wonder she didn't lose the baby. Thank God it was out of sight before the motor cut.'

Albert shook his head, 'Pity the poor sods it landed on.'

John turned to Robert, 'I don't deny you lot have had it bad, but it's been no picnic here. The buggers nearly wiped out the club a while back; lucky I wasn't on a late shift. Now they're sending even bigger stuff over.'

Robert and Albert stared at him.

'It's not my fault I failed the medical.'

Alice liked listening to the grown-ups and Nana let her put margarine on the slices of bread as Aunt Connie cut them. It made her feel grown up.

'I'd better get the knitting needles out,' Gladys said, 'would you like me to teach you to knit?'

Alice grinned, 'What can I make?'

'I think this baby would like a little scarf; that's nice and easy.'

Alice put her arms round Gladys' waist, 'I love you, Nana.'

Chapter 14

February 1945

The following day Robert and Helena took Alice to see Grandma Carlton for afternoon tea; Edgar was not there. The dining table had been set as spring weather had made it too cool to sit in the garden. An extra cushion was put on Alice's chair so she could reach. She stared at all the gleaming silver ornaments and sparkling glass. She touched the plate in front of her; it was so thin she feared she might break it. Tiny sandwiches, cut in triangles, with no crusts were offered by a young woman in a black uniform, with a small white pinafore. Alice tried to take two until she realised Grandma was not just watching her, she was frowning. After sandwiches they had cakes with crystallised fruit on top and biscuits which Cook had made.

Alice watched Grandma cut her cake into small pieces instead of biting into it. When Alice tried to do the same, the cake fell to bits and she was left with crumbs on the table as well as her plate. She decided it was nicer having tea with Grandpop and Nana even though the food wasn't so delicious.

The grown-ups talked, but it was all about the war. Alice waited, but no-one took any notice of her.

'Can I get down now, please, and play outside?'

'Alice, well-behaved, little girls do not ask to leave the table until everyone has finished eating. Now listen to what your Daddy is telling me.'

'Surely, Mother, the conversation is hardly suitable for a young child.'

Mary Carlton stared at Helena, but said nothing. Alice sighed; she would just have to be bored. She started picking at the lace edge on the starched white tablecloth until Helena put her hand over Alice's. Finally, the grown-ups had finished.

'Would you like Bill to show you round the garden?'

'Yes, please, Grandma.'

'You must be careful not to trample on any of the plants. If you ask nicely, he may let you have a cabbage to take home. In the spring you will be able to have some flowers.'

Alice grinned; perhaps Grandma wasn't so bad after all. She turned quickly and made for the door.

'Don't run, we don't want any accidents,' Mary called after her.

Alice liked Bill; when she was younger, he'd put her in his wheelbarrow and wheel her round the grounds.

'When are you coming to help me plant up the vegetables, young lady?'

'Can't we do it today?'

'Let's wait until next month.'

Alice nodded, 'Grandma said I could have a cabbage to take home.'

'Do you like cabbage?'

Alice nodded, 'Can I pick one?'

Together they walked round the garden. Bill had a sharp knife; he carefully sliced the stem and handed the cabbage to Alice. He took her hand and they walked down the side of the house.

'See here,' he pointed to stems with sprouts on them. 'How about some of these?'

'Fairy cabbages,' Alice said and wrinkled her nose, 'Not sure I like those much.'

'Oh, Alice, you don't know what you're missing. Feel how cold they are, they've had some frost and that makes them taste extra good.'

'Can I have just one stalk, please.'

Bill handed her the knife, and held her hand in his, 'Carefully now, cut the stem just there. You're a proper gardener now.'

Red cheeked and breathless, Alice rushed back to the house.

'Look, Mummy, these are for you.' She thrust both sprouts and cabbage into her lapthen rushed over to Mary, grabbed her hands and kissed her on the cheek. 'Thank you, Grandma, I've had a lovely time.'

'I'm glad to hear it, child.'

'Can I give some of the cabbage to my other grandma?'

Mary smiled, 'That would be very kind.'

The Underground was crowded and she had to sit on Helena's knee while Robert stood. When the doors opened, Alice turned to look out to the window. People were milling about, but few people wanted to get on the train. There were piles of blankets along each platform.

'It's very smelly, Mummy, it's not nice down here. Why don't they get on the train?'

'These poor people may not have anywhere else to go, but they are safe here if the naughty men fly over.'

Alice nodded and held her nose, 'Poo,' she said and giggled.

Walking down Redburn Street, at dusk, Robert and Helena had Alice between them and, holding a hand each, swung Alice up in the air until she squealed with delight.

'It is so good to hear her laugh; the only sounds I hear are from bombs or bullets.'

'Alice has never known peace, isn't that dreadful.'

'At least we're making progress once we get closer, we can hit 'em hard.'

'It's naughty to hit people – that's what Grandpop says.'

Helena and Robert looked at each other, but didn't reply.

Once Alice was in bed, Robert and Helena sat in the kitchen. Robert would be going back on the day after tomorrow, he didn't tell Helena where and she wasn't sure if it was for security or because he didn't know. She couldn't imagine what it was like for him to have no idea of what to expect from day to day. In some ways, she felt the same.

'I want to go to Mum and Dad tomorrow, spend some time there. I'll be packing up in a bit and I've no idea when I'll see them again.'

'Take Alice, let them have you both to themselves; I wouldn't mind. I should go to work anyway; they've let me have time off but…'

'Darling girl, I'm so lucky to have you. I'll tell you what, come to Mum and Dad when you finish work; Mum would love to cook us all a meal, a proper family do.'

'Well take round what's in the cupboard, I feel guilty eating their rations. You'd better take some of the cabbage and sprouts; Alice is determined to share them out.'

She stood and cleared away their tea cups. She felt his hand on her shoulder and then she was in his arms. If only they had more time, they would have grown together. If only he wasn't going away, if only she wasn't carrying another man's child. Tears spilled down her cheeks as she rested her head on his shoulder. He stroked her back and crooned soft words in her ear.

'Don't cry, my darling, I'll soon be back, just you wait. It's just one last push, that's all it will take; just think of the celebration we'll have when it's all over.'

'Let's go to bed.'

Robert laughed, 'I hope you don't make a habit of saying that.'

Helena shook her head and blushed as she took his hand; together they crept up the stairs.

Helena was exhausted after a hard day; the war might be lurching towards an end, but there was no reduction in the production at the munitions' factory. She knocked and waited and smiled as she heard Alice's voice.

'Mummy's here, Nana's teaching me to knit, see what I've done.'

Robert stood in the hallway, 'You look exhausted, get yourself in front of the fire.'

'Look, Mummy, it's growing.'

She held up a needle with wonky stitches on it.

'That's lovely, darling.'

'Nana says she'll teach you to knit if you like.'

This was family life as she had never known it, warm, cosy, no large rooms to feel lonely in. She sat down and slid her shoes off. Gladys handed her a cup of tea.

'I know we've had an early celebration of Christmas, but Robert will be away on the twenty fifth so we want you both to come to us for the real thing.' Albert Warren said, 'unless you have other plans… to see your own family that is.'

Helena smiled; what a good man he was. 'That'd be lovely, but I'm trying not to have Alice out in the evenings too much; she hasn't got a very strong chest.'

'We've thought of that haven't we Mother. We've talked it over with John and Connie; she will be dropped off first and then he'll come to collect you both.'

Helena felt her skin crawl. She dared not say why she disliked John so much; it would only cause trouble.

'We've got to look after our grandchildren and their mothers,' Albert said.

'Soon enough we'll have two grandchildren,' Gladys smiled.

The following morning, early, Robert left. Alice cried and clung to him. Helena had watched as he walked away along Redburn Street, his army boots echoing a tattoo which sounded like a dead march. Whatever happened, she wanted him to come back.

Chapter 15

March 1945

After weeks of unrelenting morning sickness, Helena and Alice walked round to Peabody Buildings; it was Sunday so, of course, they were expected. Today must be the day; she must not wait any longer. She walked into their sitting room, sat down and took a deep breath.

'I don't want to get your hopes up, but I just might be expecting. It's a bit early to tell; perhaps I should give it another month. I haven't written to Robert yet; I want to be sure.'

Albert laughed, 'Wonderful, news, the more the merrier, isn't that right Mother?'

Gladys smiled and pulled Alice on to her lap, 'You're going to have a little brother or sister, won't that be nice.'

'And a cousin too?'

Everyone laughed and Helena felt a warm glow of contentment, she was doing the right thing; she would make everyone happy. Robert had already said he wanted another child. After careful calculation, her baby would be due soon after John and Connie's. She didn't tell Gladys and Albert that; it wouldn't match with when Robert was on leave. Provided the baby didn't come early, everything would be fine.

Sometimes she felt anxious about Cyril and wondered if she should contact him to say she had had a miscarriage, but that would be wrong and might tempt fate. She must not deny the existence of the child she was carrying. It would be best to do nothing; she would never see him again and Alice would soon forget about their trip to the country.

'You are very kind to me,' Helena said, 'perhaps next Christmas Robert will be home so we can all be together.'

Life settled into a comfortable routine; months slid by and summer weather lifted Helena's spirits. Loving letters from Robert arrived regularly; they comforted her. Two weeks either side of the due date wasn't unusual so if she took things easily, she might be overdue as she had been with Alice. Ten days late and everything would be fine as long as the baby wasn't too big.

The weather had been harsh after Christmas with icy roads and pavements so Helena stopped working at the munitions factory earlier than she'd planned. Gladys and Albert arranged for John to collect her and Alice each Sunday. She felt at peace with herself and looked forward to Robert's next leave. Somehow, they would make a go of it; she owed it to Robert.

News of the war had fluctuated so much she'd given up reading the newspaper. The horror of Belsen and the German's attack in the Ardennes had left her in despair. Her father, Gilbert, was German; was that why he killed himself, did he know what was going to happen? Did she have the right to bring another innocent child into the world? Wouldn't they all be better off dead?

She had watched as spring brought new life to the gardens on the Embankment where she and Alice walked most afternoons. Soft air had stroked her skin, enabled her to rise out of the darkness and bloom with life after so much death and destruction. The bombing had stopped; everyone she met looked relieved and cheerful. Spring winds tugged at her coat, but Robert would be home soon and all would be well.

Mary wasn't looking forward to her visit; there was no telling what Helena would have decided to do. How on earth could her two daughters be so different? Frances had never caused the slightest concern and if Helena had an ounce of common sense none of this mess would have happened. She hoped Alice would be having her afternoon rest by the time she got there. At least then they could talk about her plans.

'I've told Robert and his parents…'

'What exactly have you told them?'

'That I'm pregnant.'

Mary raised her eyebrows, 'I see.'

'So, they think it's Robert's.'

'Yes, well it seemed….'

Mary raised her hand, 'All I hoped for each of my children was a contented and successful life with a suitable partner. I didn't want any of you to have the kind of solitary existence I had to endure, brought up by servants. You must do what you think is best; I can't be involved directly.'

'I suppose Edgar wouldn't like it…'

'I don't like it. Accept you may find yourself alone with Alice, if things don't go as you hope, also accept that this baby's father may disappear. I would never see you homeless so I am willing to make financial provision for you, should you need it.'

Helena put her hand to her mouth; her mother was right about Cyril. She wouldn't be able to rely on him if things went wrong with Robert. Mary stood to leave and Helena knew the matter would never be discussed again.

'Just think, Mother two new little souls come September,' Albert said.

'Looking at the size of her, it makes me wonder if they've got the dates wrong. She shouldn't be showing this early.'

'Can't be, we know when Robert came home.'

'Umm,' said Gladys, 'You know Freda's girl, next door but two, she saw Helena out one night with a man.'

'You never told me.'

'You'd have said I was imagining things.'

'Well, let's not jump to any conclusions, perhaps it was her brother.'

Chapter 16

Tuesday 8th May 1945

Mary had listened to the wireless all day; finally the war was over. Churchill had spoken to the nation as only he could, praising all the servicemen and women, but reminding them the battle would not be finally won until Japan was subdued. Her heart ached for the dead and wounded, the families shattered, including her own.

She wondered if Helena had heard from Robert. The last mention of the Eighth Army had been the previous Wednesday when British troops entered Venice. Mary had said a silent prayer for Robert's safety, for Alice's sake. There had been no recent news from Matthew other than the report of his submarine, 'Tapir', sinking a German submarine off Bergen, Norway. That was a month ago and she'd heard nothing.

Frances rang and held the phone to her office window so Mary could hear the church bells and cheering of the munition workers. Edgar would be sailing to American in the autumn; at least she need not worry about his ship being attacked.

There was to be a victory parade on Thursday through the centre of London; perhaps she and Frances should go, take part in the rejoicing. Both of them had done war work and there would be plenty for the WVS still to do after the war ended. Mary felt she was emerging from a long dark tunnel. There was work to do, help the homeless, distribute clothes, furniture, make families whole again. But first there must be a general election.

Edgar sat in his favourite armchair; his eyes were closed. Mary watched him; he was tired all the time.

'Isn't the news heartening, my dear?'

Edgar shook his head, 'The fighting is over in Europe, but the country is bankrupt. That is the price of victory, Mary. Rationing will go on for years.'

'We are so lucky we can manage, but what about people with nothing.'

Edgar shrugged. 'Now the Lease-Lend agreement has been cancelled, most of what we grow will have to be sold to pay for imports we can't grow.'

'I must have a word with Bill, see if we can increase what we grow and distribute it to the needy.'

'I admire your generosity, but what we produce is a drop in the ocean.'

Helena heard from Robert; he was now in Austria, working as an intelligence officer.

Darling Helena,

How are you, Alice and the bump?

There is so much to do here; so many men sucked into the web Hitler created. Most of them had no say in what atrocities they were a part off. I'm sorry for many of them, but it's the top men who deserve everything they get. I'm

working flat out to identify the buggers.

Enough of that, you and our children are what matter. I hope you are taking good cares of yourself with plenty of rest.

I hope to be back soon.

Love and hugs to you and Alice. I can hardly wait for the next member of the family to arrive.

Yours always, darling

XXXX

Alice was excited; Nana had made her a special dress. It looked like a Union Jack. For weeks she had hunted down pieces of material in red, white and blue. Friends and neighbours had been recruited until enough had been made to produce what Alice called 'Her Union Jack Dress'. There was to be a party in the area where families dried their washing. All the children made decorations which were hung from the washing lines. Excitement made Alice giddy. She spent more time with Grandpop and Nana because her Mummy needed more rest.

On the day of the party, the sun was shining; it was an omen. Her Daddy would be coming home soon and it wouldn't be long before Mummy's baby come to see her.

'Guess what, Alice; someone from the newspaper is coming to take some photos. Shall we put you in the middle of all the children as you have such a special dress?'

'Yes, please, can we send it to Daddy?'

'We'll buy the paper when it comes out and save the picture for when Daddy gets home.'

Alice clapped her hands and raced onto their balcony. 'All the tables are out ready for the party, should we go down?'

'Let's help Nana with the sandwiches first. You can help me carry them down.'

'When's Mummy coming?'

'She'll be here soon; Uncle John and Aunt Connie are picking her up.'

'I wish Daddy was here.'

'I know, sweetheart, but at least he's safe. We don't have to worry about those nasty men anymore.'

Chapter 17

September 1945

Helena woke with a start; the pain of her womb contracting was unmistakeable. She lay very still and watched the clock; she needed to know how often the contractions were coming. She had been so careful and now was a week after her proper due date; she smiled and whispered a silent prayer of gratitude. The threatened induction, which would have given the game away, would not be necessary.

It was early in the morning, but not too early to ask her neighbour to call the midwife. She checked Alice was asleep then crept downstairs and was relieved to see lights on at her neighbour's house; someone was up and about. Helena leaned against the door and waited for another contraction to release its grip.

'I've gone into labour, Betty, would you let the midwife know, please.'

'Not a day too soon, I reckon that's a big, bouncing boy you've got there.'

Helena shuddered, was the baby going to be too big?

'I'll send my lad round to her house.' She hurried indoors and Helena leaned against the wall as Betty's son, still clutching a slab of bread and jam, hurried away down the road.

'Do you want me to call anyone to be with you?'

Helena paused. She didn't want Gladys to come round, not yet.

'Would you mind calling my mother?'

Betty nodded, 'I'll have Alice, if you like, until your Mum arrives.'

'She hasn't had any breakfast.'

'Don't worry about that.'

The contractions were coming quicker and stronger; Helena prayed the midwife would arrive soon; everything was happening too fast. Would she be left to deliver the baby by herself?

'Come on now,' Betty said, 'I'll walk back with you, we don't want this baby born on the street, do we.'

As Helena opened the front door, she could hear Alice crying.

'Mummy, Mummy, I couldn't find you.' She clutched at Helena's legs, 'I didn't know where you'd gone.'

'Let me make that call to your mum,' Betty said and hurried away to the phone box.

'I want you to be a big girl and stay with Betty for a little while until Grandma gets here.'

'I want to stay with you.'

Helena stroked Alice's hair, 'You know Mummy's got a baby in her tummy.'

Alice nodded.

'Well, sweetheart, that baby wants to come out now, to say hello.'

'He can't say hello to me if I'm at Grandma Carlton's, can he?'

There was the sound of hurrying feet in the hallway.

'I've rung her,' Betty said, 'She said something about going to Cambridge with your step-father, but when I explained, she said she'd be over as soon as she could get things sorted out.'

'I don't want to go to Grandma Carlton's.'

'Come on now, Alice, you don't want to upset Mummy, you can stay with me for now. I'll get you some breakfast, you must be hungry.'

'The pains are getting stronger.'

Betty's took Alice's hand, 'Come on sweetheart, you can see Mummy later.'

As they left the house, the midwife arrived.

'Are we glad to see you,' Betty turned to Alice, 'This is the nice lady who will look after your mummy.'

'Good,' said Alice, 'when can I see my new baby brother?'

'What if it isn't a baby boy?'

Alice pulled a face, 'I think my Mummy and Daddy want a little boy.'

Betty smiled, 'And will you help Mummy look after him?'

Alice nodded.

'Hello, little'un, what are you doing here?'

Alice put her fingers in her mouth and twiddled her hair with her other hand.

'She's come to stay with us for a little while until her grandmother comes to pick her up.' She turned to Alice, 'Now you know who this is, he's my husband, but you can call him Uncle Bob if you like. I'm going to get you some breakfast.'

Alice nodded. She didn't want to wait for Grandma; she wanted to stay with Grandpop and Nana. After she'd eaten, when Bob and Betty weren't watching, she slipped out of the room and tiptoed up the hall. She could just reach the doorknob to let herself out and ran home. The door was shut, but she could hear shouting, it was Mummy. The lady she'd seen was supposed to be helping Mummy not hurting her. Alice banged on the door with her fists.

'Let me in, I want my Mummy, you're hurting my Mummy.' She kicked at the door; she was frightened, perhaps Mummy was frightened too. At that moment Betty came running towards her.

'Sweetheart, what are you doing?'

'I want my Mummy.'

They both turned to see a car draw up; Mary Carlton got out.

'A nasty lady's hurting Mummy.' Alice grabbed Mary's hand, 'Help my mummy.'

'Now come along, child, there is no need for all this fuss. You need to blow your nose and wipe your face, where's your handkerchief?'

'Someone's hurting Mummy.'

Then there was silence, finally broken by the wailing of a new-born baby.

Alice ran to Betty, 'Has my little brother come to see me?'

'There you are, Alice, your new baby has arrived, safe and sound.'

'Can I see him?'

Betty gave Alice a hug then turned to Mary. 'Will everything be all right now?'

'I hope so, I'm so glad I got here in time.' She took Alice's hand in hers, 'Shall we go to see this baby of yours?'

Alice nodded. Mary paused on the steps to the front door, 'Thank you for all your help; you have been very kind.'

'Well, you know where I am if you need anything.'

Helena lay back on the pillows cradling her son. She examined his face and tried to remember what Alice had looked like when she was born. Robert had said all babies looked like Mussolini. At the time, she thought it a tactless thing to say, but typical of him. She stroked her son's head which was covered with a fine, fair down. Alice had been born bald and remained so for many months. The baby had much fairer skin than Alice, it made Helena feel uneasy.

'All I need to do now,' the midwife said, 'is to weigh this young man. Then we can wash and dress him.'

Once on the scales, the baby yelled his displeasure.

'Good pair of lungs there,' the midwife said, 'and he's just short of nine pounds, Mother. It's a good job you didn't wait any longer to have him.'

Alice had been seven pounds and one ounce; how could Helena explain the difference; weren't babies usually the same size? She knew so little, in weight particularly; he should be smaller. She started to cry, exhausted by it all.

'Would he have been much lighter if he had been born two weeks earlier?'

'Oh, yes, all babies do in the last month is put on weight.'

The midwife tickled the baby under the chin and smiled at him.

'Better get you dressed young man; I think there are people waiting to see you.'

She fingered the tiny garments that had been laid out; hand-knitted vest, flannelette nightdress with an embroidered yoke, hand-knitted cardigan, bootees and mittens.

'You've been busy.'

'It's not me; it's my mother-in-law.'

'How lovely, wish I'd had a mother-in-law as handy as that.'

Helena smiled, but said nothing.

Once mother and baby were settled, the midwife packed away her things, 'I'll let your visitors in and check who will be staying with you. I'll call back later this evening.'

Helena listened to the sound of feet hurrying up the stairs. Alice hurtled into the room and jumped on the bed.

'Careful, my darling,' Helena said, 'you'll knock us both over.'

'Mummy, Mummy, why were you making that noise? I could hear you outside, but no-one would let me in, Mummy, I was frightened.'

'Sssh, everything is fine now. Why don't you say hello to your little brother?'

'What are we going to call him?'

'Shall we wait until Daddy comes home?'

Alice nodded and took hold of the baby's hand. 'Mummy, look he's holding my finger.'

Helena was aware of Mary standing in the doorway; her face gave away nothing; at least she couldn't say much, not in front of Alice.

'He looks a fine chap,' Mary said, 'Now we need to sort out arrangements for the next few days.'

'Alice could stay with you, couldn't she?'

'Unfortunately, that will not be possible; I have planned to join Edgar in Cambridge tomorrow. I should have gone with him today so I'm hoping to drive down early in the morning once we have got you and Alice settled. I suggest Susan comes over for a few days, to keep an eye on you both.'

'Can't I go to Grandpop and Nana, please?'

'I think that would be much the best arrangement, she would be nearer to you and I'm sure she wants to spend time with you and the baby.'

Helena smiled, as always, Mother was right; it was the best arrangement.

'Alice, I want you to go to get your bed things and a change of clothing. I will take you to your grandparents once I'm sure Mummy and baby are settled.'

Alice rushed out of the room.

'She seems to get on well with Robert's parents.'

'They are very good to her, Mother, but she's fond of you too.'

Mary raised her eyebrows. 'One can only hope they don't spoil her too much.'

Alice rushed back into the room with an armful of clothes and her toy rabbit, Benjy.

'There's a small case under the bed, Mother.' Helena said.

'I want you to fold everything neatly and put it in here,' Mary said as she dusted the case with her handkerchief. 'Then you can kiss your Mummy and wait downstairs for me.'

The two women listened to Alice clatter down stairs. Mary leaned over to stroke the baby's head while Helena held her breath and waited.

'What are you going to do?'

'Nothing.'

'Isn't he too big to pass off as an early birth?'

'I won't discuss it.'

Mary shrugged. 'I'll thank Betty properly for her help and ask if she will keep an eye on you. You need to inform Robert of developments or are you just going to present this child to him when he does get home.'

Helena closed her eyes, but it didn't stop her tears.

Mary and Alice arrived at Peabody Buildings; Mary had not been there before, in fact, she had never been introduced to Robert's parents. She held Alice's hand as they climbed two flights of not very clean, concrete stairs.

'You can see Grandpop's budgie, he's called Joey.' Alice said. She wriggled her hand free from Mary's and ran along the balcony to number eighty-four. She banged on the door and shouted through the letterbox. 'Nana, Nana, I've got a new baby brother.'

The door opened as Mary reached it. 'I'm sorry to call unannounced,

I'm Helena's mother.'

'Is it right? Helena's had the baby already?'

'Yes, earlier this afternoon, a boy.'

Gladys Warren put her hand to her throat, 'I didn't think it was due just yet.'

'The midwife seems to think all is well.'

Gladys nodded, 'I'm sorry, leaving you standing here, come in, please.'

Mary watched the diminutive woman hurry up the hallway. This was going to be difficult. Whatever the difference in their origins, Mrs Warren had the high moral ground as far as Helena was concerned; awkward questions were going to be asked.

'This is my husband, Albert,' Gladys said, as Mary walked into a small, overcrowded sitting-room. Albert grasped Mary's hand, 'I believe you are the bringer of good news.'

Mary smiled, Mrs Warren might be prickly, but Albert wore a most attractive, welcoming smile; perhaps Robert took after his father.

'Would you care for a cup of tea, Mrs Carlton?' Gladys asked.

'Thank you, no, unfortunately I must get home… I wanted to bring you the news and sort out arrangements for Alice.'

'Which hospital is Helena in?' 'She's at home, she was delivered at home.'

'But the baby must be very small.'

'I do assure you everything seems to have gone to plan. Would it be possible for you to call for yourself, put your mind at rest? I can drive you over there if you like.'

'Thank you, you're very kind, but our son-in-law will take us over later.'

'I can make arrangements for our maid, Susan, to stay with Helena for a few days until she is strong enough to manage on her own.'

'I'm sure there is no need for that, thank you. Now then, Alice, say goodbye to your grandmother; give her a kiss.'

Mary smiled to herself as the front door was closed behind her. She had never been dismissed in such a peremptory manner; Mrs Warren was a force to contend with. She drove home and repacked her suitcases. Would there be time to drive to Cambridge tonight; she'd probably miss the award ceremony, but at least she'd be there.

'I'm going over tonight, Dad.' Gladys said. 'Are you coming?'

Albert shook his head. 'I want to see the baby as much as you do, but I don't think we should all crowd round so soon after the birth; Helena is bound to be exhausted.'

'I'll get John to drive me over.'

'Why not give it a day or two?'

'I want to see this baby.'

'We all do, but John will be tired after work. He's on his feet all day, are you being fair to him?'

'I'm going with or without John.'

Albert sighed, once Gladys made up her mind, there was no shifting her. She was determined to find trouble, and in this instance, Albert feared there was something to find.

'I didn't think Helena's baby was due until after ours,' John said.

'It wasn't.'

Gladys clutched her handbag and stared out of the window. She had no intention of discussing anything with John. When they arrived, the front door was on the latch. Gladys called upstairs, but there was no reply.

'Put the kettle on, John, I'll go upstairs to see what's happening.'

Gladys found Helena asleep with the baby in his crib beside her bed. She lifted the crib blanket and stared, this was a full-term baby and a large one at that. She clung to the crib; her feelings were a mix of exultation and fear. She had been right to have suspicions, but how would Robert react? Since he had been in the army he had changed and there were times when his anger made her afraid. She had longed for a little boy to spoil, not just for her, but for Albert too.

'I've made a pot of tea so do you both want a cup?' John shouted from the kitchen.

Helena woke with a start, and the two women stared at each other. Helena looked at her watch. 'The midwife will be here soon,' she said.

'Good,' said Gladys, 'John drove me over, now do you want a cup of tea or not.'

'Yes, please.'

'We've got some talking to do.'

'I'm too tired to talk now, but isn't it wonderful that he's such a good size even though he came earlier than expected.'

Gladys opened her mouth, but no words came; she hadn't expected that.

'Here you are, ladies. As no-one answered, I've brought you both a cup.

How's the little mother, then?' He grinned at Helena and glanced into the crib. 'He's a fine-looking lad, just like his mum.'

'You might as well wait downstairs, John; the midwife will be here soon. Thanks for the tea.' Gladys said to his retreating back.

'You don't have to wait, Mum, the neighbour said she'd pop in once the midwife has been and my mother's maid it coming to stay for a while.'

'I'll wait.'

As Gladys sipped her tea; she could prove nothing. Robert had been very cool when she suggested, in a recent letter, that Helena was not all he thought she was. He would be home in a month, perhaps it would be best to bide her time.

'While we're waiting for the midwife, I'll fetch some more clothes for Alice.'

The sound of footsteps on the stairs brought Gladys back into the bedroom.

'Now, Mrs Warren, how are you feeling?'

Gladys watched while the midwife examined Helena and checked the baby. He squawked when he was lifted out of his cot.

'Have you fed him yet?'

Helena nodded.

'No problems there?'

'No, but he's sleepy, just like Alice was.'

The midwife smiled, 'Big babies can sometimes be a bit dozy, be thankful he didn't wait any longer. I suppose you're the proud grandmother.'

'He's certainly a fine fellow,' Gladys said. 'We didn't expect him to be so big.'

'Oh? Well, according to the notes, he's nearly two weeks overdue.'

Chapter 18

September 1945

Mary Carlton took Susan to Chelsea, the following day. Regardless of what Gladys had said, the maid would stay for a week after which, Mary would need her at home.

Helena sent a letter to Robert which would be forwarded to his unit, somewhere in Europe, to inform him of the baby's arrival. Two days later Susan rushed up stairs.

'The post has come; it's for you, from the military.'

Helena grabbed the letter and ripped it open. 'He's on his way; compassionate leave!'

She leapt out of bed and hugged Susan.

'How wonderful, how can we celebrate?'

Helena laughed, I haven't used up all my rations for this week, take the coupons and see what you can get.'

Helena sat back in bed, she felt so happy it hurt; nothing could harm her or her baby now. The episode with Cyril had faded until it seemed no more than a dream. Her future was with Robert, Alice and the baby. She would take no notice of what the midwife had said in front of Gladys. Robert would believe her, he loved her. However, in the middle of the night, when she sat up in bed to feed her wailing son, fear ran an icy finger down her spine. In the bleak early hours, she stroked his head and rocked him, whispered words of comfort, as much to herself as to him. Did she have the chance of a happy future? As she lay in the dark, her inner voice warned her something awful would happen.

With morning light, Alice climbed into bed with her, they both listened to the baby snuffling and making mewing noises like a kitten;

only then did she feel at peace.

'Your daddy will be home soon.'

Alice squealed with delight.

'I love you Mummy and I love Daddy and I love my little brother, will he have a name soon?'

'Yes, sweetheart, you can help us choose.'

Her world was complete, how silly she was to worry. There was nothing to fear.

Robert strode up the road, now he had a son, a boy for his mother to make a fuss of. This would be his way of giving her someone special to love, make up for the babies she had lost, before he was born. Stephen, the boy would be called Stephen, a noble name, Stephen Albert Warren, it had a ring to it.

He opened the front door, 'Helena, Alice, I'm home.'

A young woman came out of the kitchen. She smiled, 'Welcome home Mr Robert, Madam sent me over to stay until you came home.'

Robert grinned at her, 'Where is my son and heir?'

'Upstairs, with your wife, they're having a rest. Alice is with your parents, her Uncle John came over to get her.'

Robert bounded up the stairs, two at a time. He burst into the bedroom, but was stopped in his tracks by the sight of Helena, her body curved around the baby. He was encircled by her arms, protected, safe. Both were asleep, he with his arms above his head, his fists curled and his head turned towards his mother's breast. He made little sucking movements with his lips. Robert touched the baby's cheek with his forefinger and watched as he opened his eyes. Helena stirred when Robert sat on the bed.

'I am so proud of you, my darling girl.' He kissed her and then bent to kiss the baby on the forehead. 'We'll have such good times together, you and me and our beautiful children. I'll teach him to play chess and cricket; we'll go everywhere together. Mum and Dad must be overjoyed.'

Helena picked up the baby and handed him to Robert.

'Give your son a cuddle.'

Susan knocked on the door, 'I thought you would like a cup of tea,' she said and walked in carrying a tray. 'The midwife will be here in about an hour.'

'Does she come every day?'

Helena nodded. 'But not for much longer. Everything is going so well, isn't it Susan; we women have managed beautifully.' She grabbed Robert's hand and kissed it

'Send the midwife up as soon as she does come, please.'

Susan nodded and left.

Robert stroked the baby's head, 'He's very fair-haired isn't he, not like Alice.'

'It will probably be darker when his proper hair comes through. I'm so glad you're here.'

'Once I've washed and changed, I'll collect Alice, shall I?'

'You'd better; she's desperate to see you.'

'Perhaps I'd better wait until the midwife arrives; I want to make sure she tells me all I need to know. I've got to look after my wife and children properly.'

'We must decide on a name, I told Alice she could help us choose.'

'I thought Stephen and Albert after my dad.'

'That's a good idea,' Helena said, 'my mother had a brother called Stephen; it was so sad, he died in the First World War.'

'We'll try to wangle it so Alice thinks she has done the choosing.'

'Then go straight away, I'll be fine. You can always see the midwife tomorrow.'

'Have you any idea how much I love you?'

Helena squeezed his hand, 'Go on, off you go, bring our little girl home.'

'I'll be quick, as quick as I can; I don't want to miss the midwife.'

He opened the front door of his parents' maisonette and Alice rushed to meet him. She gripped him round the legs so he couldn't walk.

'Daddy, Daddy, you're home.'

Gladys and Albert stood in the hallway.

'What do you think of your grandson?'

'Dad hasn't been round yet, not been so good.'

'I'm sorry to hear it Dad; I'll bring him round here as soon as the midwife agrees,' Robert said, 'He's a fine specimen isn't he, Mum?'

'Well, he's certainly a good size,' Gladys said.

'Cooee, Mrs Warren.'

'Hello Sister, do come in.'

'You're looking like the cat that's got the cream.'

'My husband's home, he's gone to get Alice.'

'Wonderful, that's the tonic all my new mothers need.'

Helena nodded, 'You know I've been wondering, as everything is fine and now Robert's home is there any need for you to call every day?

'It's only five days since the birth. Mind you he has gained his birth-weight already and a bit besides. '

'So, you'll leave it to us then, you see Robert wants to be in charge and do everything himself.'

'Well don't be surprised if that doesn't last, men soon get tired of dirty nappies.'

'I promise I'll call you if there is a problem.'

'I want to see you at the clinic next week just to check all is well.'

'I promise.'

Robert and Alice were walking up the road as the midwife cycled towards them.

'You run ahead, Alice, I just want to check with the nurse that Mummy's all right.'

The midwife stopped. 'You must be Mr Warren; your wife is so pleased to have you home. In fact, she tells me you want to do me out of a job.'

Robert frowned.

'She said she can do without me now as you want to take charge.'

'Is that wise, Sister, don't you have to keep a special eye on premature babies?'

'Whatever makes you think your son is premature? If anything, he was overdue. Doctor was going to inducing labour if nothing happened soon.'

Robert felt colour drain from his face, what the hell was going on?

'Thank you, Sister,' he said and walked slowly back to his house.

Alice came clattering downstairs, 'Mummy's feeding my little brother; she says can she have a glass of water, please.'

His mother has hinted that something had been going on and he had dismissed it. What if she were right? It seemed there was a discrepancy of best part of a month. What was he going to do? The most important thing was to get Alice out of the way as soon as possible; he'd take her back to his parents this evening, find out what Mother knew.

Chapter 19

September 1945

Helena got out of bed, changed Stephen's nappy and put him back in his crib.

'Mummy can I help you change his nappy next time?'

Helena nodded.

'When will he have a name?'

'Soon, darling.'

'Shall I ask Daddy?'

She must wait for him in the bedroom; his face would show if Gladys had said anything. She got back into bed and rocked the crib while Alice sat on the bed beside her. Whatever else was going on, she must not show she had anything to hide.

She listened to Robert walk upstairs and held her breath. He placed a glass of water on the bedside table.

'I think it would be best if I took Alice back to my parents tonight, we have a lot of talking to do.'

'No, Daddy, I want to stay here, with you and Mummy.'

Robert tried to pick her up, but she threw herself on the floor and wriggled under the bed. He grabbed her legs and tried to ease her out, but she screamed so loudly she woke the baby. 'I want to stay here, it's not fair.' She burst into tears.

Robert grabbed her and held her in his arms; he rocked her until she was calm.

'You know Grandpop hasn't been too well.'

Alice nodded.

'Well Nana asked me if you would go and help her because she's getting old and can't manage on her own. I thought you might like to do that.'

Alice looked at Helena who was soothing the baby.

'I think it would be very kind of you to help Nana. We can decide on the baby's name when you come back, 'Can't we, Daddy?'

Robert didn't reply and she watched in silence as he left the room, taking Alice with him. She felt sick. Stephen, now settled and asleep, was such a beautiful baby, but what trouble his existence would cause. Robert would never accept him, she knew that. If he was prepared for them to stay together, he would make her life unbearable. If they didn't stay together, where could she go? Her mother would, be obliged to put Edgar first and there was no-one else. She lay back on the pillows too numb to cry

When Robert and Alice arrived at Peabody Buildings, John was there.

'Do me a favour will you, John, take Alice out for an hour, she could do with some fresh air. I need to speak to Mum and Dad.'

John raised his eyebrows then turned to Alice, 'Come here my lovely little niece, let's go and have some fun.'

Robert waited until he heard the front door shut.

'What's been going on Mum?'

Albert rested his hand on Robert's arm, 'Don't let's get upset about anything yet.'

'No Dad,' Gladys said, 'you may be willing to sweep things under the carpet, but I'm not, it isn't fair to our boy.'

'I spoke to the midwife today; she told me the baby was at least two weeks overdue.'

Gladys glanced at Albert, but said nothing.

'By my reckoning that means he was due at the beginning of October. When I came home last time, she must have been pregnant already.'

Silence clogged the air. Albert leaned back in his chair and closed his eyes; Robert put his head in his hands.

'What are you going to do, son?'

'I don't know, I really don't know; she's spoiled everything.'

Helena walked down stairs slowly. She would go to the kitchen, make a meal. Robert hadn't said what time he would be back, but at least she could prepare things, ready for cooking. She walked into the kitchen, but her legs were shaking so much she had to sit at the table. She rested her head on her arms, too weary to think straight.

She woke with a start, when the front door slammed, and hurried to the sink to fill the kettle; she must behave as though everything was normal. Robert stood in the kitchen doorway, the expression on his face made any pretence on her part pointless. She had always told him he had beautiful eyes, but now they stripped her mind bare as though he could see inside her head.

There would be no excuses, he would have no compassion; she had made a fool of him and must pay the price; there was nothing left.

'How long did you think you would be able to deceive me?'

Helena wished he would hit her, anything to discharge the tension that crackled between them.

'How long?' he repeated and she noticed his hands were shaking.'You are a tart, a trollop, a fornicator. And what is worse, you used my parents to look after Alice so you could go out and open your legs for anything in a uniform.'

'No, it wasn't like that.'

'You were seen. One of Mum's neighbours said her daughter saw you out at some music club.'

'That was with Matthew, he's my brother, in case you've forgotten. It was the last time he was on leave.'

Robert pointed to the ceiling, 'So where exactly did he come from?'

'I was so lonely and scared and I had no-one to turn to. The rocket attacks, night after night, I was terrified.'

'You could have turned to my parents.'

'No, Robert, I couldn't. Your mother has never liked me and when you aren't here she makes her feelings very clear.'

'She warned me and I didn't believe her, I can't even be sure Alice is mine.'

'How can you be so cruel? Of course, she is yours, she looks like you; you know that.'

'Don't you think I've had opportunities; I thought you were worth waiting for.'

'Once, Robert, once, he got me drunk; I didn't know what I was doing.'

'So that makes it alright, does it?'

Helena shook her head, 'No nothing's alright; It never will be.'

They stood as far apart as the small kitchen would allow and listened as seconds ticked away.

'What are we going to do?' Helena asked.

'More to the point, what is the father of your son going to do?'

'He doesn't know I've had the baby.'

'Really… incidentally who is this man who's managed to wreck my life?'

'Cyril… can't remember his other name…..'

'So where did you meet, on a street corner.'

Helena thought her head would explode; she screamed again and again until Robert slapped her. She held out her arms to him, 'Please, Robert, please, no-one need know.'

'I'm not prepared to live a lie. I thought I had a son, but I don't and I can't make-believe.' He turned and left the house, slamming the door behind him.

Rain beat down, washed pavements and turned gutters into rivers; wind lashed into Robert until his face streamed with raindrops and tears. He put his collar up and bowed his head. He should have put his trench coat on; he'd lost track of time, but he must have been walking for hours and it was dark. The streets were deserted and anyone with sense was at home in front of a roaring fire. At least Alice was safe and warm and asleep in bed. She was the only one who mattered now. He would go to his parents because he had to talk to someone. He opened his parents' front door and walked into the living room. It was in darkness; his parents were in bed.

'Who is it?'

'It's only me, Dad, go back to sleep.'

He heard footsteps on the stairs; Gladys hurried in.

'Oh! Son, where have you been, you'll catch your death. Take your jacket off, sit by the fire, I'll stoke it up, it won't take long.'

Robert listened to his father's laboured breathing as he came down the stairs, one step at a time; he had no right to disturb these elderly people. Albert stood in the doorway, trying to catch his breath. Gladys knelt at the hearth and shovelled coal onto the embers.

'Put the kettle on Dad,' she said as she undid Robert's shoes, removed them and his socks. Not only was his jacket soaked, so was his shirt. Gladys hurried upstairs and came back with Robert's old woollen dressing gown, the one he used before he married Helena. He'd laughed when Gladys refused to throw it away; now he was glad. He felt himself relax; here he was safe, no-one could hurt him here.

Albert handed him a large mug of tea. 'I've put a shot of whisky in, to keep the cold out.'

Robert clasped the mug with both hands and felt circulation return to his fingertips. His shoes were steaming on the fender and his mother had taken the rest of his clothes away. He leaned back, drifted towards sleep, it must be the whisky or exhaustion that made him feel drowsy.

'You're not going back tonight,' Gladys said, 'I'll make up the camp bed.'

'Helena admitted the baby isn't mine.'

'What do you want to do?' Albert asked.

'Well, if you ask me…'

'No, Mother,' Albert said, 'Robert and Helena must decide what is best for them and for the children.'

'Dad, I've only got one child and she's upstairs.'

Gladys left the room and the two men listened to her banging about in the kitchen.

'She's taken it very badly.'

Robert nodded. 'It's a bloody mess.'

'You know, when I came back after the first lot, I didn't know what I'd find; none of us did. I know it doesn't make it any easier, but couldn't you even consider accepting the child as your own, for Alice's sake. You don't want to turn her world upside down as well, do you?'

'Do you honestly mean you would have accepted a child who wasn't yours?'

'Yes, Son, I do. And I'd have made sure more children were born after that, children who were mine. There's nothing like a house full of children to keep a woman faithful.'

Robert sat back and closed his eyes.

'You'll have to go back to sort things out.'

'There's nothing to sort. I'll sign on, be a career soldier and of course I'll divorce Helena. I'll apply for custody of Alice, but as she's so young, I may not get it.'

'Robert, for God's sake don't do anything hasty. You and Helena have had so little time together, give yourselves a chance.'

'Anyone would think you were on her side.'

'It's not a question of taking sides; I'm thinking of Alice. She doesn't deserve this.'

Robert stared into the fire and let his tears flow.

'Daddy don't cry.' Alice stood in the doorway; she held her arms out and walked towards him. 'Why are you sad?'

Albert struggled to his feet, 'Now then my chick what are you doing up?'

She snuggled against Albert, 'I heard Daddy… I thought he'd like to see me.'

'Of course, he's pleased to see you, but it's raining outside and he's drenched, look. He isn't crying, big boys don't cry.' Albert ruffled Robert's hair. 'Isn't he a silly billy to go out without his raincoat.'

He eased Alice onto Robert's lap, 'A quick cuddle then back to bed.'

'Don't you like my little brother?'

Robert hugged her.

'I'll take her upstairs, Dad.'

He sat in the dark and stroked Alice's hair until her breathing slowed and she relaxed into sleep. He didn't want to destroy Alice's childhood, but whatever his dad said, he would not live with the deceit and that was that. He owed it to Helena to tell her so and the sooner the better.

'Can I borrow some dry things, Dad? I'll go back, but I'm not making any promises. I'll provide for Alice, but that's all.'

Chapter 20

September 1945

Helena stood alone; she listened to the silence, a house in mourning. Nobody needed her, everyone would be better off without her. Alice was safe with her grandparents, but what about Stephen, she had fed him, he would not need her for a while. Perhaps he could be adopted maybe she should leave a note for Cyril, but what could she say?

Robert would come back sometime, but she couldn't face him again. There was no choice for her, he'd seen to that. Stephen could not stay where he was, but who could she leave him with? Betty, such a good neighbour, she would keep him safe for now. If she left her front door open and pushed a note through next door, she'd get away without any explanation. She found a crumpled piece of paper in her handbag and wrote

Betty, please look after Stephen. Thank you and God bless. Helena.

She ran upstairs to check Stephen was still asleep, kissed his forehead and left. Downstairs it was a wet, miserable night; she didn't bother with a coat just grabbed her note and left the front door ajar. As Betty's kitchen was at the back of the house, it was unlikely anyone would hear the letter box rattle. She knocked twice, ran down the road and turned the corner so she would not be seen. The drumbeat of her heart made her felt faint; she had to lean against a wall until she felt calmer.

The deserted streets suited her, echoed her sense of loss, ensured no-one would try to stop what she was going to do. The river beckoned, she had always loved walking along the Embankment, first with Robert, after they first met, then with Alice in her pram. Now it was different. The Thames looked sullen, swollen with torrential rain, rain that would bring life, but not for her. She watched thunderous clouds which threatened to block the Moon's light. The world would be a better place without her, then the sun would shine.

Her footfall was drowned by the roar of wind and rain. She leaned against the Embankment wall and checked no-one was about. A break in the cloud showed the river in full spate; it would not take long. She removed her clothes, folded them as her nanny had taught her when she was a child. Naked she had come into the world and naked she would leave it. Wind tugged at her hair and stung her rain-chilled skin. She stared at the Moon and remembered the night, nine months ago, when that same Moon witnessed her adultery. Such an ugly word, it gave no credence to her feelings at that sublime moment when a new life was created. No-one would understand so what was the point of trying to explain?

She climbed onto the Embankment wall; wind and rain beat against her, willing her to take a step into darkness. She jumped. The shock of hitting the water knocked her breath away. She felt herself dragged lower by the current, she couldn't breathe. But wasn't that what she wanted? One deep breath of the rank-smelling water and she would feel no more pain, but her head broke the surface; it was too late, she couldn't force her body down again. She was buffeted and dragged along by the undertow. Bits of wood and other detritus smashed into her face and body, she used her arms for protection, but why bother? One good blow on the head and she would have her wish.

Her body was already numb with cold, but she felt pain on the side of her head. She had crashed into some kind of mooring pole. She welcomed the pain, she was slipping away from life, the cold had gone and she felt warm again, at peace. She smiled in the darkness; she must look like Ophelia in the painting she had often seen in the National Gallery, all she needed was flowers in her hair.

She spread her arms wide as though she were flying until something grabbed at her hair. Something was tugging at her scalp, she couldn't move. Her long hair was snagged on rotten planks which were wedged against metal steps attached to the Embankment wall. They must be used by river workmen. She was stuck and when the tide turned, she would be left hanging by her hair. She called out.

P.C. Brown was patrolling his beat, wishing he were at home in bed on such a foul night. He stopped, had he heard a noise? Probably his imagination, but he shone his light over the Embankment wall. He stared at the dark surface below him, something white flashed; it looked like a bare arm waving. Someone was there, in the river. The water was perishing cold; no-one in it would last long. He climbed over the gate and leaned on the rail.

'Anyone there?' he shouted.

There was someone, a woman; his boots rang against the wrought iron steps as he ran to the water's edge, he leaned over and grabbed her arm.

'Leave me, leave me, I want to die. Untangle my hair, let me go.'

'Don't be so bloody silly, woman.'

He managed to manoeuvre her round to the bottom of the steps, but she fought him off until he slapped her face. Exhausted, she collapsed as he dragged her onto the steps. He draped his mackintosh cape over her naked body. She sobbed as he worked to free her.

'Now then, love, it can't be as bad as that.'

'Please, just leave me.'

'Can't do that, my sergeant would go mad. How could I tell him I just left you to drown? You'll get me in big trouble you will.'

He stood between Helena and the water as he dragged her to her feet. He wrapped the cloak even tighter and then half walked and half carried her up the steps. He lifted her over the gate and, still hanging on to her, managed to climb over. He manoeuvred her to the kerb, fumbled in his pocket for his whistle which he blew as soon as he saw a passing taxi cab.

'Here mate, take us to Charing Cross Hospital, I've just fished this one out of the river.'

Jane, Betty's daughter, found Helena's note; she took the scrap of paper to her mother.

'There was no-one there, but I found this, there's a name and address on it.'

'I don't know anyone called Cyril,' Betty said. She turned the paper over, read it and handed it to Bob.

'For Christ's sake, Betty, haven't you done enough for that woman? I'm not having my wife used as a skivvy.'

'Something serious must have happened; I'll go and see.'

'I thought her husband was home on leave, it's his responsibility, not yours.'

'I know love, I won't be long.'

Betty was surprised to find the front door open and the house in darkness. She called out, but when there was no answer, she went upstairs to check on Stephen. He was asleep in his crib. She picked him up and marched back to her house.

Bob looked up from his paper.

'It's an absolute disgrace; this poor little scrap, alone in an empty house. I think it's a matter for the police.

'First sensible thing you've said all evening. I'll go round to the station.'

'Had you better go to the midwife too, unless Helena comes back soon, we have nothing to feed him with.'

'If you ask me, that woman is totally irresponsible and by the sounds of it I'm going to be soaked, it's lashing down.'

Helena was bundled into the Accident and Emergency department and given a hospital gown.

'What's your name, dear?' A well-upholstered, middle-aged nurse put an arm around Helena's shoulders.

'Don't be nice to me, I don't deserve it.'

'Now then, we're not having any nonsense, but we do need to know your name, that's not too difficult, is it?'

'I don't want you to find out what I've done.'

'I don't believe a nice young lady like you could do anything too terrible.'

Helena slumped against the nurse and cried.

Where did you leave your clothes, dear, did someone attack you?'

Helena shook her head, 'I don't want to live anymore.'

P.C. Brown popped his head round the curtain, 'Is she O.K.?'

The nurse raised her eyebrows, 'I think she could do with a cup of tea, do us a favour dear, get a nurse to bring one with plenty of sugar.' She turned to Helena, my name's Janet, Janet Thompson, what's yours?'

'Helena.'

'There's a good girl, now how old is your baby?'

'How… how do you know? He wants to get rid of me.' She started to struggle, but Janet Thompson held her tight.

'Let go, let go.'

Two doctors and a nurse rushed in.

'Now come on sweetheart, we want to help you. Who wants to get rid of you, did he throw you in the water?'

'No, please let me go, I want to die, nobody wants me.'

'I'm sure your baby does.'

Helena lashed out, 'Leave me, just leave me alone.'

Someone grabbed her arm while nurses held her down. She watched as a tired looking man in a white coat filled a syringe.

'Now stay still, dear,' he leaned over her, 'I'm going to give you something to make you feel better.'

She screamed as the needle went into her arm, tried to struggle, but could feel her energy fade away, her body relaxed and she slept.

Janet spread a blanket over her and stroked her face.

'Do we have to inform the police? Whatever the problem is, criminal proceedings for attempted suicide won't help.'

'We have no choice,' the doctor said, 'if the court's involved it will be easier to get her somewhere safe.'

'She told me her name was Helena and she's recently had a baby.'

The doctor sighed, 'Probably what tipped her over the edge.'

Robert arrived to find his front door open, what the hell was she playing at? He closed it behind him and went from room to room; finally, to their bedroom. There was no sign of Helena or the baby and his crib had gone.

He sat on their bed; perhaps she'd gone to her mother. He'd go to the phone box and call. It would mean admitting he had no control over his wife and no idea where she was; it was hardly likely to impress Mrs Snooty Carlton.

He heard a knock at the front door, perhaps it was Helena, perhaps it was why she had left the door ajar, she'd lost her key. A young boy stood on the doorstep.

'Mum, sent me to see if anyone was in.'

'Who's your Mum?'

'We live next-door, we've got your baby.'

'Christ… right, I'll come straight away.'

He locked the door and followed the boy.

The kitchen was full, Betty, husband Bob who had returned from the police station, their daughter Jane and the midwife who was feeding Stephen. Robert felt all eyes on him as he walked in.

'Mr Warren,' the midwife said, 'I have no idea what is going on here, but my concern is for your baby and his mother.'

Robert felt his face redden, now was not the time to go into exactly whose baby Stephen was.

'I have no idea what has happened, I went to my parents and when I got back Helena and the baby had gone.'

'I've been to the police station,' Bob said, 'we thought there might have been an accident. The sergeant said he would send someone round.'

'I found a note,' Jane said, 'from Helena.'

Betty handed the scrap of paper to Robert. He read both sides and slid the paper into his pocket.

'What time was that?'

'Couple of hours ago.' Bob said, 'What I want to know is what is going to happen to this baby if your wife has disappeared?'

'I'll see if she's gone to her mother.'

The midwife sat Stephen up on her lap and patted his back. 'This baby needs to be cared for properly. Do you think you can take on that task, Mr Warren?'

'Helena was breast-feeding him…'

'I'll show you how mix up a bottle,' Betty said, 'anyway I'm sure Helena will be back soon.'

The midwife handed Stephen to Betty and stood up, 'I'm not happy about this, Mr Warren, I will be round in the morning. I'll leave the bottle and this tin of milk powder; he'll probably need another feed in four hours or so.' She gathered her things and left.

'Would you mind if I leave Stephen with you while I phone her parents?'

'Don't be long,' Bob said.

Robert ran down the road checking his pocket for change as he went. He listened to the phone ringing.

'Hello, Mr and Mrs Carlton's residence.'

Robert pressed Button A and heard his coins clatter into the money box.

'Hello Susan, it's Robert Warren, may I speak to Mrs Carlton?'

'She's giving a dinner party, Sir. I don't think I can interrupt. The guests should be leaving soon.'

'It is very important; you see Helena had disappeared.'

'Oh Sir, I'll speak to madam at once, but Miss Helena isn't here.'

Robert pressed his forehead against the glass of the telephone box. The whole thing was a nightmare. He waited and tried to work out what he could say; did Mary know the baby wasn't his, had Helena confided in her mother? That didn't seem likely. Since Helena wasn't there, would Mary know where she was?

'Hello, Robert.'

'I'm so sorry to disturb you, but Helena has gone missing, has she been in touch with you this evening?'

Mary sighed. 'I'm sorry, I've heard nothing.'

Chapter 21

September 1945

Mary Carlton sat at her dressing table. She removed her pearl necklace and earrings, unpinned her hair, brushed it. She watched Edgar in her mirror; he had been quiet, preoccupied. Had the business with Helena and Robert upset him?

'I think this evening went very well, my dear.'

'Except for that phone call; we must make it clear to the staff, we will not have our evenings disturbed because some people feel entitled to speak to us whenever they choose.'

Mary flinched. Something was wrong; Edgar never used to be so harsh. She decided not to tell him who had called or why. He would find out soon enough and be appalled, but not surprised by Helena's reckless behaviour. He didn't understand that for a woman the umbilical cord was never completely severed. Even though Helena had always been a trial, the blood tie could never be ignored.

'I'll drive over to Chelsea tomorrow and see how things are with Helena.'

Edgar didn't reply.

She got into bed and sat, self-consciously, beside her husband. She suspected she was seldom in his thoughts now.

'I think the lecture tour of the States will go ahead after all.'

'How wonderful,' Mary said, 'what could be better. Let's have a holiday afterwards; I've been quite worried about you. You have been working too hard recently.'

She smiled and placed her hand over his. Edgar didn't remove his hand, but neither did he give any indication that he was aware of her.

Mary shivered, was she always fated to be alone?

Helena slept through the journey from Charing Cross to Friern Barnett Psychiatric Hospital. When she woke, she felt groggy and disorientated. A doctor appeared; she closed her eyes and ignored him. He rested his hand on her shoulder, but she pushed him away.

'Helena, I'm Doctor Jennings, I want to help you. Your baby will be missing you, so will your husband.'

'No, he won't.'

'I'm so glad the policeman found you in time.'

'I'm not.'

'Can't you just give us your husband's name; he'll be so worried.'

'Leave me alone, I want to die.'

Other patients, woken by the noise, began to moan and cry out. Dr Jennings went to put his arm round Helena's shoulders, but she grabbed his hand and bit it. He winced and pushed Helena away.

'Now will you leave me in peace?'

Dr Jennings wrapped a handkerchief round the wound on his hand.

'Nurse,' he called, 'I think she needs to get some sleep.'

The nurse appeared with two colleagues and a heavy canvas garment. Helena fought hard, kicking and lashing out at anyone within reach, but finally, her strength exhausted, the staff managed to buckle her into the strait jacket. There were smears of blood on her face and she was gasping for breath. Nurses helped her to her feet.

'Is she going to be all right here, or do you want her in the 'rubber room'?' the staff nurse asked.

'I doubt you'll have any trouble tonight, but for her own safety, we'll move her.'

The doctor followed as nurses led her away. The padded cell was the size of a single bedroom with thick padding on walls, ceiling and floor; there was no furniture, no window only an observation hatch in the door.

As the door was opened, Helena sank to the floor.

'Why have you brought me here?'

The doctor knelt down, 'You'll be safe here, Helena, you can have a good night's rest and I'll see you in the morning.'

The nurses lifted her and placed her in a comfortable position on the floor. It felt soft and she was so tired all she wanted to do was sleep. Nothing mattered any more. She scarcely felt the needle in her thigh and was asleep before the strait jacket had been unbuckled and removed. She dreamt she was moving higher and higher towards the Sun, now she was bathed in its heat and light; she had her children with her, they were laughing, clutching her hands, but where was Robert?

She whimpered in her sleep, a man moved closer, a man with his face covered; she stretched out her arms, pulled away the cover. Was it Cyril, she wasn't sure; she couldn't remember his face? He clutched at her then took Stephen in his arms and turned away.

'He's mine,' the man said.

She tried to follow him, but Alice dragged her back.

'I want my Daddy,' she said.

Helena screamed. She heard the clatter of running feet and the sound of a key turning in the lock.

Someone took hold of her shoulders, held her close, rocked her gently; she was a baby again.

'Hush dear, try to sleep.'

'He took my baby away, find my baby.'

'I want to report my wife missing,' Robert said to the station sergeant.

'Wait over there, Sir, and I'll get someone to speak to you.'

An officer took him to an interview room.

'My name's Greenwood, D.C. Greenwood, I believe your wife is missing. When did you last see her?'

'It was about four o'clock this afternoon.'

Greenwood raised his eyebrows, 'It's only ten past ten now, Sir, what makes you think she's missing? She could have gone to see a friend and forgotten the time.'

'My wife had a baby last week and when I got home this evening not only was she not there, neither was the baby. Fortunately, the neighbours had received a note put through the door, by my wife, asking them to look after the child.'

'Do you have the note, Sir?'

Robert felt in his pocket and handed over the scrap of paper. The policeman read both sides.

'Who is Cyril?'

'I don't know.'

'Could he be a friend, someone your wife would visit?'

'I don't know, Officer.'

'There's a telephone number here, Sir. I think the best thing I can do is to give the gentleman a ring.'

Robert waited alone.

D.C. Greenwood returned, 'I've managed to get through to a Cyril Davies. He couldn't help us much; he said he hadn't seen your wife for some time.'

'She's not with her parents, I've already checked.'

'Did you have a disagreement about anything?'

'Not really.'

'So, you last saw her at four o'clock, how did she seem?'

'A bit tired and tearful so I took our daughter to my parents so Helena could get some rest.'

'So, you took your daughter to your parents at four o'clock.'

'No, we went over earlier and then I came back about three o'clock.'

'And how was your wife then?'

'Quiet, not herself.'

'And you went out again at four o'clock knowing your wife was not quite herself?'

D.C. Greenwood watched as Robert used a handkerchief to dab at the perspiration trickling down the sides of his face.

'I've done nothing wrong. As far as I knew there were no problems when I went out. I just thought she was overtired. She's the one who's gone off.'

'Quite so, Sir, but abandonment of an infant is a very serious matter. It is most fortunate that you have kindly neighbours, who were willing to care for your son. What did you do when you left the house at four o'clock?'

'I went for a walk.'

'Doesn't that seem a strange thing to do when you wife was…' The policeman flicked through his notes, '… tired and tearful? Wouldn't it have been better to stay in and keep an eye on her?'

'I suppose so, but I didn't expect this.'

'No, Sir, I'm sure you didn't. Now while I was 'phoning Mr. Davies, the desk sergeant checked local hospitals to see if your wife had been admitted. No Mrs Warren has come to light yet, but we'll keep checking.'

Robert nodded.

'I want you to go home and check your wife hasn't returned. If she hasn't will you be able to cope with the baby or can he stay with your neighbours?'

'They said they'll look after him, but I've got to return to my unit the day after tomorrow.'

'I'm sure we will have got things sorted in the next day or two, but just in case we haven't traced her by tomorrow, we could do with a recent photograph.'

'Thank you, Officer.' Robert walked to the door and turned. 'May I have my wife's note back, please?'

'I'm sorry, Sir, this is evidence; as I said, abandonment of a baby is a

103

serious offence.'

'Could I just see it for a minute?' Robert scribbled Cyril's name and address on the back of an envelope he found in his inside pocket.

'Good night, Officer.'

Robert left the police station, turned up his collar and walked out into the night. Although it had stopped raining, it still felt raw. His footsteps echoed down empty streets.

Chapter 22

September 1945

Robert called at Betty's house where Stephen lay sleeping. She had collected his things, all the paraphernalia needed for one small baby.

'Thank you for all you've done, Betty. I'm sorry Helena caused you so much trouble.'

'Don't worry love, that's what neighbours are for.'

On leaving Betty's, Robert found a policeman and Mary Carlton waiting for him.

'Give me that, Sir,' the policeman said and he took the crib from Robert. Together all three went into the house.

'I won't keep you long, Sir, Sergeant sent me round. He's spoken to your wife's doctor and no action will be taken against her for abandonment of the child. We understand she has been admitted and is receiving treatment.'

Robert nodded and flicked a glance at Mary. It was impossible to tell, from her expression, how she was taking the news.

'The only problem we have is did your wife throw herself in the river or was it an accident? As I expect you know, it is a criminal offence to attempt suicide.'

'Yes, I do understand. I didn't know that's what she did. I've not seen her or her doctor yet so I don't know.'

Stephen, disturbed by the voices, gave a plaintive wail; Mary hesitated then picked him up. The two men stood in the hallway. 'I'm sure it was an accident, Sir

'Yes, I'm sure it was.'

Robert saw the policeman out. By the time he came back Stephen was yelling loudly.

'Betty showed me how to prepare a bottle; I think I'd better do it now.'

Mary walked up and down with Stephen in her arms until she heard a knock at the door. Cyril and a woman stood on the doorstep.

'I presume you have come about the baby.' Mary stepped back to let them in. Robert came out of the kitchen and the two men stared at each other.

'Cyril Davies, I presume, and is this your wife?'

'No, Gwen's a friend. After last night's call, I thought I'd better come over.'

'Really, who told you where we live?'

'I've been here before, I walked Helena home once.'

Mary jiggled Stephen up and down, but the screaming continued. Gwen smiled and held her arms out.

'If you give me the bottle, I'll feed him. Shall I take him to the kitchen? It will give you a chance to have a talk.'

'We need to sort out a sensible arrangement.' Mary said.

'Yes,' Cyril paused and turned to Robert. 'I know you must hate the sight of me, but I had a call from the police last night; I felt I had to do something.'

'Like what? You've had your fun, now face up to your responsibilities.'

'Sit down, Robert,' Mary said, 'getting angry achieves nothing.'

'I won't have this man's bastard in my house.' He moved towards Cyril who stepped back.

'Since he's yours, take him.'

'Do we not have to consider Helena's feelings about this? Stephen is her baby and he is also my grandson.'

'For heaven's sake, Mary, she's in a psychiatric hospital.'

Robert stepped towards Cyril, 'Thanks to you, she threw herself into the Thames; my family has been torn apart.'

'I'm so sorry,' Cyril said, 'I thought he'd been taken to the hospital, to let them sort things out? I beg you, please don't. I grew up in an orphanage; I don't want the same for him.

'Robert and I will go to the hospital and speak to Helena's doctor. I really don't think we can make any other firm decisions yet.'

'The first decision I'm making,' Robert said, 'is for you to take your child with you.'

Cyril nodded and stood up. 'Let me speak to Gwen.'

She walked into the sitting room, Stephen in her arms.

'You take him and what he's wearing, what you need to feed him and nothing else. The crib and all the other clothes stay here. They were my daughter's things and I want them.'

'We won't take up any more of your time, Mr Warren; Stephen will be safe with us.' Gwen said.

'Let me give you our telephone number, please contact us as soon as you have some news. Perhaps it would be a good idea if we had your number in case we need to contact you.'

Mary stood up and stroked Stephen's cheek. 'That won't be necessary; I'll keep in touch.' She pressed twenty pounds into Gwen's hand.

'You'll have a lot to buy.'

Gwen smiled, 'We'll take the baby to see Helena, if the doctors agree. It might help her get better, you know, seeing how much her baby needs her.'

Mary smiled, 'I will be in touch, I promise you.'

'How come,' Robert said, 'I'm always made to feel this mess is my fault.'

Helena opened her eyes and wondered why she was on the floor, at least it was soft. She stretched out her arms, the walls were soft too. When she looked round, she was in an empty room. Her head was throbbing in fact she ached all over. She struggled to her feet and took some deep breaths then leaned against the wall; what happened?

Her hair had an oily, musty smell; she remembered being in water somewhere; but where were her clothes? She groaned and licked parched lips. What little light came from a small window was suddenly reduced and Helena realised it wasn't a window, if was some kind of hatch in the door. Someone was looking at her, she was being watched.

'Help me,' she croaked.

A key turned in the lock and a nurse came in.

'Hello, dear, feeling a bit better?'

Helena slid to the floor and cried.

The nurse knelt and put her arm round Helena's shoulders. 'Don't cry, you're safe now, we'll look after you.'

'Where's my baby?'

'Doctor's spoken to your husband, he's on his way over, I dare say your baby is with him.'

'I won't see him; he wants to get rid of me. I won't see him.'

'I can hear doctor coming now, he'll sort things out; don't you worry.'

'Now then, Mrs Warren, I'm Dr Kennedy, has nurse told you your husband is on his way?'

Helena struggled to her feet, 'I've done a terrible thing and my husband will never forgive me. Please let me go.'

'You know, Helena, having a baby can sometimes make a woman feel unsure of herself, unable to cope, but you have your husband and in-laws to support you as well as your own parents and I'm sure that with some rest and perhaps something to make you feel calmer, all your worries will fade away.'

'Promise me you won't make me see him.'

'We can't make you see anyone, but wouldn't it help to talk things over?'

'You don't understand, my baby isn't Robert's, he found out yesterday.'

'I see.'

It was midday when Robert and Mary arrived at the hospital. Patients were having their lunch and Helena's doctor was in a meeting. They could find nothing to say as they sat in a deserted corridor where the smell of stale bodies and overcooked cabbage did little to lift their spirits.

Dr Kennedy took them to his office.

'This is my wife's mother, Mrs Carlton.'

'I'm glad you've both come, Helena is very ill. I believe she will have to stay with us for some time.'

'May I see my daughter?'

'I don't think they would be wise at the moment, for either of you.'

'Why?' Robert asked.

'It would be distressing for her… and for you as well. My consultant wants to talk to you; he will be here soon.'

While Robert gazed out of the window, Mary felt the hand of her dead husband on her shoulder. She remembered his erratic behaviour, the depressions, followed by the lifting of his spirits to dizzying heights when he was capable of anything. Manic-depression the doctors had called it. For Mary, with her horror of emotions expressed, it had been a nightmare from which she only escaped when he killed himself. Would it have been different if she had been more understanding, more forgiving of his indiscretions?

Only after his death could she allow her feelings for Edgar to blossom and, in time, be made public. Now Gilbert had come to haunt her. Helena had inherited her father's instability; the facts could no longer be hidden. Mary closed her eyes and willed herself to hide her despair. She heard movement, someone had come in. She gathered her thought and sat upright, ready for whatever was to come.

Robert sat forward to listen to a middle-aged man with a pronounced air of authority. He we, according to his name tag, Mr Brownlow, presumably a consultant. Mary could see the veins in Robert's neck were throbbing; perhaps he needed help from Mr Brownlow too. She felt weary and detached from the whole business. As she watched, she thought, not for the first time, what a pompous young ass Robert was. Poor Helena, he couldn't have been easy to live with, but then neither was she. All hope the marriage would give Helena stability was dashed. He was no more able to control her behaviour than anyone else.

'What do you mean I must leave my wife alone?'

'Mr Warren your wife is in a state of great distress, she refuses to see you.'

'Have you any idea of the distress she's caused me?'

Mr Brownlow shuffled his papers, 'I do understand there is a problem, but your wife is my patient, you are not. I must do what is best for her.'

'What are you suggesting I leave the country so she can carry on her illicit affairs? I'm the victim here; I've not done anything wrong.'

Robert slumped in his chair and put his head in his hands.

'I am not sitting in judgement on you or your wife, but I beg you to accept that she be left to find a way out of her present condition with, of course, our help. The only reason I needed to see you was to sign papers to commit your wife into our care.'

Mary gasped, 'What are you saying?'

'I believe, Mrs Carlton, that your daughter is schizophrenic.'

'But that's madness, isn't it,' Robert said.

'No, Mr Warren, but it is a serious mental illness. There is, however, every reason to suppose her condition will improve with treatment.' Mr Brownlow pushed papers towards Robert, 'Please will you sign these.'

'What am I going to do, I have a daughter and I'm due back at my unit very soon.'

'Perhaps this is something you can discuss with Mrs Carlton,' Mr Brownlow turned to Mary, 'Grandparents have an important role in situations like this.'

Mary knew Robert would not ask her to care for Alice and she was relieved because she knew Edgar would never tolerate it.

Mary drove Robert back to his parent's home; there was little to say. She left him to tell his parents the latest developments. She wondered how much she should tell Edgar. Thank goodness they were going to America soon; hopefully, by the time they returned, matters would be resolved. Life was like walking a tightrope; whatever she did, someone would be upset. The house was quiet, as usual, and Mary took a deep breath as she stood in the hall. It was good to be home. Some people might thrive on crisis, but Mary knew she was not one of them.

Alice would be safe with Robert's parents; Stephen would be safe with

Cyril's friend, Gwen, who seemed sensible. That left Helena and Robert, he'd got his parents, but who did Helena have? Beautiful, wayward and unbalanced, Mary felt a flutter of sorrow in her heart, but what could she do? Edgar had been so strange recently. She sighed; for months she had stopped herself acknowledging her fears. She could not do anything to upset him and must rely on Mr Brownlow and his staff to do their best for Helena.

She would go to Edgar's study to see if he was ready for afternoon tea. She loved this time of day when he discussed his writing with her. She found an envelope on the desk, addressed to her; he was bound to be back soon. She would order tea and he could join her later.

She tore open the envelope; after the first few sentences she put the letter down. Her hands were shaking and she gasped; there must be some mistake.

Dear Mary,

I feel our relationship has changed, particularly recently. When two

people marry, they expect to spend the rest of their lives together. However, people do sometimes drift apart for a variety of reasons.

She was trembling, she had to sit down; this was more than she could bear. She had not changed, he had. The signs had been there.

....we have grown apart and do not make each other happy any more. I admire you in so many ways, you have a fine mind and have offered me more support, in my work, than I deserve. You are a gracious hostess and have organised social functions with flair.

Even though it is not considered appropriate for

110

women to enjoy the physical pleasure of married life, I have found you to be a passionate and generous lover.

I fear, for both our sakes, our future lies apart. I am confident you will understand and agree that my decision to leave is the best one for both of us. With that in mind, I will stay at my club for two weeks before I sail to America to start the lecture tour.

It is my intention to sell the house which, as you know, is in my names. I will, of course, give you as much time as possible to find a home of your own. With your generous private income, I feel sure you will have no difficulty in finding a suitable property.

I will, of course, tell my solicitor to inform you of all decisions made that might affect you. I wish you well and feel sure we will both be able to look back on our marriage with few regrets.

Edgar

The letter slipped through Mary's fingers and fluttered to the floor, she leaned back in the armchair. She could hear the ticking of the clock on the mantel-piece; it competed with the thudding of her heart. It felt as though pins were being stuck in her eyes, she blinked and suddenly, for the first time since she was a tiny child, tears streamed down her face. Her limbs had lost all strength and she could not wipe the tears away; nothing mattered anymore. She didn't hear the knock on the study door.

'Good afternoon, Madam,' Susan said, 'shall I put the tray on the little table?'

She got no reply and waited.

'Oh, Madam, whatever is the matter?'

When there was still no reply, Susan put the tray down and ran to the kitchen.

'Quick, quick, Cook, come quick, Mistress has been taken bad, looks like she's had a stroke or something.'

Chapter 23

September 1945

Robert slumped in his chair and let his tears fall unheeded.

'What's happened, Son?'

'I went to the hospital with Helena's mother. They told me to stay away from her, Dad, said I'd upset her.'

'That might be best for Helena, at the moment.'

'The doctor said he thinks she's schizophrenic.'

'Poor girl.'

'What about Alice, where can she go?'

'First things first, she stays with us, she can live here as long as is needed. That's one problem solved.'

'Helena is going to be in hospital for heaven knows how long. What are we going to tell Alice?'

As far as Helena is concerned, your hands are tied; do as the doctors say, feel sorry for her.'

'Dad, she wanted to pass that baby off as mine.'

'I know, lad, that was wrong, but don't sit in judgement'

'Where is the baby?' Gladys asked as she handed Robert a cup of tea.

'With his bloody father.'

'Good riddance.'

'No,' Albert said, 'that child didn't ask to be born, it isn't his fault. We've all made mistakes, no-one's perfect.'

Robert stood up, 'No, Dad, I'm not having it. The police tried to blame me and now the doctors are blaming me. What did I do? I need you to be on my side; I've no-one else to turn to. I tried to contact Mary, but apparently, she's not well. She was all right this afternoon. We're just getting the brush off, Dad.'

'The poor woman is bound to be upset with the news.'

'Sssh,' said Gladys, 'You'll wake Alice.'

'The doctors said leave Helena alone so I will; I told you, I'll stay in the army. If Helena is schizophrenic, she's no fit person to care for my child. I'm bound to get custody.'

'So, you'll be abroad, Helena will be heaven know where, what about Alice? You know Mum and I will care for her, but she needs her parents; we won't live for ever.'

'What else can I do? I've terminated the tenancy and told Mary's servant girl to let her know Helena's possessions need to be removed.'

Albert sighed, 'All this makes me sad, I've always liked your Helena; I hope you never come to regret what you're going to do.'

'Well, I for one think you are doing the right thing.' Gladys said, 'But it's a crying shame if you have to sign on again just when the war's nearly over. I hoped you'd be home near us, not being sent round the world, clearing up other people's problems.'

'I'll go upstairs and check all this shouting hasn't woken her up, none of us want her upset.' Albert stood and walked slowly out of the room.

Alice loved staying with Grandpop and Nana and the best bit was the bed, it had been Daddy's bed before he and Mummy got married. The mattress was made of feathers and she had to use a stool to climb into it. She wriggled until the feathers were settled inside their casing; it was like floating on a cloud. The feather eiderdown was up to her chin, she felt safe.

She put her head under the covers and clutched Benjy tightly, he was her best friend. Aunt Connie had given him to her when she was a baby. His rabbit ears were getting a bit frayed now and Nana had stitched him up several times when his stuffing came loose, but to Alice he was still the best companion in the world.

Under the covers, she could shut out the noise of the grownups, downstairs. She heard Daddy shouting and it made her shiver. She didn't know what was wrong and no-one would tell her. She listened carefully; someone was coming up. She popped her head out of the covers, but kept her eyes shut in case it was Daddy; she didn't want to make him cross. The door opened and she peeped with one eye, but light from the landing showed it was Granddad.

He leaned over and kissed her.

'You're supposed to be asleep, little chick.'

'Why was Daddy shouting?'

'He's a bit upset.'

'Is it because of Mummy?'

'Yes, you see she isn't very well and she's had to go to hospital so the doctors can look after her.'

'Will she be back soon?'

'I don't know, sweetheart.'

'Can't Daddy take me to see her?'

'Doctors don't like too many people visiting…'

Can I see Stephen then?'

'Not for a while.'

'Is Stephen not very well too?'

She waited and watched her granddad's face, but he wouldn't look at her.

'Some nice people are going to look after Stephen until Mummy gets better and you are going to stay with us, won't that be lovely.'

Alice put her arms round Albert's neck and hugged him. 'I do love you, Grandpop.'

She paused for a moment. 'If I'm coming to stay with you and Nana, why can't Stephen come here too?'

'Because….. Nana and I are both old people and it would be too much for us, looking after a small baby.'

'I'd be ever so good. I'd help you feed him and change his nappies and things.'

'We'll have to think about it won't we. Now it is definitely time for you and Benjy to go to sleep.'

'Daddy will be going away soon, won't he?'

'Yes, but you can write to him and draw him pictures; he'll love that.

Chapter 24

October 1945

Helena was taken along the hospital corridor with a nurse holding her arm. Life was without hope; she didn't care what happened. Her breasts were engorged and sore, but where was Stephen? She had wept when the doctor told her she was not well enough to care for him and now she was being given medication to dry up her milk. She had wanted death and she wanted it still, she had lost everything and she couldn't fight any more. Her legs were leaden and she shuffled along like an old, old woman.

When they arrived at the treatment room, Helena stopped. She looked at a row of wooden beds; each one had a patient lying on it, strapped down.

'What's going on?' She clutched the nurse's arm.

'Now come along, dear, this will make you feel better.'

She heard a woman whimper and watched as metal things with pads were placed either side of her head. Without warning, she writhed and strained against the straps, then lay still. Doctors moved down the line of beds; there were screams and cries of despair as one by one the treatment was applied.

Two orderlies lifted Helena and placed her on the end bed. She felt the straps being tightened around her abdomen, arms and legs.

'Open your mouth,' a nurse said and something tasting of rubber was pushed between her lips, 'it will stop you biting your tongue.'

Helena trembled; it was her turn next. Doctors and nurses surrounded the bed, she was trapped, was this what it was like when prisoners went to the electric chair?

'Right, Sister.'

One of the doctors held the electrodes against Helena's temples while everyone else stood back. She opened her mouth to scream, but felt a blow to the head and everything went black.

She rose to consciousness like a deep-sea diver and gasped when she opened her eyes. She had no idea of where she was or how long she had been lying there. The bright lights hurt her eyes and her wrists and ankles were sore. She tried to move, but was still restrained. Her body felt limp, lifeless. She moved her head, but all she could see was the row of beds.

'Wide awake now, are we?' A passing nurse patted her hand, 'You see it wasn't so bad, was it?'

Helena looked at the nurse, but didn't recognise her.

'Where am I?'

'In the treatment room, you'll be going to go back to the ward soon. You lie still for a while and rest.'

'Will you undo these straps, please?'

'Not yet, dear, we don't want you falling off the bed.'

Stephen was registered with the local council-run crèche. Once Cyril explained his circumstances and referred to Helena as his wife, Mrs Wilson agreed to enrol him the following day.

'I'll take Stephen to see his mother and register his birth tomorrow.'

On arrival at Friern Barnet, Cyril went straight to the ward Sister's office.

'I warn you now, Mr Davies, Helena is still very ill however she has had her first session of E.C.T. which should help.'

Cyril looked blank.

'Electroconvulsive therapy, a jolt to the brain, she's still a bit tearful, though doctor thinks that's a good sign. Please wait in the visitors' room while I get her.'

Stephen was still asleep when Helena appeared. Cyril stood up as she shuffled towards him. She glanced at Stephen and then back at Cyril, but said nothing.

'Hello, Helena, I thought I'd bring Stephen to see you.

Helena moved closer.

'Why don't you hold him?'

Unsure, she turned to the nurse who smiled and nodded.

Helena placed her hand on Stephen's head, stroked his hair.

'I'm so confused, nothing makes sense; is this baby mine?'

'Yes,' Cyril said, 'this is Stephen.'

He placed the baby in her arms and held them both close.

She kissed her son's head and smiled, but when he stirred, she panicked and tried to hand him back to Cyril.

'He's just getting comfortable; why don't you loosen his blanket, he's probably a bit warm in here.'

Helena took Stephen's hand in hers then bent over him; she held him against her breast, rocked him and started to undo her nightgown, ready to feed him. The nurse knelt at Helena's feet.

'Everything is going to be all right. I don't think he's hungry at the moment, he just wants you to give him a cuddle.'

Helena nodded and gently rocked back and forth, crooned softly.

'He's going to be fine, Helena; I have found a really nice nursery for him.'

Helena looked up. 'He's mine so I want to have him with me.'

Another nurse opened the door,

'You are a lucky girl, Helena; let me have a look at your baby.'

She stroked Stephen's head.

'He's a beauty, but I think it's time you had some rest.' She nodded to Cyril, 'This will have done her good.'

Helena stood and turned to Cyril, 'Thank you for bringing my baby here, but I've got a little girl too... haven't I, where is she?'

'Alice is with Robert's parents, she's fine.'

There were tears in Helena's eyes, 'I want to see Alice.'

'Please don't cry, I'll have a word with your mother, get Alice here as soon as I can.'

He slipped his arm round Helena's waist and she leaned against him, he could feel her breath on his cheek.

'I'll come again soon; shall I bring Stephen?'

She nodded and left the room.

He watched as she walked down the corridor with the nurse, but when Stephen gave a hungry cry, Helena didn't turn round.

Chapter 25

October 1945

Alice held Grandpop's hand as they walked along the King's Road, Nana walked on the other side, holding his arm. They were visiting Aunt Connie and Uncle John. Their baby would be arriving soon, but Alice was too unhappy to think about new babies. She had sat on Daddy's knee before they came out.

'Be a good girl for Grandpop and Nana while I'm away,' he'd said.

'When can I see Mummy and Stephen?'

Nana had whisked her off her Daddy's knee and hurried her out of the room.

'Get your coat; we're going out,' she'd said, 'say bye - bye to Daddy.'

Now Daddy had gone away, Mummy was in hospital and no-one would tell her where Stephen was. She only had Grandpop and Nana left.

Visiting her aunt and uncle was boring; there was nothing to do. They didn't have a garden like Grandma Carlton. She had to sit quietly and be good while the grown-ups talked. Uncle John was at work and Aunt Connie was stretched out on the settee. She looked much fatter than Mummy was before Stephen was born; perhaps she was having two babies.

Grandpop whispered, 'Go to see if Uncle John is coming up the road.'

She went to the window and looked down at the street; she watched people walk past and wondered where they were going. A man waved at her and she waved back.

'Uncle John's home,' she said.

Connie frowned and struggled to haul herself upright.

'I suppose he'll be wanting his tea.'

'Don't worry, dear, I'll get it while you rest.' Gladys was up, and in the kitchen almost before she'd finished speaking. Connie looked at her father and raised her eyebrows.

He shrugged, 'You know what she's like.'

John came in, hearty and red-faced. 'Good to see you, Dad, where's the little woman? In the kitchen I expect, best place for 'em, well only one place better.' He rubbed his hands together and gave Albert a knowing wink.

'Hello, hello, who have we here, I do believe it's my pretty little niece.'

He picked her up, hugged her and gave her a smacking kiss that left a wet smear on her cheek. She smelt his breath which was sour and sickly; she wrinkled her nose.

'Now, John don't get her over-excited or she'll never sleep tonight.' Gladys stood in the kitchen doorway wiping her hands.

'I'll get a bit of tea for all of us, but it won't be ready for a while.'

'There's not much in the cupboard, Mum. When is the rationing going to stop; it doesn't seem much of a victory, for us all. I just fancy a nice bit of steak.'

'You women and what you fancy when you're expecting. I think it's your imagination. Now what about you, little lady?' said John, 'I bet you'd like to go on the swings.'

Alice nodded.

'I'll take her down to the gardens, how long have we got?'

'About half an hour, now be careful with her John, don't swing her too high.'

'I'll look after her like she's my own. Now come on or we won't have time.'

Albert watched from the window as John and Alice crossed the road, Alice looked back and waved. Albert blew her a kiss.

The swing was in a private garden in the centre of the square. It had metal railings round it and dark laurel bushes to shut out prying eyes. In the middle was a grassed area with some benches and down a path stood a solitary swing. The garden could only be used by the residents of the square all of whom had a key. In the centre of a bustling city, it was an oasis of calm where mothers and nannies could bring their charges to play in safety. At this time, it was usually deserted; the residents' children were at home having their tea.

Light was fading and it wasn't warm, Alice shivered. John opened the gate which creaked as he shut and locked it.

'Are there any bogey men here?' Alice asked.

John laughed and picked her up, 'Of course there aren't.' He hugged her tightly and again, she felt his breath, hot on her cheek.

'Are you cold?' he asked.

'A bit.'

John carried her to a bench and sat down with her on his knee. He rubbed her hands with his. 'That'll warm them up.' He rubbed her back and then slipped his hand inside her coat, he rubbed her chest and tickled her neck. She giggled.

'Where else are you ticklish, I wonder?'

His hand moved down to her legs, 'Are these legs cold too?'

Alice nodded. As he rubbed her legs, her skirt rode up until her knickers were showing. She tried to pull her skirt down, but his hands were in the way. Then he hugged her so her face was pressed into his coat. She looked up at his face; he was sweating even though it wasn't warm, and he seemed out of breath.

'Can I go on the swing now?'

John didn't answer.

'Please can I go on the swing now, Uncle John?'

He looked down at her and smiled. He carefully smoothed her skirt over her thighs, stroking them as he did so.

Together they walked back to the apartment, but Alice refused to hold his hand.

Chapter 26

October 1945

Mary called the number Cyril had given her; Gwen answered.

'He's gone to the hospital with Stephen; he thought it might help Helena.'

'I see; there have been developments, what time are you expecting him back?'

'Fairly soon, shall I ask him to call you.'

'No, I will call again, thank you.'

The phone went dead.

'Stuck up cow,' Gwen said to herself. Mary Carlton obviously had no intention of having her precious privacy disturbed.

Stephen had been given his bottle and Cyril and Gwen were eating when the phone went again.

'Good evening, Mr Davies, my son-in-law has removed all his possessions from the house he and Helena were renting. He has given up the tenancy and I believe he will be leaving the country soon, reporting back to his unit. I thought you should know.'

'What about Helena, where will she go when she comes out of hospital?'

'Mr Davies, whatever the circumstances, Stephen is my grandson. I need to know your intentions towards him and my daughter.'

'I took him to see his mother today; she was quiet, but seemed pleased to see us. She was asking to see Alice.'

'Do you think a mental hospital is an appropriate place for a child of barely four?'

'Probably not, but at least she would know where her mother is.'

'I'll write to Robert's parents to see what instructions he has left. I warn you I think it unlikely they will agree to Alice going anywhere with you.'

'I realise that, I thought you would be able to take her.'

There was a lengthy pause and Cyril smiled.

'Has the baby's birth been registered yet?' Mary asked.

'No, but it would be helpful if you would do that for me as I have to go back to work.'

There was another pause, Cyril smiled, Mary wasn't used to being given orders.

'Should I give your name as the father?'

'Of course, and he is going to the local council crèche for the time being so be assured he will be well cared for.'

'I'm relieved to hear it.'

'Also, I intend to marry Helena one day and I will care for her and Stephen. If necessary I will care for Alice as well.'

'I admire your determination, Mr Davies, and wish you success. I will visit Helena tomorrow and hopefully will get more information from her doctor.'

As Cyril ended the conversation, he saw Gwen turn away and go to her bedroom. He knew what she would do now.

Stephen began to cry and Cyril went to the kitchen to make-up another bottle.

Helena lay on her bed and thought about Cyril's visit. There was a tiny seed of hope somewhere inside her; perhaps things were not so black. She wasn't sure if it was the treatment or the visit which lifted her spirits. Of course, there would be more treatment sessions; if she were going to get better there would be no escape from that ordeal.

Stephen was beautiful, but so was Alice; would Robert try to stop her having contact? Since she was in a psychiatric hospital, he was entitled to claim she was unfit. She must get better, but how would she cope on her own with two young children? Surely Cyril must think a lot of her, why else would he visit? If she stayed with him, Robert would never allow Alice to stay too. What on earth was she going to do?

Chapter 27

October 1945

John arrived at his in-laws unexpectedly, on Saturday morning.

'Connie isn't at all well, can you come round? I don't know whether to get the doctor or not.'

'I'll have to bring Alice with me. Albert's gone to the cobblers; he could be ages. I'll write a note for him, Alice put your coat on.'

'I want to stay here, Nana.'

'Don't be silly, get your coat.'

No one spoke, in the car. Alice sat in a back seat and clutched Benjy. Everything was muddled up, she felt scared; when would she see Mummy and Stephen?

Once at the flat, Gladys knew Connie was in labour.

'Get an ambulance, John, and keep Alice with you until we get Connie sorted out.'

John held Alice's hand as they ran to the phone box. Alice waited outside with her fingers in her mouth; she wanted her daddy.

'We'll tell Gran the ambulance is on its way.' They hurried back; Alice had to run to keep up. When she heard Connie's screams and groans, it reminded her of Mummy, she put her hands over her ears and tried not to cry.

'For goodness sake, John; why have you brought her back here?'

Alice watched John's face flush. 'What was I supposed to do?'

'Use your common sense, take her to the park.'

'Looks like we're in the way here,' John said, 'come on Alice we'll go to the bloody park.'

Alice heard a sharp intake of breath from Nana and smiled; grown-ups were not supposed to swear.

She watched as Uncle John unlocked the gate, she felt cold inside and her legs didn't want to take her any further. She held Benjy tightly as John grabbed her hand. She watched him lock the gate behind them.

'We must celebrate now, Alice, you're going to have a new cousin.'

Alice watched him and tried to move away, but he kept touching her and laughing; she didn't like it. He took her to the swing and pushed her until she was breathless and squealing with excitement. Perhaps she'd just been silly; she'd ask Grandpop when she got home.

'Push me, push me, Uncle John, I want to go over the bar.' Her skirt was billowing and she didn't care. Then he let the swing slow down until he could grab her in his arms.

'Let's go play hide and seek in the bushes, we can hide together.'

'It's getting dark and no-one's here.'

'There might be, let's find a good place and when someone comes near, we can jump out and say, Boo.'

Alice shivered, 'I wish Grandpop was here.'

John held her hand and hurried down the path, 'Here's a spot, quick before the bogey man finds us.'

'But there aren't any bogeymen, you said so.'

He pushed his way past a large laurel bush; it was shielded from the path by other bushes and from the road by railings and a hedge. A branch caught Alice's leg and tripped her, she whimpered as John picked her up and held her tightly to his chest. She could hear his heavy breathing and feel his hot breath on her face; that same, familiar smell made her retch. He tried to kiss her, but she turned her face away. His wet lips slid across her cheek and left a snail trail of saliva.

'Put me down, please, Uncle John. I want to go home,' she whispered. She could feel her heart thudding and there was a roaring in her ears.

Slowly John let her slide down his chest and stomach until she felt something hard pressing against her. John held her there; she was trapped in his arms. She opened her mouth to cry out; with her first cry he dropped her and grabbed her by the back of the neck. He forced her face into the material of his trousers so she couldn't breathe. The roaring in her ears got louder. She tried to hit him, but he grabbed her wrists. She gulped for air.

'Hold it,' he hissed.

He held her with one arm and fumbled with his trousers. She struggled to get free, but he grabbed her neck again. Her legs buckled; he forced her to her feet.

'Hold it,' he pulled her hand towards him. She could feel something

125

hard in his trousers, like a piece of wood. It was too dark to see.

'Hold it,' he said and forced the hard thing into her hand. He was grunting and his grasp of her wrist made her yelp. He moved her hand backwards and forwards, faster and faster until he groaned. The grip on her wrist and neck relaxed, but Alice was too scared to move. She waited.

'We'd better get back,' John said, 'don't want to be late.'

Alice cried, 'I've got my coat dirty; Nana will be cross.'

John knelt and, by light from the street lamp, used his handkerchief to rub away the stain on the front of her coat. They walked back along the path towards the gate.

'I don't think you should say anything to Nana about what you did today; you don't want to make her cross, do you?'

Alice shook her head. She only had Grandpop and Nana left, she must not make them cross.

'You see, Alice, if Grandpop and Nana find out you've been naughty, they'll have to send you away. I don't want that to happen, Alice, so I promise I won't say anything.'

Alice didn't reply; his voice seemed to be coming from a long way off. It was then that she realised she didn't have Benjy under her arm; she dared not tell Uncle John, he might change his mind and talk to Nana. Perhaps it was because she'd been naughty, now even Benjy didn't want her any more.

It rained heavily that night and Benjy was soaked. A stiff breeze shuffled the dank, rotting leaves from last winter. Throughout the night his outline was blurred as more and more leaves came to rest. Finally, he was completely covered.

That night, for the first time, Gladys and Albert were woken by the sound of Alice screaming in her sleep. Only two days after that, Alice was taken ill and diagnosed with measles. A bed for her was made-up downstairs and the room was kept dark to protect her eyes. Alice felt safe, she didn't have to go to school, but best of all, she didn't have to see Uncle John. Nana had explained they couldn't visit until she'd got rid of the spots.

Chapter 28

October 1945

Gladys took her responsibilities very seriously indeed. Looking after someone else's child was daunting particularly when that someone was Robert. She knew Albert thought she worried too much, but the child was too quiet, with no appetite and now the nightmares were a regular occurrence. Albert often sat with Alice on his knee, but when he tried to talk about her nightmares, she seemed unable to explain what was frightening her. Gladys was at a loss.

After a harsh winter, Albert's precarious health had deteriorated to the point where even the morning and afternoon walk to school was a challenge.

'I can go to school by myself... I don't want to make Grandpop poorly.'

Gladys smiled and hugged Alice, 'You're a good girl and we've got to keep you safe until your Daddy comes home.'

'Can I see my Mummy then and Stephen?'

'I don't know, sweetheart, but I've had a good idea. You know we used to take you out at the weekend, to the park well, so Grandpop doesn't get so tired, I'm going to ask Uncle John if he will take you instead. Don't you think that's a good idea, Grandpop?'

'No, please don't make me go, please.' Alice burst into tears and ran from the room. Gladys hurried upstairs to find Alice hiding under the bed. 'Please, Nana, don't make me go. I want to stay here with you.'

When Alice did crawl out, she put her arms round Gladys' neck and clung to her. That evening Gladys went upstairs to find Alice standing in the corner with her nose pressed against the wall.

'Come on, sweetheart; let's get you back into bed.'

Alice refused to move; her body was rigid, she was shivering.

'What's the matter, lovey?'

After a long pause, Gladys knelt and took the child in her arms.

'You can tell me.'

'I've been a naughty girl.'

'It's all right, my love, you've stood there long enough. You can get back into bed now. Give your Benjy a cuddle.'

'He's run away; he doesn't love me anymore.'

Gladys led Alice back to bed. She climbed in and, without a word turned on her side; her fingers slid into her mouth, she gave a sigh and slept. Gladys stroked the child's hair and waited until she felt warm again then tip-toed downstairs.

Albert folded his newspaper. 'You've been a long time.'

'I reckon she's been sleepwalking; have you seen that rabbit of hers?'

'Perhaps she was looking for it.'

'What, freezing cold, standing in the corner?'

'I wonder if she left it at Connie's.'

'I don't know,' Gladys said, 'but suppose she'd tried to come downstairs, she could have broken her neck. What are we going to do?'

'I don't know, love. I think she's pining for her mum, her dad and her little brother. Robert doesn't want her to have contact with Helena and the baby for now, but.'

'I don't blame him.'

Albert sighed, 'Well in my opinion he'll have to change his mind about that when Helena's better. She's the child's mother.'

'I won't go against Robert's wishes.'

'Maybe, it's seeing Connie with Pauline, that's doing it.'

'You're not suggesting I don't go to see my other granddaughter, are you?'

'No, but try to involve Alice more with the baby. Let her hold her, give her a bottle, make her feel useful.'

Gladys raised her eyebrows, 'You know what Connie's like; she scarcely lets John get near, never mind Alice.'

Albert took Gladys' hand in his; it was gnarled with swollen knuckles and veins like blue ropes under the skin, the medals for work, the reward for struggling against the odds.

'We'll just have to do our best for her, won't we?'

Chapter 29

December 1945

Alice lay in bed and listened to the sound of Grandpop and Nana in the kitchen. It was a school day and Alice could feel her stomach churning. She knew Nana would insist she eat breakfast even though she felt sick every morning. Perhaps if she didn't get out of bed and said she felt poorly, they would let her stay at home.

'Come on Alice,' Albert called, 'your porridge is ready.'

Alice sighed, if she didn't go down, Grandpop would come up to get her and that made him puff and would make Nana cross. After what Uncle John had said, she watched Grandpop and Nana more and more. If they couldn't look after her, where would she go? Every night she prayed that they would not send her away. It was then she missed Benjy, then when she most wanted to hug him, but he was gone.

She walked downstairs counting as she went; Gladys hurried out of the kitchen.

'Hurry up now, or Grandpop will have to walk quickly to get you to school on time.'

She slid into her chair and looked at the steaming bowl; she blinked back tears. If she didn't eat it, Nana would be cross and she mustn't make Nana cross. She didn't want to make Grandpop hurry, but she didn't want to go to school in case Grandpop and Nana went away and she had to stand at the school gates for ever. If she didn't go to school, her teachers would be cross. She wanted Mummy and Stephen and Daddy; where were they?

She picked up a small spoonful of porridge and put it in her mouth; she tried to swallow, but couldn't. She knew Grandpop was watching her, she must not upset him.

'Have a sip of tea to wash it down, my chick,' he smiled, 'then I'll have a spoonful and then you can have a spoonful.'

She blinked away her tears and swallowed.

'There's a good girl, let's give Gran a surprise, finish before she comes for the bowl.'

'That wasn't so bad,' Gladys said when she came out of the kitchen, 'get washed and dressed, Grandpop will wait here.'

Alice held Albert's hand as they walked along the balcony, towards the stairs to the street. She kept swallowing; she didn't want to be sick like yesterday. She tried to concentrate on what Grandpop was saying, but she could feel perspiration bubble on her forehead; she whimpered and let go of his hand. Without warning porridge hit the concrete wall with such force that it splashed their legs.

'I'm sorry, Grandpop, I'm sorry.' She clung to him and the smell of bile clotted the air. Together they walked back along the balcony. Gladys sponged down Alice's legs and coat and wrapped two plain biscuits in a piece of paper. 'Have these with your milk, once you feel better.'

When they arrived at school, Alice's teachers were waiting. She had run home so often it seemed the only way to keep her safe.

'Good morning, Alice, Mr Warren.' Miss Armstrong, Alice's teacher smiled. 'Now then dear, you go and play for a few minutes while I talk to your Grandpop.'

'She was sick again,' Albert said.

'Have you any idea what's upsetting her?'

'She won't say. We think she's missing her mum and of course her dad won't be home for a while.

'We'll keep a close eye on her, just let us know if she says anything that might help and we'll do the same.'

They stood for a moment and watched as Alice stood alone in a corner of the playground. She didn't seem to have any friends, and of course the dreadful squint after her bout of measles didn't help.

Chapter 30

December 1945

Mary listened to the news; for once she was comforted by the latest reports. Allied submarine losses had been fewer recently, largely due, apparently, to a shortwave radar system. It was now possible to detect U-boats surfacing, to recharge their batteries, several miles away from Allied ships. Mary had no idea how radar worked, but she thanked God for it. Food convoys were getting through at last, although food shortages were as bad as ever. All she wanted now was to hear from Matthew.

She walked round the ten-roomed apartment on the top floor of a magnificent mansion in Holland Park. The furniture she had removed, from what Edgar had so charmingly referred to as his house, looked right, suited her new property. Although she would miss the house they had shared, she felt comfortable in her new home.

She wondered if he had ever regarded the home they had shared as theirs or if she was never more than another part of the fixtures and fittings. Rage and bitterness left a foul taste in her mouth. She had let the servants believe it was her decision to leave. If Edgar decided the staff, many of whom they had had for years, were to lose their employment, he could tell them himself.

It was her intention to have every room decorated as she wanted, a luxury she had never before enjoyed. However, such freedom of choice drew attention to her single status. She had decided not to employ any servants even though income from her father's estate ensured she would live comfortably with plenty to spare.

She would, for the first time in her life, fend for herself. Of course, she would continue with the voluntary work; the war may be over; clearing up the carnage would take years. Running her home alone would easily fill the days that stretched before her. Her only hope was that at least two of her children would want to share some part of their lives with her. Mary read the letter from her beloved son, Matthew.

Hi Mother,

The sailor will soon be home, and in one piece, but before I return to Blighty, I'm going to the States to meet up with some pals. Hope you don't mind.

I should be back by the end of the month.

Love

Matthew.

Mary did mind, but would never say so. She had hoped to up-date him on her move, but she had no address; how would she let him know? Frances had promised to move back to London once the war was over, but would her friend Andrew prove to be an obstacle? Mary would have to be patient; she didn't want to become a possessive mother. She had sent her new address to friends and relatives without making any reference to Edgar. They would have the wit to draw their own conclusions.

She was surprised to receive a reply from her second cousin, Phillip. She regarded him as a neurotic man whose problems were usually self-inflicted. After a short and disastrous marriage to a Hungarian 'countess', he had been left with a precocious daughter and no home. The divorce had been acrimonious and exhausting for all concerned. Mary had smiled when she learned that, after months of wrangling over who owned what, the exasperated judge decided the forks from a set of silver fish cutlery should go to the wife and the knives to Phillip. He, of course, had been outraged.

Mary reread his letter. He was obviously in a difficult situation, but did she want to share her new home with someone she found rather trying? If she didn't take him in, the opportunity for companionship would be lost. If it didn't work, she could always tell him to leave. She leaned back in her favourite chair and gazed out of the window. She was high up enough to look out on the tops of trees that grew in the gardens below. The sky was clear and she watched pigeons come to roost.

There was enough space for Phillip and Patricia to have a bedroom each and a good sitting-room. She need not spend too much time with them and she had her sanctuary here in this lovely room where she could shut herself away. While she cherished solitude, there was a difference between choosing it and having no alternative. There was the added bonus that if they did come to stay, expenses would be shared. Yes, she would do it.

Chapter 31

December 1945

Helena had been in hospital for ten weeks; she'd had enough of her fellow inmates. How could she persuade her doctors she was sane when all around her were behaving so irrationally? It was the other inmates making her do stupid things. Mary visited occasionally, but Helena found it difficult; the two women had never been close and Helena knew she would be blamed for Edgar's departure. She wondered what Mary would do about the huge house in EdgwareeathHeath. One thing was certain, she would neither be asked to live with Mary, nor would she wish to.

Cyril came every weekend with Stephen, but there was still no sign of Alice. Helena wondered if Robert wanted his daughter to forget her own mother. Despite the horror of the ECT treatment, Helena had to admit she felt much calmer. The diagnosis had been changed from schizophrenia to manic depression. Her doctor had reassured her that a mix of drugs would help to keep her on an even keel, sodium amytal and largactil had been mentioned. All things considered life did not seem quite so bleak.

Helena smiled; Cyril would be here soon, he said he wanted her to live with him. She wondered if she really loved him, certainly her feelings were not like those she had once had for Robert; perhaps that was a good thing. Such an all-consuming love was like fire, dangerous, destructive; it had destroyed them both. Someone, she couldn't remember who, had told her Robert was staying in the army. Surely that would strengthen her right to care for her little girl; where else could Alice go?

At last Helena was given permission to leave the hospital and have a weekend with Cyril. She inspected his sitting room; she walked round slowly touching the shabby furniture, gazing out of the window.

'It's not much,' he said, 'in time, we can do it up.'

She put her fingers on his lips, 'Don't, anything is better than hospital.' She put her hand to her mouth, 'Oh, that isn't very kind, I didn't mean it like that.'

'It can't be easy living with all those crazy people.' He grinned at her.

'Don't forget, I'm one of them.'

'This is the beginning of something better, see how you cope'. He held her close, felt her hair brush his cheek.

'I want to etch every detail of how you look, right now, into my memory. So, when I'm a doddery old codger, I will be able to recapture this moment.'

Helena shivered, hadn't Robert said something similar? How did he feel now, would he ever forgive her? Poor Robert.

'I have never wanted anyone as much as I want you.' Cyril held her hand, 'Come with me,' he said and led her towards the bedroom. Stephen started crying.

Helena smiled, 'He needs his feed.'

He watched as she hurried to their son, 'You are well worth waiting for.'

The Eighth Army, under General McCreery had entered Klagenfurt on 8th May. Robert and his comrades had been busy ever since, sorting out a city filled with refugees, defeated German soldiers and Yugoslav troops who wished to claim the city as their own. He was billeted in Tentschach Castle where Benito Mussolini had stayed in 1943. Robert was billeted in one of the turret rooms; he liked the isolation in the evenings where he could stare out of his window and dream of a better life.

He had been interrogating German troops who had served in the death camps. The horror made him stop thinking about his situation and concentrate instead on the thousands of poor sods left to die. News had come through about Josef Kramer, the commandant at Bergen-Belsen; the bastard had been hanged. That night he treated himself to a glass of schnapps.

The letter from his mother, received not long after he left England, had enclosed a picture from Alice. She had drawn herself in the middle of the page, alone. She had written her name underneath and added some kisses, but according to Gladys, the child had refused to draw anyone else.

Chapter 32

December 1945

When John walked Alice back from the park, it was nearly dark and she was crying.

'Now stop upsetting yourself, you don't want to make Nana cross, do you?'

As John opened the front door, Gladys, in coat and hat, hurried towards him.

'You're very late; Albert will be waiting for his tea.' She looked at Alice and then at John.

'What's happened? I told you to be careful with her, has she hurt herself?'

'You know your trouble, Mum, you make too much fuss of this child. She's got to take the odd bump or two. She's all right; don't you think I checked myself when she fell off the swing? What kind of man do you think I am?'

'She didn't bang her head, did she?' Gladys turned to Alice, 'Did you bang your head?'

Alice stared at the floor.

'You're all right, aren't you, I look after you, don't I?' John said and patted Alice on the shoulder.

Gladys struggled to get Alice into her coat. 'Right, I'll be off, goodness knows what Albert will be thinking, worried sick probably.'

As they walked down the road, Gladys noticed that Alice was limping.

'Why are you walking like that, did you hurt your leg?'

Alice shook her head, 'My bottom's sore.'

Gladys stopped and took out her handkerchief to wipe Alice's face, puffy with tears.

She gently removed the child's wire-rimmed glasses and cleaned them.

'Did you fall off the swing?'

Alice nodded.

'My word,' Albert said, 'I'm glad you two are back.'

He glanced at Alice and then at Gladys who shook her head,

'Come and have a cuddle with your old Grandpop,' he said and lifted Alice on his knee. She snuggled down against the woolly cardigan Nana had knitted. She put her fingers in her mouth, but winced as she wriggled to get comfortable.

'It's all John's fault; he let her fall off the swing, she was in a terrible state when he brought her back. I'm not sure we should let him take her out again.'

'I don't like Uncle John,' Alice whispered.

'If you've had a nasty bump,' Albert said, 'would you like a nice warm bath in front of the fire?'

Alice nodded. She put her fingers back in her mouth and closed her eyes. Albert put her on his armchair and went to fetch the tin bath.

'Shall I have a word with John?'

'One of us will have to,' Gladys said, 'I'm not happy about this. Heaven only knows what Robert will say when he gets home.'

While Albert brought bowls of warm water, Gladys undressed Alice as she lay in the armchair. When she got to Alice's knickers, she saw blood.

'No wonder she said her bottom was sore.' Gladys examined the knickers; there was no sign of mud or earth, just blood. Alice was drowsy with sleep and Gladys didn't want to wake her. She would wait until the child was safe in bed before she said anything to Albert.

After the bath, he made some cocoa and walked upstairs with Alice, waited until she'd drunk it and settled her down for the night.

Gladys was sitting, white-faced, in her chair when he came down.

'Do you think John has interfered with her?' She showed Albert the knickers. 'She cried when I tried to wash her... down there.'

'Surely there must be some other explanation; he's a married man for heaven's sake, married to our daughter. Why would he do anything to a little girl like Alice?'

Gladys slumped forward, 'Look, there's no dirt, just blood; how could that have happened? Surely if she hurt herself when she fell, there would be earth or grass stains.'

'I suppose so.'

'We can't say anything; just make sure we never leave Alice alone with him again.'

'What about Connie and Pauline?'

'She wouldn't thank us for wrecking her marriage, with the baby and everything.'

'Perhaps we're wrong,' Gladys said.

Albert nodded and went to the sideboard to pour two small tots of brandy, 'For medicinal purposes,' he said, 'let's just hope we're wrong.'

Alice's nightmares continued and finally Albert and Gladys brought Alice into their bed so they could comfort her during the night.

Once Pauline was born, it had become a regular arrangement with John and Connie for them to bring her over for a visit on Sunday afternoon, for tea. Albert walked into the kitchen.

'I'm going to say something today,' he said.

Gladys nodded and continued setting the tea tray. 'Where's Alice?'

'In her room.'

'Would it be best to leave her there?'

'No, she's going to sit with me. I don't want her to feel we're shutting her out.'

'Suppose there's a row, you know what John can be like.'

'You just leave it to me, but I want you to open the door when they arrive so I can keep Alice close.'

Albert struggled upstairs, resting halfway to get his breath back.

'Now then my little chick, we are going downstairs and I am going to tell you a story.'

'Is Uncle John coming?'

'Yes, but you are not going out with him ever again. You are going to stay with Nana and me.' He hugged her. 'Now, I'm going to ask your Auntie if you left Benjy for her to look after.......he'll be wondering where you are.'

'He doesn't love me anymore, Grandpop, he ran away in the garden.'

'We will just have to try to find him then.'

They were halfway down the stairs when there was a knock at the door. Albert hurried into the sitting room, grabbed one of Alice's books and sat her on his knee.

'Hello, Dad,' Connie said and leaned over to kiss them both.

'Grandpop used to read me stories, didn't you, Dad?'

John stood in the doorway; Albert glanced at him and was pleased to see he looked uncomfortable.

'I'll put our little treasure on the settee shall I, Dad?'

'Yes,' said Albert and he put his arms round Alice's shoulders. 'I need to speak to you later, John.'

John sat down beside his daughter's crib.

In the kitchen Gladys opened a tin of pineapple chunks and poured evaporated milk into a small jug.

'Oh,' said Connie, 'John's favourite.'

Gladys made no comment.

'How's Alice after her fall?'

'She's all right now, but you might as well know she won't be going to the park with John anymore.'

'That's a bit hard on the kiddie isn't it; she enjoys going on the swing. You can't protect her from every bump or scratch.'

Gladys had the bread knife in her hand, as she turned she pointed it at Connie.

'I'm telling you she's not going out with John again and that's an end to it.'

'Have your own way, Mum.'

Connie pulled a face and went to set the table. John was sitting staring into space and Albert was reading to Alice. The air was heavy as though thunder storms were brewing.

'What's wrong, Mum?' Connie said as she stood in the kitchen doorway.

Gladys paused. 'Your Dad's not at all well; Dr Costello says there's nothing more he can do. He can't cope with this upset.'

'What upset; is it something I've done?'

'No….it's nothing you've done.'

'So, it's John then, is it?'

Gladys picked up a plate of bread and margarine and a home-made cake. John leapt to his feet when he saw her.

'Give me those, Mum, is there anything else to bring through?'

'It's all right, I can manage.'

Throughout the meal, Albert and Gladys made a fuss of Alice and encouraged her to eat. Connie ate in silence. When Pauline stirred, John picked her up.

'Come and see your little cousin,' he said and beckoned to Alice who backed away from him.

'Leave the child alone,' Albert said.

'Can I make up her bottle,' Connie asked and she and Gladys went to the kitchen.

John put Pauline back in her crib, 'What the hell's going on? All because she fell off a bloody swing, what happens if she has a really bad fall? Christ almighty.'

Gladys stormed into the room, 'Don't you use your foul language in this house.'

'I do think you're making a bit of a fuss, Mum.' Connie said as she lifted the now screaming baby from her crib.

'I'll get her bottle,' Gladys said.

'Listen John, I don't care what you think of the way we care for Alice. Robert gave us a lot of responsibility and I think you know why she will not be going out with you again.'

Connie was rocking Pauline who continued to scream. 'What's going on, Dad?'

'I don't want to say anymore.'

'You can't leave it like that.'

'I've had enough of this,' John said. He pushed his chair so hard it fell over. Alice started crying and clung to Albert. John leaned over her.

'What have you been saying? Telling fairy tales, I wouldn't wonder.'

Albert pushed Alice behind him as he got to his feet.

'She said nothing, she didn't need to.'

Gladys hurried in and handed Connie the bottle. She stood beside Albert, white-faced and shaking.

'I think you had better go home now,' Albert said.

'But I've got to feed Pauline,'

'You can do that when you get home, my dear, it won't take long.' Albert turned to John.

'Please go.'

Thick veins in John's neck stood out blue against his florid skin. He moved closer to Albert. 'You...stupid...old...man.'

He raised his arm across his chest and Gladys cried out as she leapt between them, she raised her hands to protect them both. John's back-handed blow made contact with Gladys' left shoulder. She fell back against Albert who staggered as he tried to keep his balance. Alice was sobbing behind the settee.

'Get out of my home,' Albert said.

Connie was crying as she gathered her belongings. She put Pauline back in her crib and tugged at John's sleeve, 'Come on John, we know when we're not wanted.'

Albert stood close to Gladys whose left arm hung, immobile at her side. They listened to the diminishing cries of their younger granddaughter as she was taken home.

'I wonder if I will ever see that little girl again.' Gladys said.

Chapter 33

December 1945

Mary read Robert's letter and sighed. She had enough to do organising the redecoration of the apartment and helping Phillip and Patricia to move in. Mary knew all Robert's furniture had gone to Cyril's when Helena left. She decided it would not be wise to inform Robert of his furniture's present whereabouts. She would pass his letter to Helena and Cyril; it was their problem now.

...As far as access is concerned, I have custody of Alice; which, under the circumstances, is only right. I do not wish to stop Alice seeing her mother, but I must protect her from any emotional outbursts. Alice will stay with my parents and if Helena wants to see her, she will see her in their home. Initially she may visit my parents and Alice at their convenience, once a month. Should the plan work well, I am prepared for the visits to be more frequent.

I will take advice from my lawyer and of course Helena's doctor. I trust this meets with your approval.

Yours
Robert

Mary was glad Alice would be allowed to see her mother, but smiled when she realised Helena would have to run the gauntlet of Gladys' disapproval. Robert was a clever man, but Mary suspected he could be vindictive when crossed. She paused; Edgar probably thought she was being vindictive too in refusing to divorce him. She folded the letter and put in her desk drawer; there were more important things to think about.

The December weather had been unsettled and it turned cold with high winds and snow. The first problem would be getting Helena and a small baby to and from Albert and Gladys' home, assuming the baby couldn't be left with someone, but Alice would want to see her little brother. Would Robert allow Cyril's son into his parent's home, Gladys was bound to tell him. Would Robert allow Alice to visit her mother and half-brother at Cyril's home? Mary sighed and wondered what other possible arrangements would be dreamed up. As she was the only one with a car, there was going to be much ferrying about. She wasn't even sure where Cyril lived.

With so much toing and froing, the problem of petrol supply became more challenging. Of course, it wasn't only petrol. Mary had seen women in shabby and inadequate clothing waiting, huddled outside shops, in orderly queues desperate to find food for their families. It didn't feel like victory.

Everything was in short supply and there was little chance of the situation improving. She would have to do a lot more shopping to cater for her lodgers until they were settled. She wondered how Philip would react if he knew that was how she referred to him and his daughter. More to the point, how was she to buy extra without more ration cards. The matter would have to wait until Philip and Patricia arrived. Whatever was decided, she would not be left to stand outside shops.

She walked round her new home checking if anything still needed doing; the whole place gleamed. She had so much to be thankful for, particularly her WVS work. During her hours at the depot there was no time to feel sorry for herself. Once home was when the black cloud threatened to choke her, then all she wanted was Edgar.

She wandered into the kitchen, made a pot of tea and some toast. She couldn't be bothered to cook for herself. She picked up the newspaper and went to her splendid living room; how she loved that room. Frost on the roof tops glittered and the air crackled with a threat of snow, but she felt safe.

According to the news; Governments were sorting themselves out with talks of an International Monetary Fund and a World Bank. Unity of purpose was what the world needed; nations needed to talk to each other. It reminded her of her days working for the government, Ministry of Ag. and Fish. It had been wonderful, a woman in a man's world. The trip to the States had been one highlight; it was there she met Gilbert. She closed her eyes and took deep breathes until the ache in her heart subsided.

From her experiences, more women leaders would help; that would be the day, she thought. Too many men believed women were chattels, either skivvies or tarts. There had been rumours of houses of prostitution being set up by crooks, in the West End; the thought made her shudder.

Chapter 34

December 1945

Alice had not seen her Uncle John and Aunt Connie or baby Pauline since that dreadful Sunday. She knew it made Grandma and Grandpop sad and wondered if they thought she was to blame. What had Uncle John said? They would send her away if she said anything about what happened in the gardens, but she hadn't said anything. It made her tummy feel strange, perhaps that why she was sick in the morning. She was scared and didn't have Benjy any more, to comfort her

She knew Gladys visited Connie when John was at work and she was at school. There was never any mention of what had happened when he hit Grandma, but she still couldn't use her left arm. Grandpop made her go to the doctor, but it didn't want to get better, that was what Grandpop said. She wondered when he would try to find Benjy, he'd said he would, but he had been so wheezy Alice was scared to remind him. If only she could go to the garden on her own, she'd have a look, but she knew she would never go there again.

It was Saturday afternoon and Alice was bored; she could hear children playing.

'Can I play outside?'

'Now what I've told you,' Gladys said, 'those children are common and I wouldn't be at all surprised if some of them have nits.'

Alice decided she had better go upstairs and play with Nana's button box; she had nothing else to do. It wasn't too bad in the winter, when it soon got dark, but in the summer, she spent hours watching from her window; always watching other children playing.

She took the lid off the wicker work container which held thousands

144

of buttons. Today she would try to sort them according to colour or perhaps she would imagine what kind of garment they came from; she could draw a picture of what the garment looked like and of someone wearing it. She liked drawing and making up stories. Sometimes she made patterns with lots of different colours, but always she returned to the window to watch the children outside.

She sat on a stool with her nose pressed against the glass and looked down at the lines of washing stretched across the square. She saw women standing on their doorsteps, talking while children careered around on carts made from orange boxes and old pram wheels or played tig. She wanted to make friends, but didn't know how.

She wondered when she would see Daddy again; it was always exciting when he was home because he took her out to the zoo or on a boat ride down the Thames. He brought her presents and once he took all of them, Grandpop and Nana as well, to Eastbourne for a holiday. Even then it had been difficult to mix with children on the beach. Nana did not approve of children who ran in and out of the sea in their knickers. She had knitted Alice a woollen costume; it stretched when it got wet and it was scratchy. At least she had been allowed to paddle and Daddy had helped her build an elaborate sandcastle.

Her world was peopled with adults, most of whom were her grandparents' generation. On Sunday afternoons they took a bus and then a walk to the Albert memorial and back. Grandpop used to come too; now he found it too exhausting. Nana had knitted her a new stuffed animal, a small bear; it wasn't the same as having Benjy.

Although Alice enjoyed doing school work, her class-mates had sorted out who they wanted to be friends with and Alice was rarely included in their games. She found grown-ups were easier to get on with and at playtime walked round holding a teacher's hand.

Gladys was surprised to receive a letter from Alice's Headmistress just before the Christmas holiday.

'Albert, listen to this, Alice has been chosen to represent the school. She's got to present money to Princess Marina's charity. Wait until I tell Mrs Fleming, she's always going on about her grand kids.'

Albert smiled, 'What a clever girl we've got.'

'Is she a real princess?' Alice asked.

'Yes, she's a member of the royal family,' Grandpop said.

'Didn't her husband die in the war, Bert?'

'That's right, poor lady.'

'Can I have a new dress, Nana?'

145

'We'll see. I think that new white one with red spots would be nice, you've only worn it once.'

'Can I have some new shoes then?'

Albert smiled, 'I think we can manage that.'

When the big day arrived, Alice and her very proud grandparents travelled by bus to the Albert Hall. Alice stared at the huge building.

'Does it belong to you, Grandpop?'

'No sweetheart, a long time ago we had a queen called Victoria, her husband was called Albert so I supposed it belonged to him.'

Alice nodded. 'Do you think I should practise my curtsy again?'

'You'll be fine, just don't fall over,' Albert said.

'I wish Robert was here.' Gladys said.

'I'll tell Daddy about it when he comes home and I'll tell Mummy next time I see her.'

It was a cheerful bus ride home; Alice sat on Albert's knee and looked out of the window at all the brightly-lit shops. As they got nearer to their stop, the shops were smaller; instead of large stores there were tobacconists, fish shops, barrows piled high with fruit and vegetables. The pavements were crowded with people hurrying to shut up shops at the end of the day's trading.

'I'm hungry,' said Alice

'What did you have at dinner-time?'

'My tummy was all fluttery so I didn't have anything.'

'Ah,' said Albert as he glanced at Gladys, 'I think our clever little girl deserves a treat. What do you like best of all?'

'Could we,' Alice paused, 'have fish and chips?'

'That would save having to cook our tea,' Albert said, 'you get Alice ready for bed and I'll walk down to the fish shop.'

'Don't you overdo it Bert.'

Alice felt happy as she watched Grandpop smile and squeeze Nana's hand.

Tucked up in bed, Alice went through her day, walking across the stage, giving a curtsey and dropping the bag of money in a large box. She could still hear the applause as cameras flashed. Grandpop had paid for a small photograph of her which he said she could give to Daddy when he came home.

Her tummy was full to bursting and Grandpop had let her eat chips with her fingers when Nana wasn't looking. She licked her lips; she could still taste the tang of vinegar and salt. Tomorrow she would tell her teacher all about it.

When Alice woke, a gap in the curtains let sunlight fall across her face. She watching patterns on the ceiling and wall; they shivered as the bedroom curtains moved in the breeze from an open window. Today she was looking forward to going to school; all the children wanted to hear about her afternoon at the Albert Hall, they would want to talk to her, ask her questions. She listened to the usual noises coming from the kitchen; Nana was getting breakfast. She didn't want to be late, but she couldn't hear voices so Grandpop must still be in bed. She would go next door and have a quick cuddle.

She heard a noise and then a crash; perhaps Grandpop had dropped the glass he kept his teeth in. She hurried next door and climbed onto the bed. Grandpop was staring up at the ceiling.

'Good morning, Grandpop.' She waited, but he didn't answer. 'Please talk to me, Grandpop?'

She knelt on the bed and leaned over to give him a kiss. As she leant against him, he slumped to one side. She gasped and gripped his shoulder and gave it a little shake.

'Please Grandpop.'

His head lolled to one side and his false teeth slid slowly out of his mouth. Alice screamed and ran downstairs.

'Come quick, Grandpop's ill, he won't speak to me.'

Gladys wiped her hands on her apron and ran up the stairs. Within seconds Alice heard Nana's cries. Alice put her hands over her ears and went to Albert's chair. She climbed into it and sat with her knees to her chin; she sucked her fingers and wiped away tears as she rocked back and forth.

Chapter 35

December 1945

Robert was given compassionate leave. The sound of his boots echoed up the stairwell and along the balcony to his parent's maisonette; he let himself in. Alice was waiting in the hallway, when he picked her up, she sobbed and clung to him.

'I found Grandpop, and now they've taken him away.'

Robert held her in his arms and carried her into the living room. Gladys came to meet him; she didn't weep until he put an arm round her. The only other sound was the ticking of the clock that Albert was given when he retired, such a short time ago. There was so much to do; Robert had never arranged a funeral. Gladys was in no fit state to look after herself, never mind anyone else, so who would care for Alice?

'I'm going to make a cup of tea; have you eaten today, Mum?'

Gladys shook her head.

'Alice, see if there are any eggs in the pantry, I'm going to boil an egg for your Nana.'

'I couldn't eat anything.'

'You are having something, Mum, so sit down and wait to be served.'

There was a knock at the door; it was their neighbour, Sally Groves.

'Thank goodness you are home; I'm really worried about your mum.'

Robert led her through to the living room, Gladys hadn't moved and Alice was kneeling at her feet, her head in Gladys' lap.' He beckoned Sally into the kitchen.

'I'm doing Mum a boiled egg and some toast.'

'Your Alice's no better; the poor little mite has had hardly anything. She was the one who found your poor father.'

'I know she's just told me. What am I going to do; I've only got seven days leave.'

'What about your Connie and John, couldn't they look after her for the time being? I don't think your mum will cope.'

'No, I suppose Mum's told you about Helena?'

Sally rested her hand on Robert's arm, 'Yes, love, I know. Shall we have a little talk with Alice? It would make your mum feel better if she knew Alice was sorted.'

'That's a good idea, let's do it now.'

He carried in cups of tea and watched as Gladys took a sip. Alice clung to him and he sat her on his knees.

'Now then Alice, Nana isn't very well at the moment and Sally has come up with a really good idea. How would it be if you stayed with Uncle John and Aunt Connie for a while; you'd be able to help with baby Pauline.'

'No, no, I won't go, I hate Uncle John, don't make me go, please Daddy.' She clung to him and sobbed.

Gladys held her arms out and Alice went to her still crying. 'Don't make me go.'

'Why don't you like Uncle John; he's really nice to you and takes you to the park; that's what Nana said.'

'He said you'd send me away... if I tell you.'

Robert sighed, 'What the hell's going on?'

'Please son, don't be cross, it isn't Alice's fault.'

'Shall I take Alice to my house while you and your Mum have a talk?' Sally turned to Alice. 'You can meet some of my grandchildren, sweetheart, you'd like that.'

Alice nodded and went to get her coat.

'I'll keep her for her tea.'

'See if she'll tell you anything. Why on earth did she think we'd send her away?'

Sally shook her head. 'I'll do what I can; I'd better let you get on now.'

As the front door clicked shut, Robert pulled up a chair. Before he could speak, there was noise from the kitchen. He leapt up and rushed to the cooker. The egg had boiled dry.

Damn and blast, 'Mother, your egg must be rock hard. Is it okay if I mash it up for you and make a sandwich?'

'I'm not really hungry.'

'Nonsense.'

Robert gave her a plate plus sandwich. 'I want to see this eaten and I

149

want to know what been going on.'

Gladys leaned back in her chair. 'Dad and I couldn't be sure, but Alice got hurt when she was with him.'

'What do you mean hurt?'

Gladys closed her eyes. 'It was the blood, you see, made us wonder.'

'What blood?'

'Well, she fell off the swing; I always thought he pushed her too high.'

'I suppose she grazed her knees, but all kids do that.'

'She was so upset and she wouldn't say…'

Gladys dabbed at her eyes. 'We gave her a bath when we got back, that's when I found the blood… on her knickers, but apart from the blood there wasn't a mark, no grass stain, earth, nothing. She said she hurt, 'down there'; how could that happen?'

Mother and son stared at each other; unspoken words hung like boulders between them.

Sally came back soon after. 'She's eaten a good tea and she said she'd like to play with Beth. How would it be if she stayed with my daughter until you can make some other arrangements? She'd only be a couple of streets away from here, got three kiddies of her own. It might do Alice good, a bit of company…'

Robert slumped down on the kitchen stool 'I should have been here.'

'Now then don't let your mother see you cry.'

'If your daughter could help out, I would be so very grateful… after what Alice's been through.'

'I'll be going round to Maureen and Fred's soon. Alice can walk round with me and meet them all.'

Alice held Sally's hand as they walked to her daughter's house. Sally's husband had died years ago and Nana had helped out then. Perhaps that was why she was helping Nana now.

'You've seen my grandchildren when they've come to visit, haven't you?'

Alice nodded, 'I never played with them before because Nana doesn't like me playing out.'

'That's because your Nana loves you so much that she wants to keep you safe.'

'She said it was because I might get nits.'

Sally laughed.

'What are your grandchildren called?'

'There's Peter, he's ten, then Andy he's nearly eight and the baby is

Beth and she's five and a half.'

'Nearly the same age as me, I'll be five next; can I play with her?'

'You certainly can, in fact how would you feel about staying with them for a little while? You and Beth could share her bed; that would be fun.'

For the first time since Albert's death, Alice didn't feel frightened. Daddy was home and if Beth liked her, perhaps they could be friends.

'Won't your daughter mind if I stay?'

'We'll have to ask her, won't we?'

Sally pulled a key out of her pocket and opened her daughter's front door. Alice felt nervous; suppose they didn't like her. When they walked in, children swarmed around them.

'Now just a minute you lot, let me introduce a friend of mine, Alice Warren. I've brought her here to see you and I want you to let her join in your games.'

The girl, Beth, grabbed Alice's hand and pulled her up the hallway. 'We're playing sardines, come on, find somewhere to hide with me.'

'What's all this then, Mum?' A large man in shirtsleeves put down his newspaper.

'She's Gladys Warren's granddaughter, she needs somewhere to stay.'

Maureen turned from the stove where she was preparing the children's tea, 'I told you Fred, the old man died.'

Fred Coleman shook his head, 'Nice old boy, what a shame; the little girl lives with them doesn't she?'

'That's the point, her Dad is home on leave,' Sally looked round to make sure Alice was out of earshot, 'Can't go to her mother, she's…' Sally tapped her forehead.

'Poor little thing, of course she can stop here for a bit.'

Sally turned to Fred. 'That all right with you, then?'

'The more the merrier,' he said and went back to his paper.

Sally stood up, 'Right I'll go and get her some clothes. What about taking her to school, she goes to the church school, shall I do that?'

'That would be a help, it's like a mad house getting my lot ready and out in time.'

Sally kissed her daughter and left; at least Robert would have one thing less to worry about.

'Are you going to let Helena know about your dad?'

Robert sighed, 'The trouble is, Mum, I bet she'd try to use it to get Alice living with her.'

'But you've got custody; it's for you to decide, isn't it?'

'The best thing I can do is get some arrangements sorted out and then tell her. I've said some dreadful things and done some stupid things; I'm sorry about that, but… I don't want another man bringing up my child.'

'So, what are you going to do?'

'Fostering perhaps, the trouble is, I did what I said, I signed on for nine years, so I won't be out until she's thirteen. Perhaps I shouldn't have been so impulsive, but…'

'I'd have her if I could, but…'

'Mum you've done enough.'

'It's not easy to find foster parents these days, not since the war. So many poor little souls with no-one left.'

Robert shrugged, 'I'll think of something. What's more important is that I am here with you for the funeral. I'll never forgive myself for leaving you to cope on your own.'

Gladys took his hands in hers. 'That wasn't your fault.'

'Does Helena's mother know?'

'I haven't told her, you're not thinking of sending Alice to her, are you?'

'I'd rather not, and besides she would be too far away from you. I want her to visit you often; you're very important to both of us.' He paused, 'I'll write to Mary, see what she suggests.'

Sally Groves arrived, 'She's settled a treat; I've come back for her clothes. Maureen and Fred are happy to have her for a couple of weeks so that gives you some breathing space.'

'I don't expect your daughter to do this for nothing, let me give you some money.'

'I don't think Alice will eat Maureen of of house and home.'

'I am very, very grateful. Now, if you'll excuse me, I'm going to the undertakers, then to the welfare people to see if they have any ideas for a more permanent arrangement.'

'I'll keep your mum company for a bit, a natter will do us both good.'

Robert turned away; sorrow threatened to choke him.

Alice thought back to what Uncle John had said; if she was naughty, Grandpop and Nana would send her away. Now she had been sent away, perhaps it was her fault Grandpop died. If the Coleman family found out what she had done, they might send her away too. She decided to say nothing about what happened in the park. She watched as Peter, Andy and Beth hurtled around in the house and outside in the street. They always tried to include her in their games, but she felt too sad to play.

The best time was if she woke in the night; then she would listen to

Beth's breathing at the other end of the bed they shared. The house, silent in the darkness, felt safe.

'Can we go to see Nana after school today?' Alice said one morning as she was eating her breakfast.

Maureen Coleman smiled, 'What a good idea, you could take her some flowers.'

Sally collected Alice, as usual, for the walk to school.

'Can I stay with Maureen and Fred until Daddy comes home? I like it there.'

'I think your daddy is making arrangements for you, you see it is a bit cramped at Maureen's and Daddy thinks you really need a bedroom of your own.'

'No I don't, I like sharing with Beth.'

'Well let's see what happens.'

When they reached the school gates, Sally kissed Alice, 'I'll see you later, have a good day. I'll let you choose some flowers for your Nana.'

'Can't I write to Daddy and tell him I don't want my own bedroom?

PART TWO 1946

When the power of love
overcomes the love of power,
the world will know peace.

—Jimi Hendrix
Musician

Chapter 36

January 1946

Peace was hard to cope with; bombing raids had stopped, but little else improved. Mary wondered if life would ever return to what it was before the war. Crime was rampant; too many British people had lost both honesty and decency. To Mary's disgust, Billy Hill, one of Britain's best-known gangsters, wallowed in publicity, given to him by newspapers, and claimed the title 'Bandit King' as though criminal acts were something to be proud of. She was more than grateful to live in the safety of a fourth flat apartment away from danger.

Mary reread Robert's letter. How foolish of him to sign on for a further nine years, probably an act of outrage against Helena and her problems. Now it looked as though his impetuous behaviour had come back to bite him. Had she been living in her old home, with servants, she could have made arrangements for Alice. She paused as she realised what pleasure it would have given her; they had much in common. Of course, it was out of the question now, Alice must not be moved too far from her other grandmother, frail and alone. She was the only link the child had with her father.

Perhaps a local family might be keen to foster Alice; she was no trouble and would be starting school soon. She would put the idea to Robert; it would be easier for Alice if she knew some of the children starting with her rather than be moved to a strange area where she knew no-one. That was the best plan; she would have a chat with Alice next time she ferried her over to her mother's, find out how she felt.

Connie Stanley did not enjoy motherhood; John made no effort to share the burden of a crotchety daughter, prone to colic. Sleep was hard to come by at night, so John offered to do night shifts on a permanent basis so he could sleep during the day. Connie spent much of her time at her mother's while he slept. It avoiding the embarrassment of telling John he was not welcome at his mother-in-law's. It was a separate life which suited Connie; it did not last.

Winter that January was severe. Energy supplies often failed; no-one could keep warm. Animals froze or died in their fields, starved by lack of fodder. There was a desperate food shortage which led to further reduction in rations. Many businesses closed down temporarily. The Gresham Club in Abchurch Street limped on, lit by candles for the few members who presented themselves; John worked there. He was a commissionaire during the day, bowing and scrapping to the toffs; how he hated it. Once on night duty, he was caretaker cum odd job man. At least, at night, no-one saw him performing menial jobs like sweeping up outside and cleaning urinals.

On a freezing morning, in January, his body was found down the cellar steps by the barman who was expecting a delivery; his head had been caved in. The police could only guess at the sequence of events. The club had been ransacked; any silverware had been taken and the thieves tried unsuccessfully to force the safe.

For once Pauline had slept so Connie was less than pleased when she was woken by loud knocks at the door; John had probably forgotten his keys. She swung the door open to find a policeman there.

'Mrs Stanley?'

Connie pulled her dressing gown more tightly, 'Is it Mum?'

'No, Madam. Is your husband called John?'

She nodded.

'Can I come in?'

She turned and stumbled through to their sitting room.

'I'm so sorry to bring bad news; is there anyone who could come and stay with you.'

'Is he badly hurt?'

The policeman paused, 'Your husband's body was found this morning, by the Gresham Club's barman.'

Connie slumped in her chair.

'He was attacked during the night.'

'Attacked?'

'He must have disturbed them and he suffered serious head injuries…. he passed away.'

Once the policeman had left, Connie took Pauline round to tell her mother.

'What am I going to do, Mum?'

'I don't know, I think you have to apply for a widow's pension; that's what Robert did for me.'

'I can't live on that; I've got Pauline to bring up.' She dabbed at her eyes and sniffed hard. 'It's not fair, Mum, when did John do anybody any harm?'

Gladys leaned back in her chair and closed her eyes; she had nothing to say.

Sally Groves shouted as she opened the front door, 'Gladys, it's only me.'

'I am so glad to see you.'

'Why, what's happened?'

'John, you know Connie's husband, has been murdered.'

'Oh,' She paused, 'Is that the one who… you know… interfered…'

Gladys took a deep breath, 'Yes, that's him.'

'Do you want to talk to Alice about it?'

Gladys shook her head, 'I can't cope with that.'

'Don't worry,' I'll talk to the kiddie, I'll see she's all right.'

'Shall I put Maureen in the picture?'

Gladys nodded and grabbed Sally's hand, 'You're a good friend.'

John's killers were never identified but various criminals, known to operate in the Cannon Street area of London, were questioned.

Alice hugged Fred the bear and whispered in his ear. 'Uncle John has had an accident; he's gone away now.' She snuggled down and rolled closer to Beth.

She slept soundly all night.

Chapter 37

September 1946

Warm autumn weather lifted Helena's spirits; she was going to see Alice today. Mother would collect her and Stephen after lunch. There was awkwardness about the visits, but it was better than nothing. Everyone would be on best behaviour except Stephen, who was becoming more mobile by the day.

Helena was irritated by Robert's arrangements; Alice needed to see her mother and brother more often than once a month. Gladys' friend, Sally saw more of Alice, took her to school; it wasn't right. It was time things changed; perhaps Mother could be persuaded to make some suggestions today.

Alice and Sally were already there when Mary arrived with Helena and Stephen.

'Mummy,' Alice hugged Helena and held out her arms to Mary. 'I'm so glad you've come; I've got lots to tell you.'

Stephen grizzled and struggled to be put down.

'I've got something for you to play with, Stephen,' Alice said and led the way into the living room.

Sally stood up, 'I'll go and make a cup of tea.'

Helena glanced at her ex-mother-in-law, shocked by her appearance.

'Sorry to hear you've not been well,' she paused; she could hardly call her Mum now.

'I've lost everyone.'

'My Dear Mrs Warren, you have had a very trying time, please let me know if we can do anything to make things a bit easier for you,' Mary took Gladys' hand and stroked it.

'We've all lost, haven't we?' Helena looked from Mary to Gladys,

'I've lost Alice.'

No-one spoke, as Sally breezed in with a tray of tea and a few biscuits. 'What would young Stephen like?'

'I've brought his bottle of juice.'

'Can he have a biscuit?' Sally offered the plate to Helena.

Helens clenched her fists; no-one was going contradict her statement or even comment on it, nobody cared how she felt. They were all ganging up on her, ignoring her.

She glanced at Mary who shook her head. No, she would not leave it, Alice was her child; she needed her mother.

'I want to see Alice at least once a fortnight from now on.'

'Now is not the time.'

'Mother, don't interfere; how could you understand? When did you see us? You were too busy being the society hostess.' Helena stared at Sally. 'Ten minutes in the evening before she swept down to dinner.'

Stephen was on the floor, sucking at a biscuit, Alice knelt beside him. She had some wooden bricks in her hand.

'Look Stephen, we can play with these.' She placed one on top of another and Stephen knocked it off.'

He chortled when Alice did it again, the adults watched, in silence.

Mary drove them back to Camden Town. She would have to be careful she didn't make things worse; let Helena make the first move.

'Why didn't you back me up, Mother?'

'Do you realise, my dear, how much damage your outburst caused today?'

'Why? Because I asked to see more of my child?'

'I understand how you feel, but you went about it in an inappropriate way.'

'Robert is just doing it to upset me.'

'You both have to think less about what you want and more about what Alice needs.'

The raised voices startled Stephen who started crying.

Mary pulled up outside Cyril's block of flats. 'I'll write to Robert, but I warn you, after today, Gladys may well say she can't cope with your visits.'

Helena struggled up four flights of stairs to the front door. Cyril wouldn't be back from work yet. She wished her new home was less dismal, but Cyril said they couldn't afford to have decorators in and he wasn't about to start painting and papering. She smiled; she would show him how to make a place look inviting. It would take her mind off Robert's determination to ruin her life.

She would ask the landlord if she could borrow a ladder and some brushes. She'd decorate the place herself. Cyril was a good man, but he was a bit of a stick in the mud. He needed to be more adventurous, make his life more exciting.

Alice held Sally's hand as they walked back to Maureen and Fred's.

'I wish Mummy didn't get so upset.'

'She doesn't mean to upset you, you know, and she has been ill.'

'Do you think my Daddy will be home soon?'

'Let's hope so.'

'Can I stay with Auntie Maureen and Uncle Fred for ever and ever; I like it there.'

'Not for ever and ever, but for the time being; will that do?'

'I heard Uncle Fred talking in the kitchen last night. He said I would be too much for Auntie Maureen when the next one arrives.'

'Oh.'

'Are they having another little girl to stay, as well as me?'

'Now don't you worry about that.'

Chapter 38

October 1946

Vera Clements had been unable to have more than one child; her husband, Douglas, had suggested fostering so their daughter, Katy, had company. The money from fostering helped as business wasn't good. Vera resented the time she had to spend on other people's children, but all her husband's pipedreams of promotion had come to nothing.

It was arranged for Alice to meet the Clements at the local Social Services clinic. Only Vera and Douglas attended as Katy was at school. Alice didn't realise why she was meeting them until Sally explained another place had been found for her.

'Please don't make me go, please. I'll never see Beth again, she is my friend.'

'You won't be too far away,' Sally said. 'We'll arrange something, you can come for tea.'

'But it won't be the same; and what about Nana and Mummy and everyone?"

'We'll talk to Vera and Douglas, see what we can arrange, Sweetheart. I'll let your grandmother have your address and Nana said Daddy will be home soon.'

Alice cried the day they came to collect her from Maureen and Fred. Douglas drove them along the Embankment towards the Royal Hospital. She and Mummy used to go that way when she was in her pushchair; sometimes Daddy was there too. Alice cuffed away her tears. Supposing the Clements didn't like her; what could she do? Run away?

The Clements lived in a large first floor apartment in Smith Street, with a garden opposite. Vera showed Alice the spare bedroom, small and sparsely furnished. Alice sat on the bed, too shocked to move. She didn't unpack her things, didn't want them to think she wanted to be there. She heard a commotion in the hallway and heard the sound of someone running up the stairs. Katy barged into the room without knocking.

'How long are you going to stay here?'

'I don't know.'

'Why aren't you with your mummy and daddy?'

'Daddy is in the army; he's gone back to Austria.'

'Has he seen any kangaroos?'

Alice paused, 'I think that's Australia.'

Katy pulled a face, 'Haven't you got a mummy?'

Alice swallowed hard, 'She's been in hospital.'

'I don't want you playing with my things; Mummy says they're for me not for other people's scruffy brats.'

Vera walked into the room, 'Good,' she said, 'you're making friends. Now put your things away, Alice, you are a big girl now, you can't expect me to do it.'

'Daddy said I could go to see my Nana soon.'

Vera raised an eyebrow, 'I'll sort something out.'

Later that evening Alice listened to the hum of voices from the living room. She clutched Fred the bear to her cheek; when she breathed in, she could smell Nana's lavender scent. She wondered how long it would take Vera 'to sort something out'.

Douglas agreed to take Alice to school each morning and Sally was happy to bring her back. That was the best part of Alice's day particularly when Sally took her to have tea with Beth and her brothers.

'There's something wrong with that kid,' Douglas said, 'she doesn't speak, doesn't eat. I don't want us accused of neglecting her.'

'She wants to know when she can see her other grandmother.'

'Where does she live?'

'No idea.'

'Get on to the welfare, let them sort something out.'

'It would have to be a Saturday or Sunday; she's at school the rest of the time.'

Douglas sighed, 'Let me guess, muggins is going to have to take her.'

'I heard Katy tell Alice not to play with her things.'

'That's a bit hard, what's the kid supposed to do, just sit in her room? I sometimes wonder if you give in to Katy too often.'

'It would be easier if you weren't gallivanting round the country so much. I'll end up taking her to school most of the time.'

'For Christ's sake, woman, you can't have it both ways. I can't drum up orders and stay at home.'

Alice looked at the strange stamp on a letter from Helena; it was French. What was Mummy doing in France, was she going to stay there?

'Dear Sugar-Plum Fairy, I have brought Stephen here for a holiday.'

Alice wondered if Cyril was with her, perhaps she would ask when she wrote back, but she couldn't write back, there was no address. She read on.

I am sending you a present, something special. I hope it fits.

It must be something to wear. Christmas was not too far away; whatever Mummy had sent her, she would wear it when Daddy came home.

She tucked the letter away in her underwear drawer and got ready to visit Gladys. Someone had arranged for her to visit every fortnight; today was the first time.

She sat in the front seat of Douglas' car. She had drawn a picture for Gladys because she didn't have any money to buy flowers.

'Can I stay until tea-time?'

'If you want, I'll pick you up at six o'clock.'

Douglas watched her as she ran up the stairs to Gladys' maisonette.

'Poor little sod,' he said as he drove off.

Alice rang along the balcony and knocked on Gladys' door. Sally Groves was there, she hugged Alice, 'Come in, come in, we've all missed you.'

Gladys stood and held out her arms.

'I'm almost as tall as you are now, Nana.'

Gladys hugged her 'How long can you stay?'

'Douglas will come at six, he said.'

'Is everything all right where you are?'

'I've got a nice bedroom... it's not as nice as here though. Douglas and Vera have a little girl, she's called Katy.'

'So, you've got someone to play with then?'

165

Alice stroked her woolly bear. 'I've decided to call him Fred, I like Fred.'

Gladys and Sally looked at each other, but said nothing.

'Right, let's get our tea, Nana has made some cake.'

Six o'clock came too soon and Sally had to take Alice by the hand to get her downstairs.

'Please can I go back to Maureen and Fred?'

'Sally kissed her, 'Once you're settled in, you'll be fine.' She put Alice in the car.

When they arrived at the Clements there was a parcel waiting for her. It had Mary Carlton's address and had been forwarded.

Katy was jumping up and down with excitement. 'What is it? Can I open it?' She started to pull at the string holding the brown paper in place.

'It's my parcel and I want to open it.' Alice picked it up and went to her bedroom, Katy followed her.

'If I can't play with your toys, you can't come into my bedroom.'

Katy ran from the room crying. Alice listened to the raised voices; she didn't care. She pulled off the brown paper and, with trembling fingers, opened a very fancy box. There was a layer of white tissue paper and underneath it was a glorious, scarlet dress. It glowed like a ruby and there was a froth of lace at the collar. Alice touched it and then carefully lifted it out of its wrappings and spread it out on her bed. The skirt was full and the sleeves long; it was a special dress for the winter. It even had a white petticoat with lace round the hem.

She wrenched off her clothes and dumped them on the floor, the soft fabric slipped over her head; it felt wonderful. She twirled in front of the mirror on the wardrobe door. The dress looked a bit big, but Alice was glad; she didn't want to grow out of it too soon. She struggled to do up the buttons at the back then rushed back into the living room to show of the best present she'd ever had.

Katy was sitting on Vera's knee, crying, both mother and daughter stared.

'It's not fair,' Katy said, 'why can't I have a dress like that instead of my stupid old green one?'

Alice wondered if she should offer to let Katy borrow it; she decided not to.

Chapter 39

December 1946

Cyril opened the door to find Helena and Steven, dishevelled and weary. He had no idea she was coming back. She started crying and flung herself into his arms while Stephen, white-faced with exhaustion gave a thin wail.

'The taxi man's waiting downstairs, Cyril, I hadn't got any money.'

Cyril stared at her, gone six weeks and now she arrives unannounced.

'What was I to do?' she said, 'We had to leave earlier than I planned because the ferries were all booked up for Christmas; I had to get back didn't I?'

Cyril sighed. 'How much does he want?'

'I don't know, I didn't ask, please forgive me.'

'We'll talk about it later. You take Stephen in while I settle up with the taxi bloke.'

As Cyril walked upstairs, he reflected on this utterly unexpected development. God only knew where she'd picked up the taxi; it had clocked up a small fortune. No point in asking; she was as high as a kite. Dr Kennedy had warned him Helena would be volatile and potentially dangerous in her manic state. He wondered when he would be able to phone Gwen; as they were both expecting to be alone, they had decided to combine forces over Christmas and the New Year. Obviously, that would have to be cancelled in time for Gwen to make other arrangements.

He thought back to the note Helena left for him.

Taken Stephen for a holiday in France.

Stephen should have been at his nursery school. Cyril was threatened with the boy losing his place there; Mrs Wilson had made that very clear. At least that problem was solved, for now. As he returned to his flat, he could hear Stephen screaming and Helena shouting. Now she was back, Cyril realised how quiet it had been without her.

Cyril was amazed by Helena's ability to dismiss her disappearance as though it were no more than a weekend away with friends.

'How on earth have you managed for money?'

Helena laughed, 'I've been teaching French students to speak English, wasn't that clever of me.'

'You could have let me know what was going on.'

'Don't make a fuss, we've come back for Christmas, darling, we couldn't leave you on your own and we've got to arrange for Alice to be with us too.'

'I've had one postcard while you were away... I didn't know where the hell you were.'

'Don't be cross, we've had a wonderful time, Stephen has said his first words, in French. What an asset if he grows up to be bi-lingual.'

'Does this mean you will take off again when I least expect it?'

'Darling, don't be an old grouch.' She leaned over and kissed him. 'We've missed you.'

Cyril watched as Stephen climbed onto a chair and grabbed a slice of bread.

'When did he last eat?'

'Yesterday, the crossing was dreadful, so rough we were both sick. You are glad to see us back, aren't you?'

Cyril looked at her, irritating, unpredictable, beautiful, she was buzzing with exuberance, the magic whatever it was still had him firmly in its clutches.

'Well, your timing is lousy; the shops are heaving with people wandering round like zombies. Christmas just around the corner.......'

'We'll have a wonderful Christmas; shall we show Daddy his presents now.'

Stephen gurgled and jumped up and down with excitement.

Cyril scooped him up; young man you are going to bed so Mummy and I can have a talk.'

He held the boy firmly as he tried to wriggle away. 'Your mum is a pain in the arse?'

Stephen giggled, 'arse,' he repeated.

Once washed, undressed and fed, Stephen fell asleep with no complaints. The next bit would be more difficult. Helena's behaviour scared Cyril a lot of the time. When manic there was no reasoning with her and sometimes, he had been frightened to go to work for fear of what she might get up to. Once her mood changed, she became increasingly depressed, scarcely moving from the armchair in the kitchen; then he was reluctant to go home from work, for fear of what he might find. For Stephen's sake he must do his best. He had phoned Mary several times after Helena disappeared to France, but there had been no reply.

He returned to the kitchen and poured himself a large gin. Helena was opening and closing cupboard doors. 'There isn't much food in, is there?'

'Enough for me.'

Helena turned then flung her arms round his neck and kissed him. 'Tell me you've missed me.'

He clutched her to him and felt desire flood through his veins like fire.

She pulled away from him slightly, her eyes sparkled.

'You have missed me, haven't you?'

'My God, you are a hussy, get into that bedroom.' He slapped her bottom; so much for the serious talk. He gulped down the rest of his gin. To hell with it, drink and be merry for heaven knew what tomorrow would bring.

On Christmas Eve Helena dragged Cyril and Stephen round the crowded shops. She felt a quiver of unease; he looked so old. Where was the man who swept her off her feet?

'Don't you think it's time we got Stephen home? He must be hungry by now.'

'Don't be silly, he loves shopping, all the hustle and bustle and bright lights.' She kissed Stephen on the forehead and for a brief moment the child was quiet.

'Helena, I'm taking him home; not only is he shattered, so am I.'

'But we haven't got the turkey or anything yet.'

'I tell you what, I'll take Stephen and the shopping you have got. Give the poor little scrap his tea and you can get everything else. I'll see you back home.'

Helena watched as he walked away with Stephen in one arm and the shopping in the other.

By the time Helena returned, in a taxi, Cyril was on his second gin. She hurtled through the front door as he opened it, laden with more than he could have carried.

'Taxi's down stairs, can you sort it.'

'You will have to learn to use the tram, Helena, we can't go on like this.'

She pulled a face at his retreating back and started to unpack.

She left the huge goose on the table and when she heard the front door slam stood smiling waiting for his reaction.

'What the hell is that?'

'Darling I've been so clever, there were no turkeys left so this nice poultry man said I could have it; he said he didn't think anyone else would to come to buy it as it was so late. Think of the money I've saved you.'

Cyril sighed and glanced at their cooker. 'How on earth can we get that in the oven?'

'Don't be so negative.'

'And how long will it take to cook.'

'How do I know; I can't do everything.'

'By the way, I've heard from your mother, didn't know she'd moved.'

'What did she say about Alice?'

'She is trying to do something about your access.'

He wouldn't tell Helena more than he had to; she'd erupt if he told her about the Clements. In her present state of mind, interference from her was bound to do more harm than good.

'But what about Christmas, that's tomorrow in case you've forgotten. Alice, should be with me. Then, when the time came, they could go to school together. I want Alice to get to know her little brother.'

'Just leave it, Helena, let me sort that out.'

'Darling,' Helena threw her arms round Cyril's neck, 'It means so much, I can't bear not being able to see her. I thought Robert had agreed to visits.'

'He has, but for the last six weeks, you haven't been here.'

Stephen had been in his pyjamas eating his supper, but he slid off his chair and banged his head on the kitchen door. He started screaming and threw himself on the floor.

'Try to play it down a bit, Helena; I think Stephen needs a bit more attention. All he hears is Alice this, Alice that…'

'Don't be so silly, he will love her like I do, she's his big sister.'

'Yes, I know but he's never met her, has he?'

Helena turned from the sink, her eyes flashed sparks. 'That is not my fault so stop getting at me.'

He stood and took her in his arms; her body was stiff, unyielding. As he held her close, he felt tension loosen its grip and she leaned against him. He kissed her.

'You take Stephen to bed; give him a cuddle while I finish the washing up.'

'I'll take him to the nursery after Christmas and explain where he's been.'

Cyril smiled, 'I'll write to your mother, see what she can do.'

Helena hurried out of the room and Cyril took a swig of his gin.

Chapter 40

Christmas 1946

Christmas lights were twinkling in the fading light as Douglas drove Alice to Nana's home. He said little, but Alice knew Katy was making a fuss over the new dress; perhaps Douglas and Vera would buy her a new one after all. She leapt out of the car once they arrived and waved as it drew away. She was staying for four whole days and, on the day after Boxing Day Daddy was taking her to a pantomime. She ran upstairs and was rosy cheeked and breathless when she knocked on Nana's door.

'Hello, Daddy,' she said.

Robert stared, 'What on earth are you wearing?'

Alice twirled round so the skirt flared out. 'Do you like it? Mummy sent it from Paris.'

'You'd better come in,' Robert said, and strode down the hallway. Alice stood for a moment, her chest felt tight and she gulped for breath. She walked into the living room where she knelt and rested her head in Nana's lap.

Robert stood in the doorway, 'Come along, child, better go upstairs and get your things unpacked and get yourself ready for bed.'

Her bedroom was unchanged. She sniffed the air; it still smelt of Nana's lavender scent. She climbed onto the bed and clutched a pillow to her chest. She thought about Benjy and hoped another little girl was looking after him. She could hear Daddy and Nana downstairs; she was supposed to be asleep, but crept to the top of the stairs so she could listen.

'What on earth was Helena thinking of? That dress makes her look like a tart.'

'Don't be too hard on the kiddie, it isn't her fault.'

'I'd better go and check on her.'

Alice scuttled back to bed. She listened to his footsteps and wondered if he meant a strawberry tart or a cherry tart; she decided she wouldn't ask.

On Christmas morning there was a pillowcase of presents for her. She tore paper off the biggest. It was a compendium of board games; she wondered if she would be allowed to take it back to the Clements. What was the point, Katy would always have to win; it would be better to leave it with Nana. She could hear voices downstairs; she'd better get up. She took the two presents she had chosen for Nana and Daddy. Grandma Carlton had helped her choose.

She went downstairs. 'Happy Christmas, Nana.'

Gladys hugged her, 'Go and speak to your Daddy,' she whispered.

There was much clattering of saucepans from the kitchen; Alice stood in the doorway. Robert had his back to her. He was different, a bit scary; Alice wondered if it was her fault. She moved closer and put her arms round his waist and leaned against his back.

'Happy Christmas, Daddy.'

He turned, knife in one hand, a Brussel sprout in the other.

'Glad to see you're up at last. I thought children always got up very early on Christmas morning. Don't tell me you're a lazy-bones.'

Alice felt herself blush. 'Thank you for the lovely present.'

'You've opened them?'

'Only one.'

'It would have been nice if we could have opened our presents together.'

'Oh.'

Robert put the knife down and ruffled Alice's hair. 'Never mind; now I must get on, there's lots to do.'

'Can't I help you?'

Robert laughed, 'Off you go, child, you'll get under my feet, you keep your Nana company.'

'Don't you want to open your present now?'

'I'll leave it till later.'

Gladys fetched a brush and comb; Alice sat at her feet and held the red ribbon that was going in her hair.

'I'll wear my red dress today with the ribbon to match.'

'Why don't you wear something else? You don't want to spill something down it.'

Alice turned, 'But, Gran…'

Gladys put a finger to her lips and shook her head.

Robert bustled in with a tray. 'How are my ladies? I've done tea and toast for breakfast and then, young lady, you'd better get dressed.'

Once upstairs, Alice looked at the clothes she'd brought with her, there was nothing special, nothing as nice as her red dress. She settled for a skirt and jumper; she wondered if she could wear the dress at the pantomime. She'd ask Nana.

'Are you sure there's nothing I can do, son?' Gladys asked.

'Alice is going to set the table for us, once she shapes herself.' He hurried back into the kitchen.

Alice wondered how many presents Katy would have, loads probably. Mummy would have got her something else, but this week was not her turn for a visit. She decided she would show Nana how well she could read and took a book from the shelf. She chose 'My Father's Dragon'. Daddy had promised he would buy the next two books in the series as soon as she could read this one without making a mistake.

At 12.30 Robert shouted from the kitchen. 'Have you set the table yet?

Alice leapt to her feet and found Nana's best white tablecloth, it had been starched and she pulled each corner into a point.

'There are serviettes in the dresser and some mats,' Gladys said. 'You know where the cutlery is, don't forget some serving spoons.'

Alice giggled; this was fun, it was what waitresses had to do. She wondered if she would get a tip. Daddy always left some change on the table when he took them out for a meal.

'Let's have you sitting down.' Robert hurried in with a roast chicken on a platter. He hurried back for dishes of vegetables and a gravy boat.

'Oh, son, it's a feast.' Gladys started spooning potatoes and sprouts onto Alice's plate and then her own while Robert sliced the bird. As soon as they both had their meat and gravy, she picked up her knife and fork and started eating.

'It's wonderful, so tender and tasty.'

Robert didn't answer, but Alice watched his face. She could tell he was cross, but what about? She sat poised with knife and fork ready not sure if she should start eating.

'Come along, Alice, don't let it get cold, Daddy's been hard at work all morning.'

'It is very rude, Mother, to start eating before everyone has been served.'

Gladys put her cutlery down with a clatter; she didn't speak, in fact, no-one spoke for the rest of the meal. Once everything had been cleared away, Robert put the radio on for George VI's Christmas message.

174

The day dragged for Alice and Nana looked miserable. The only relief was opening the presents as soon as the King's speech was over. Alice watched Gladys tear off the paper.

'Oh, Alice. It's lovely, such a pretty bottle.'

'Grandma said 4711 is very popular, Nana.'

Gladys unscrewed the top and sniffed. 'Lovely, it will be a nice change from lavender.'

Alice smiled and handed a small parcel to Robert. He weighed it in his hand and pursed his lips. 'It isn't a football, is it?'

Alice laughed and hugged him, 'Don't be silly, Daddy.'

He tore a corner of the paper and peered inside; he smiled. 'Just what I needed.' He pulled out two white handkerchiefs and pretended to blow his nose, loudly on one of them. He grinned at her, 'I'll save the other one for later.'

Alice wondered if Connie would bring Pauline over, but it hadn't been mentioned.

'Can we play Ludo or something?'

'Oh, let's do that, Robert.'

As the day faded into night, they finished their game and Alice had a bath in front of the fire. Daddy could carry the tin bath all by himself, but Grandpop had always used a saucepan to fill and later bail it out. She kissed Nana and Daddy and went up to bed. Perhaps tomorrow, at the pantomime, would be good fun.

It wasn't. As she had not brought anything nice enough to wear to the theatre, she wore the red dress which made everyone cross.

Chapter 41

After Christmas 1946

When Alice returned to the Clements, she hung her dress in the wardrobe. She ran her fingers down the soft material; it reminded her of Helena which, in turn, brought back faded images of her baby brother except he wouldn't be a baby any more. He wouldn't know her and she wouldn't know him. He was probably with Mummy and it wasn't fair. Daddy was going abroad tomorrow and Mummy had no plans to visit. Alice brushed away tears; if only Grandpop hadn't died.

Alice heard Vera calling her for tea so she carefully pushed the dress into the wardrobe so the skirt didn't catch in the door.

'Have you tidied up your room?' Vera asked.

Alice nodded and sat down; she took no part in the conversation between Katy and her parents. It was all about a party Katy was going to; Alice hadn't been invited. She didn't mind, somehow nothing mattered anymore.

'We can have a nice afternoon shopping, just the two of us, Alice.'

Alice was surprised, but at least Katy wouldn't be with them.

The following day was cold, with the threat of snow, when Vera and Alice left. They would go to the West End, as the sales were on, and then have tea out. The afternoon passed in a blur of people, lifts, crowds and sudden changes of temperature. They plunged out of one over-heated, overcrowded store onto cold, wet streets only to repeat the process until Vera decided there was nothing else worth buying.

Alice was exhausted by her efforts to keep Vera in sight in the seething masses. She tried to take an interest in the items Vera inspected although none of them would be for her. At last, Vera called a halt and looked for a tea-room. Alice had never seen her so cheerful perhaps it was because she liked the things she'd bought. Alice wondered if she would feel the same when she had money to spend. Perhaps it was different for grown-ups.

As they sat in the tea-room, Alice wondered if people thought she was Vera's little girl, she wouldn't mind if they did. The journey home was jolly too, everyone seemed happy despite the icy weather. Alice had to stand up so an elderly woman could have a seat. Vera put an arm round Alice's waist, it felt good.

'Lean against me,' Vera said.

It was still raining when they got off the bus. Alice helped Vera with her parcels as they hurried home. It was dark and street lights reflected off slush in the road and raindrops on Alice's glasses made everything sparkle. She breathed out hard and laughed at the cloud of condensation made by her breath.

The house was in darkness. 'I thought Douglas and Katy would be back by now.' Vera paused. 'I expect you'd like a nice warm bath after being out in the cold. You can use some of my bubble bath.'

Alice smiled and went to her room to undress.

'Don't hang your coat in the wardrobe tonight, Alice, it's wet. I'll put it on the airer.'

When Alice went upstairs, she was surprised to find her wardrobe door half open. It was an awkward catch and she always had to push it hard until it clicked. She went to shut it, and stopped, her heart was pounding. The afternoon treat had been a trick. She remembered Vera's arm round her waist and shuddered.

Why were they being so mean to her? Alice felt hot and her body shook; Douglas and Vera and Katy had done a bad thing. She'd tried to be good, but it didn't help. She heard the front door open and listened as Douglas told Katy to be quiet. They should have come back earlier and then the dress would have been put back and she would never have known. She walked slowly downstairs, holding the banister rail, she was trembling with rage. She hated them. When she pushed open the kitchen door, they looked at her, but nothing was said. Katy stood by the stove in the white petticoat and the red dress was draped over a chair.

Alice wanted to hit them, make them cry; it wasn't fair.

'Have you had your bath, dear?' Vera's voice sounded shaky.

'Why is my dress here?'

They wouldn't look at her. Katy started to snivel and Douglas put his arm round her. Alice pushed past him and grabbed Katy by the arm.

'Stop her, Doug,' Vera said.

'You have everything,' Alice grabbed Katy's other arm and tried to shake her. 'I can't even play with your toys, I hate you, I hate you.'

Alice's grip on Katy's arms was too tight for Douglas to pry her fingers off. Katy started screaming.

'Mummy, she's hurting me, stop her Mummy.'

A kitchen chair was kicked over in the struggle and there was a crash of crockery as it was swept from the table. The red dress lay crumpled on the floor. Alice was sent reeling by the force of Douglas' hand connecting with her cheek. She stumbled and fell. She clutched the dress to her chest and lay still.

Katy was sobbing as she showed Vera the finger and nail marks on her arms.

'She's drawn blood, Doug; I'm taking her to the doctor.' She turned to Alice who hadn't moved. 'You're a vicious little cat, that's what you are.'

As Douglas half-lifted, half-dragged Alice to her feet, she screamed, 'It's my dress, it's mine.'

He shook her sharply, 'Stop making such a bloody row.'

Alice struggled to free herself and kicked him on the shins; he grunted with pain and letting go of one arm, he walloped her bottom.

'Get her up to her room, Doug. I'm going to the doctor.'

'For God's sake, woman, she's got a few scratches, the doctor will laugh you out of the surgery.'

'What sort of father are you? Anything for a quiet life, no wonder you're always passed over for promotion.'

He grabbed Alice, who struggled to free herself, 'Do what you bloody well like,' he shouted over his shoulder as he tried to manhandle Alice out of the kitchen, 'you usually do.'

'And you can tell the welfare lot we don't want that brat here anymore.'

He flung Alice on her bed, 'Calm down, enough is enough, I'm sorry, I didn't mean to hurt you.'

'It's my dress,' was all she said.

He stared at where he had left a hand print across her cheek, it had started to bruise.

The following morning Alice was told to pack her things; Douglas drove her to a children's home until other arrangements could be made.

PART THREE 1946-1947

They say everything you go through
In your childhood
Builds character and inner strength

—Curtis Joseph
Canadian ice hockey player/coach

Chapter 42

January 1947

The bruise on Alice's face was a perfect imprint of Douglas Clements' hand. The following day her teacher asked what happened and then contacted Mary. Alice was placed in Girls' Village Home, Barkingside Ilford. It was the nearest Barnardo children's home with a vacancy.

There were lots of little cottages and each had a house mother. Annie Jones was Alice's house mother; she looked kind. She sat beside Alice and put an arm round her shoulders. Alice wept and Annie waited until the tears stopped.

'You will be safe here, Alice and I hope you will get to know the other girls, they are older than you, but they are a friendly lot.'

'But I'm not an orphan, why have I been sent here?'

'Lots of kind people are going to talk to your family so we can decide what is best for you.'

'Do Mummy and Daddy know I'm here?'

'Your Grandma knows and has told your Daddy.'

'What about Mummy and Nana?'

Annie paused, 'Your Grandma will talk to Mummy and Daddy will talk to Nana. Don't you worry. Now it is nearly lunchtime come on let's meet the others; she took Alice by the hand.

There were four girls sitting round a large kitchen table; they were all in their teens. Alice stood in the doorway; they were so big, like grown-ups. Why couldn't see go to Fred and Maureen?

'Your Grandma is on her way; that will be nice, you can show her round.'

Mary arrived after lunch and demanded to see whoever was in charge;

181

Annie Jones met her.

'Alice is my granddaughter and I am deeply concerned by the present situation. Why was she brought her? She has family who love her; she should not be in a children's home, no matter how well run, when she has family.'

'I understand the foster home arrangement broke down and it was decided it was best for everyone if Alice was placed elsewhere.'

'You have told me nothing I cannot work out for myself. What happened?'

'It might be best if you spoke to Alice. I'll take you to her room.'

'Precisely.'

The bruise on Alice's cheek had not faded much.

Mary stroked Alice's cheek and kissed her.

She turned to Annie Jones, 'Is this anything to do with it?

Annie looked uncomfortable.

'In addition to family, my granddaughter stayed for some time with a loving family. Why did no-one consider placing her there for a few days? At least she'd have been with people she knows who are fond of her.'

'Are they registered foster parents?'

'I doubt it; but, was the person who assaulted Alice, registered? It seems Alice would be safer with me.'

'As I understand it, Mrs Carlton, Alice's father is her legal guardian.'

'I'll get this sorted out, my dear. Leave it to me.' Mary turned on her heel and swept out. Annie and Alice stared at each other for a moment; neither spoke.

Chapter 43

January 1947

Mary usually invited Phillip to have coffee with her after their evening meal. This weekend both Philip and Patricia were out for the evening. It was a relief to have some time to think. What was she going to do about Alice? The child had been moved about like a piece of lost property; to place her in a home for wayward girls was a disgrace. Robert had promised to send a letter authorising Mary to act on his behalf; either the letter had gone astray or it had not been written.

In addition, there was another letter from Cyril; Helena was demanding to see Alice more often, that wasn't going to be easy. After Mary's visit to Barnardo's, Robert had been contacted. He had decided to make his own arrangements for Alice. She was to be placed with a Mr and Mrs Williams in Potter's Bar. Mary had been told nothing and wondered if her role in Alice's life was to be terminated.

Mary gazed out of her window, she watched the wind tussle with trees just coming into leaf and remembered her own childhood. Her mother had died giving birth to her, but she had been the youngest of a large family and had brothers and sisters to play with and there had been servants to care for her and give her stability. Alice had nothing.

She wondered what Robert's plans were; there was no sign of his leaving the army. She walked down the hallway to the smallest room in the apartment. She called it 'The Cabin'. It reminded her of a sea voyage taken many years before. It would be ideal for a young child and Patricia would be company for her. She must write immediately to make the suggestion to Robert. She could also include reference to Helena's access to Alice.

Patricia's divorced parents were determined to outdo each other in how much money they spent on their only child. A policy, Mary felt sure, they would come to regret. Patricia attended a private school which seemed to teach little, in favour of play and model-making. Despite her privileged background, Mary could see no purpose in private education. If a child was bright, she would do perfectly well in a state-run school. Phillip had always been an intellectual snob so there was no point in her discussing the matter with him.

She heard the front door slam and heard voices; she continued stirring the sauce for their evening meal and wished it were Matthew who would walk through the door. Patricia raced into the kitchen, cheeks glowing and breathless with excitement.

'We made model villages this morning, mine's called Fogley and my teacher said it was the best in the class and I'm going to be an architect like Daddy.' All was said without a pause for breath. Mary smiled.

'Well done. Your meal is nearly ready; you'd better wash your hands.'

'What are we having, Aunt Mary?'

'Cod with parsley sauce, creamed potatoes and cabbage.'

'I hate fish...and cabbage'

'It's extremely good for you and if you are hungry enough, you will eat it.'

Patricia pulled a face and stalked out of the kitchen. Mary sighed; the child had probably gone to soften up her father. She gave a brisk final stir to the sauce, not a lump in sight. Mary smiled; no spoilt child was going to dictate the diet in this home; neither would her father.

The meal was eaten in silence; Patricia sulked and pushed her food around the plate. Mary suspected Phillip wanted to remonstrate with her for cooking something Patricia didn't like. Perhaps he decided such action could put his present home in jeopardy and so said nothing.

'Patricia and I will do the washing up for you, Mary,' Phillip said.

Patricia started crying and pushed her plate away. 'I want Mummy, she doesn't make me wash up; it's not fair. It's not my fault you and Mummy hate each other.'

Mary left the room without a word. If Phillip was willing to let a child manipulate him, more fool him. She went to her sitting room, tuned in the wireless to the Third Programme and welcomed the serenity of Vaughan Williams' music. Edgar would be broadcasting later, a lecture on Communism.

She had mixed feelings about listening to his broadcasts. When she heard his voice, she felt there was still contact, some common ground. Afterwards she felt drained of hope and filled instead with a bitterness she could taste. If she didn't listen, she was racked by grief and guilt; by denying his existence now, she was denying the past they had shared. She walked to the door and locked it; she did not want any interruptions.

As she tuned the radio to the Home Programme, the phone rang, it was Robert.

'As you know, Mary, I have made arrangements for Alice to live with a friend of mine and his family.'

'Are you referring to the Williams' family, because I knew nothing of this.'

There was a pause and Mary wondered if the line had been cut.

'Oh, I apologise, I thought I'd informed you. The thing is they are moving north at Easter. Is there any chance Alice could come to you until I can make more permanent arrangements?'

'What do you want me to do about her education? She can't keep changing schools.'

'I leave to you. I thought it best to give you time to sort things out you. If she moves in with you at Easter, she will start at the beginning of the summer term. I'll send written permission for you to act as Alice's guardian.'

At least that was a step in the right direction. 'What about her mother....'

There was a pause.

'If she wants to see her mother, I've no objections, but I don't want her to stay there overnight. Would it also be possible for you to take Alice to see my mother from time to time? My father's death has hit her very hard. Seeing Alice would be so good for her.'

Mary sighed. 'I'll do what I can.'

'Thanks, let me know what it will cost to feed and clothe her.'

'We can sort that out when you come home on leave.'

'That won't be for a while yet.'

'No matter; I must go now.'

Mary poured herself a small brandy and cupped the crystal glass in her hands. The rich aroma took her back to better times. All that was missing was the smell of Edgar's cigars. She glanced at her watch, his programme started ten minutes ago. She turned up the volume so his voice filled the room. She closed her eyes and imagined he was sitting opposite her, so close she had only to stretch out her hand.

Chapter 44

Easter 1947

Alice sat on the green trunk her father had used during the war; it was all she had to remind her of him. Once again it held all her possessions. She felt sick and scared.

Jean Williams sat beside her on the trunk and held her hand.

'It's going to be all right, Alice, once you settle in.'

'Can't you take me with you?'

Jean hugged her. 'You'd be too far away from your family if you came to Scotland with us. We are all going to miss you so much. I'll give you our new address, so promise you'll write, Louise and James will want to keep in touch. Perhaps you can visit us when your Daddy comes home.'

Alice nodded. 'I don't think Grandma Carlton likes children very much.'

'Well, she must like you a lot, because she asked your Daddy if you could go to live with her.'

'Did she?'

'She certainly did.'

Alice gave a watery smile, but then she heard the toot of Grandma's car. Jean took her hand and they went to the door. Grandma Carlton smiled and held out her hand to Jean.

'Thank you for looking after my granddaughter, I know she has been happy with you; I will always be grateful.'

Jean went for the green trunk and Alice watched as she and Grandma dragged it out of the house. The two women manhandled it into the boot; Alice tried to stop her tears.

I'll get our new address, Alice. Please don't forget to write, we'll need your new address too.' As Jean went indoors, Mary put her arms round Alice and hugged her.

'Alice, I don't know what you like to eat so would it be a good idea if, before we go home, we go shopping so you can choose something nice.'

Alice nodded.

'There you are,' Jean said, 'addresses and everything, shall I ask Grandma to keep it all safe.'

'Yes, please.'

Alice waved to Jean who stayed on the pavement until the car turned the corner and was out of sight.

Alice thought Grandma's apartment was very grand. She went to her new bedroom; the walls were pale blue, the colour of the sky on a summer's day. The carpet was grey and so were the curtains; it was a plain room, no clutter, no fuss. The bed was built-in with cupboards underneath and a small table with a lamp stood beside it. She had few clothes so the single wardrobe was big enough. She knelt on the bed and looked out of the window. The room was at the back of the house and looked out on the backs of a similar row in the next street. Between the rows, there were trees and gardens. It was nothing like Nana's maisonette, surrounded by disused air-raid shelters and lines of washing.

She had never lived so high up and when she looked down, she felt dizzy. She leaned on the window sill and watched pigeons glide and swoop. They perched on the top most branches of plane trees almost on a level with her window. When she lay back and stretched out on her bed, all she could see was the sky; it did feel a bit like being at sea, that must be why Grandma called it 'The Cabin'. She stood on the bed and bounced gently; it was just right.

The sun was low and would soon be setting behind the trees; for a while the room glowed with golden light which transformed it into a warm, welcoming refuge. Alice liked it; perhaps it wouldn't be so bad living with Grandma.

Matthew's letter arrived two days after Alice moved in; why did life play such cruel tricks? Phillip and Patricia had established themselves and Alice had settled in. Now Matthew had dropped a bombshell. He was coming home, next month, with an American wife. Would they be able to stay with Mary until they could find a place of their own?

She could hardly ask Phillip and Patricia to leave and she wouldn't consider altering the arrangements for Alice, the poor child had gone through enough. Through no fault of her own, she would not be able to have her beloved son live with her. Her frustration and dismay temporarily blotted out the other bombshell... a wife. Why hadn't he told her, had he thought she would object. His secretive behaviour was hurtful; surely, he didn't think she wanted to interfere with his life, but then perhaps he did.

Maybe it was a blessing she couldn't offer to take them in; it would reassure the newly-weds she had no intention of making a nuisance of herself. What she could and would do was sort out one of two furnished flats they might like to rent. She would go to the local property agent tomorrow. She must let Frances know her brother was coming; perhaps she would drive up to London for a visit. Again, there was the problem of space. She had better buy a collapsible bed just in case.

Shortage of food continued to be a problem, now even bread was on ration. The dock workers had gone on strike, leaving a cargo of meat and other food stuff to rot, on the docks. Mary was appalled by the waste. Despite winning the war, hunger haunted the country. Now she was cooking for four and although they each had ration books, it didn't make the choice of food any easier. Mary studied the recipe for Wooton Pie which had been published in the newspaper. That would be a change.

'Alice, do you like vegetables?'

'I don't like Brussel sprouts much. Aunt Connie said they were fairy cabbages, but it still didn't make them taste nice.'

Mary laughed, 'I'll let you into a secret, I don't like them much either.' She handed Alice the recipe. 'Is there anything else you don't like?'

'I don't think I've had parsnip before, but I'll try it, if you like.'

'We'll go to the market and we may be able to find some bananas.'

'I've seen pictures, but I've never had one.'

After a successful shopping expedition, Mary and Alice peeled and chopped and made potato pastry for the pie.

'I think I can manage now, dear, go and wash the pastry bits off your hands.'

'Shall I lay the table afterwards?'

'That's very kind of you, my dear, although we do not lay the table, we set it.' The words were spoken quietly and delivered with a smile.

Alice nodded.

'There will be four of us tonight. My cousin, Phillip, and his daughter, Patricia, share the apartment with me; they will be home soon.'

Alice collected the cutlery; Daddy had shown her the right way to do it. She knew Mary was watching her so she must do it properly.

'We'll get you into school by next week, Alice, we want you to do well.'

The front door banged.

'There they are.'

Patricia rushed into the kitchen, but stopped dead when she saw Alice.

'Now then you two,' Mary said, 'your dinner is nearly ready. Patricia please show Alice your room and get to know each other. I'll call you in about ten minutes.'

Patricia's room was much bigger than Alice's and filled with toys and clothes, but Alice didn't mind, she preferred 'The Cabin'.

'I wish I could grow my hair long,' she said, 'but mine doesn't seem to want to grow.'

'My Daddy say's my hair is my best feature,' Patricia took a brush from her dressing table and brushed the dark brown hair which hung to her waist.

Alice thought it must be nice to have a best feature; all she had was a squint although her glasses were making it better.

'My Mummy wants me to have my hair cut but Daddy says she can't 'cos he's in charge.'

Alice smiled; at least she wasn't the only one whose parents didn't like each other.

'Where do you go to school?' Patricia said. 'I go to St. Catherine's.'

'I'm not in school at the moment; Grandma's going to sort that out.'

'Then why are you wearing a school uniform, haven't you got any other clothes?'

Alice felt herself blush; she hoped Patricia wasn't going to be like Katy Clements.

Chapter 45

May 1947

Helena put the telephone down with a bang.

'That was my bloody mother, wanted to let me know Alice is living with her and asking us if we were coming over for tea later.'

'That's good, isn't it? It will make it easier for you to see her.'

'That's not the point, that bastard, Robert, would rather my daughter live with an old woman than with me. I can't believe it.'

Cyril watched Helena storm about, too agitated to sit down. Secretly he thought it was an excellent arrangement, but he wasn't going to tell Helena that.

He put his arms round her; such physical contact sometimes calmed her; he was her human strait jacket.

'Now come on, don't get upset; don't let Robert feel he's got the upper hand. I'll check with Mary and if we all go over, Stephen can get to know Alice.'

Helena rested her head against his shoulder, 'You're probably right.'

'We'd better prepare Stephen and try to drum some manners into him. He's a bit wild you know…'

Helena stared at him and he held his breath. This tall, slender woman with fine features was like a thoroughbred race horse. She kept him permanently on edge yet his desire for her showed no signs of diminishing. He was middle-aged and longed for a quiet life, but he realised that as long as Helena was in his life, there would be no peace; without her there would be no life.

Stephen opened the kitchen door, 'Go out.'

'Hey, hang on, you're too old to go out on your own, and we're going over to see Grandma.'

Stephen stood with a mutinous expression on his face. 'I don't want to go to Grandma's'

'Don't be silly,' Helena said, 'And for heaven's sake, will you stand still while I sort out your hair.' She tugged at the knots and tangles while he squirmed and complained.

'When did he last have his hair combed?' Cyril asked.

Helena banged the comb on the kitchen table, 'Do it yourself.' She shouted and stormed out of the room. Cyril glanced at the kitchen clock; they should have left half an hour ago.

'Well,' Helena said as she opened the kitchen door, a few minutes late 'I'm ready.'

'Then ring your mother and explain we're going to be late.'

'For Christ's sake will you stop making a fuss; we'll take a taxi.'

'And are you going to pay for it?'

'Money, money, that's all you think of.'

'It's the lack of it that bothers me; you can spend it faster than I earn it.'

She smiled and sidled over to him, 'Don't be a meanie. Anyway, you've got to be especially nice to me now. I'm pregnant.'

Cyril sat down; he felt his stomach lurch. How long had she been home, no more than six weeks? He thought back to Stephen's conception and wondered if he was the biter bit; Helena had been very vague about her time in France. Was he becoming cynical and suspicious?

'So, I've left you speechless for once, aren't you glad.'

'Of course, I am,' Cyril said, 'it's just come as a bit of a shock.'

'What's pregnant,' Stephen asked.

Helena took his hand and placed it on her stomach. 'There's a baby growing in there, a new baby brother or sister for you.'

'I hope it's a brother, I don't like girls.'

'We'll have to wait and see,' Helena said.

'If there's a baby in your tummy, how is it going to get out?'

'We definitely do not have time to go into that,' Cyril said, 'Come on, if we hurry, we'll catch the 3p.m. bus and we'll only be an hour late.'

191

Chapter 46

May 1947

Alice put on her new school clothes, a white blouse, grey skirt and cardigan. She had some new black shoes with buckles. Grandma had decided that her raincoat didn't need replacing. At least she would not have to wear that horrid velour hat any more. Alice took the hat out of the wardrobe and stroked it. Grandpop and Nana had bought it for her. Grandpop said it was very smart. She never told them other children laughed at her for wearing it. She put it back in the wardrobe; she wouldn't throw it away, not yet.

She would be starting at her new school on Monday. It was the fourth one she had attended in four years and though she hated being moved, at least she had not been anywhere long enough to make any special friends, no-one special to say goodbye to. She'd said goodbye to Nana, but that was ages ago. She'd ask Grandma for some writing paper and she'd send Nana her new address.

Grandma was in the kitchen; Alice walked in and did a twirl to show her new clothes.

'You do look nice, and it's a good fit. Hang it up carefully.'

Alice raced off to her room, changed into some old clothes and raced back.'

'Is your uniform hanging up?'

Alice blushed, 'It's on my bed, but it isn't creased. Can I leave it until I've iced the cake?'

Mary smiled and shook her head, 'I don't know.'

'Shall I wear my red dress this afternoon; Mummy hasn't seen me in it yet.'

'Yes, good idea, but put your apron on.'

'Can I do it now?"

Mary watched as Alice spread the chocolate icing.

'You have done a splendid job, Alice. Get yourself changed and we can wait for your mother; she'll probably be late.'

'Darling,' Helena said as she swept Alice into her arms, 'you've grown so much I hardly recognised you.' She turned to Stephen, 'Come and say hello to your lovely big sister.'

Stephen hid behind Cyril and didn't speak; Cyril grabbed his hand and pushed him forward.

'My mummy has got a baby in her tummy and I want a baby brother,' he said.

Mary appeared and ushered them into her sitting room. Alice had put out some of her old books and some paper and crayons for Stephen; he ignored everyone but Helena. He clung to her like a limpet, either on her knee or clutching at her legs. Each time Helena tried to speak to Alice, Stephen interrupted. Finally, Cyril grabbed the boy and tried to interest him in some drawing. Stephen howled and Mary suggested they went to the kitchen for tea.

'Alice has made a lovely chocolate cake,' Mary said.

'Don't like chocolate cake,' Stephen said.

'Good,' said Mary, 'all the more for us.'

Stephen stamped his feet.

'Don't upset him, Mother,' Helena said.

Mary raised her eyebrows.

Alice was shocked. Stephen was so naughty and Mummy didn't seem to mind. He took sandwiches, but he didn't eat the crusts, he kept getting down from the table. Alice watched the grown-ups in amazement. Cyril looked flustered and grabbed Stephen as he tried to leave the table again. For the rest of the meal, he sat on his father's knee.

'I want cake,' he said.

Mary sighed, 'I thought you didn't like chocolate cake.'

Stephen shrugged and pulled a face. Helena cut a slice and gave it to him. Alice watched as he licked off the icing and crumbled the cake onto his plate; no-one spoke.

Cyril cleared his throat, 'I think we'd better get this young man home, he's tired.'

Alice listened to the clatter of Stephen's feet as he ran downstairs, and went to helped Mary to clear the mess.

'I don't think Stephen likes me very much,' she said.

'Perhaps it's because he doesn't know you very well.'

'I wish my Daddy would come home.'

'It isn't easy for you, is it?'

Alice shook her head; she could feel tears gathering. She didn't want to cry in front of Grandma in case she was sent away.

Mary smiled, 'I tell you what we'll do, we'll sit by the fire in the sitting room and we'll have a bit of supper later, some buttered crumpets would be nice. Meanwhile shall we see if we can finish that crossword?'

'That would be lovely,' Alice said.

Chapter 47

September 1947

Summer had moved into autumn with blue skies and gentle breezes. Alice had settled in her new school and would soon be moving into a new class. At last, she knew where all her family members were and had contact with them, especially her father. He'd be home on leave soon. However, the problem of Stephen and his behaviour would have to be tackled. Mary had said she wanted to talk to Alice about him.

'Do you think Stephen is jealous of you?'

Alice shrugged, 'He's just so unkind all the time; I'm trying to like him.'

Mary smiled, 'I had brothers, but I was little and thought they were a pest.'

'Did you tell them so?'

'No, they were bigger than I was.'

'Do you think he will ever like me?'

'Don't forget, young ladies grow up more quickly than boys. You are a very sensible young lady. Just keep on as you are; one day he will realise he is very lucky to have you. Meanwhile, I have arranged for Cyril to take Stephen to the playground on the Heath when Mum comes here to visit you.'

'But that means you won't see Stephen.'

'Don't you worry, a little bit of Stephen goes a long way. He'll be better when he's older, calmed down a bit.'

Alice nodded and continued with her cross-stitch. It would be nice to see Mum without any outbursts from Stephen. Now Helena was calm and relaxed during her visits; Alice wondered if it was because there was another baby in her tummy. Each time Helena came to Mary's apartment,

Alice placed her hand on the bump to see how things were progressing; on a recent visit, Alice had felt the baby moving.

'Would you like me to make something for your baby?'

'Oh, darling, it's our baby,' Helena said clutching Alice to her until she could scarcely
breathe, 'yes, please make something; that would be wonderful.'

'As the weather is so settled, I thought it would be a good idea to take the children on a picnic in Kew Gardens fairly soon, before they go back to school.'

Helena smiled, 'Thank you, Mother.'

The following week, Mary collected Helena and Stephen from Kentish Town and Phillip said he and Patricia would drive over and meet them outside the Gardens. Alice felt giddy with excitement; the only person missing was Daddy, but she knew if he were at home, he wouldn't be invited.

They found a secluded spot, uncultivated and away from the hot houses and pavilions. Dappled shade under the trees and lush ferns growing in feathery clumps gave an air of mystery and magic. The grown-ups sat on rugs while the children crept, barefoot, in the undergrowth. The drone of bees hung heavy in the still air as the children picked fern fronds. The girls made headdresses and capes, wings and wands.

'Don't want to play,' Stephen said and swished fern fronds at the girls' legs.

'Well go and sit with the grown-ups then,' Patricia said, 'we don't want to play with you anyway.'

'No.' He threw himself on the ground and cried.

Alice put her arm round him, 'Come on you could be the king of the fairies; I'll make you a crown.'

Stephen smiled.

'If he's king of the fairies, I'm going to be queen.' Patricia pulled a clump of fern and twisted it into a headdress. 'You can be our servant. Alice smiled; she didn't mind.

'I'll be the good fairy who grants Kings and Queens their wishes.'

Patricia pulled a face, but said nothing.

Sunlight came in shafts through the trees, flickering, sending sparks of gold on all it touched. Alice was bewitched, she seemed to float in the warm air; Stephen took hold of her hand and her heart thumped with delight. Everything was beautiful, the real world didn't matter. Make-believe was better.

Too soon the sun dipped behind trees, a light breeze rustled the grass and long shadows made them shiver.

'Come along children get your shoes on, time to go home,' Mary said.

The spell was broken and Stephen snatched off the crown of ferns, stamped it flat and stomped off to Helena.

Patricia ran to her father, 'It's not fair, do we have to go home now?'

Alice looked up and watched branches move, changing the patterns of light and shade. The world of make-believe beckoned and she didn't want it to end. This had been the best afternoon she had ever had; she wanted to stay here forever. Her feet were cold and she hurried to find her shoes and socks. She'd write to Dad and tell him all about it, but she'd better not mention Mum or Cyril.

Chapter 48

October 1947

Mary checked her hair in the mirror and stepped back; she looked elegant enough to meet royalty. Matthew and his new wife would be arriving any minute. Her relationship with her son would be different now, she would have to share him. He would be Emma-Jane's husband first and Mary's son second. It would be difficult for her to take a backward step, but she must, otherwise she ran the risk of losing him entirely.

She thought about Frances, so independent and apparently disinterested in family life. The cat who walks by itself as Kipling always claimed and then there was Helena. She leaned closer to the mirror. 'Of course, he isn't all I have, what nonsense.'

'Grandma, what time are Uncle Matthew and Aunt Emma-Jane arriving?'

Alice had been standing quietly in the hall, neat and tidy, and Mary wondered how long she had been there.

'Soon, child, have you finished your homework?'

'Yes, I've been reading, I've got a new Doctor Dolittle book.'

Mary smiled, the child was no trouble, in fact she was a comfort. She glanced at her watch again, time was standing still. Apart from Alice, the apartment was empty; Phillip had taken Patricia to her mother's house. He always returned from these access visits in a foul mood and Mary had no idea what he did between dropping the child off and picking her up again. One thing was sure the 'Countess' would never consider inviting her ex-husband in for a cosy chat.

The doorbell rang; Mary hurried to the door and there he was, smiling. Standing next to him was a tall, dark-haired girl with eyes the colour of topaz.

'Come in, my dears, come in.' Mary put her arms tightly round Matthew's neck and drew him to her, frightened to let go in case he was an apparition. After a moment Matthew eased himself out of his mother's grasp.

'I want you to meet Emmy.'

He turned to his new wife, 'Don't you believe all mother says about me and don't look at pictures of me on a bear-skin rug.'

'I'm pleased to meet you; Matthew has told me so much.'

The two women touched cheeks and smiled.

Mary pushed Alice forward and Matthew knelt down, 'I do believe this is my little niece, come and give your uncle a kiss.'

Emmy shook Alice by the hand and they all went through to the sitting room.

'You must be ready for tea; I've been busy baking and Alice has helped.'

Emmy looked round, 'Gee, honey this is just so beautiful.'

Mary watched as this stranger touched the wood of the desk, rich brown and highly polished: she listened as Emmy admired the rich upholstery: marvelled at the Chinese carpet and the cream silk walls. Sunlight warmed the room and made it glow as the sun slipped behind the trees.

'Unfortunately, the meat ration has been reduced again, so there is less choice for our afternoon tea; ham is unheard of.' Mary smiled and went to get the tea trolley.

The clatter of crockery broke the spell; when she returned with the tea trolley it was laden with white linen napery, bone china and an array of sandwiches, scones and cakes. The silver teapot reflected light, made patterns on walls and ceiling.

Once everyone was seated, given tea and something to eat, there was silence. Alice watched the grown-ups watching each other.

'Now, Mother no interrogation, please. I've warned Emmy you would want to know everything about everything.'

Mary felt herself blush, 'That's unkind, Matthew, I just want to know a bit about how you met and when you decided to get married and…'

'Mother, all in good time, let us get our breath back.'

Mary wondered if he was hiding something; she certainly wasn't going to ask any more questions in front of Emmy; a time would come soon enough.

'By the way, thanks for looking out some accommodation for us but we've decided to rent a house in Wimbledon, it's Archie's, he been posted abroad so it's ideal.'

Mary nodded.

'I really didn't see myself in a condo?' Emmy said and smiled an all-American, broad, perfectly white, unblemished smile. 'Keep Off', that smile said, 'You ain't gonna run my life, lady.'

'What's a condo?' Alice asked.

'Emmy smiled, 'It's what you call an apartment, it's short for condominium.'

'Where did you live in America? Alice asked.

'In New York, near Central Park.'

'Of course,' said Matthew, 'we hope to buy, no point in renting, it's the deposit that's the problem.' He looked at Mary and smiled.

'More tea, Emmy, my dear?' Mary asked.

Emmy passed her cup. 'I believe your Princess Elizabeth is getting married soon.'

'Yes,' Mary said as she poured more tea, 'it will be quite a celebration after the war. We are so good at public ceremonies, aren't we Matthew?'

Matthew nodded 'I want to get sorted a.s.a.p. because I start work next week, really landed on my feet'

'Could we go watch the wedding?'

'If you want to stand on the street somewhere to watch the parade as it goes past.'

'Not in the church?'

'That will not be possible; it is for important guests and visiting dignitaries.' Mary smiled. 'And are you intending to work too, my dear?'

'Of course, but once we're settled, we hope to start a family.'

Emmy placed a perfectly manicured hand with bright red nails, lightly but proprietorially on Matthew's arm. He smiled at her then flicked a glance at his mother whose face was devoid of expression.

'Since when did you want to be a mother, Em? You always said you valued your independence and your figure too much.'

'I have you to thank. As soon as I met you, the thought of a miniature Matthew seemed awfully appealing. Besides my mom always said she could never have too many grandchildren.' She turned to Mary, 'Don't you agree?'

Mary smiled, but her mind raced backwards to the time, five years ago when Matthew came home on sick-leave from the navy. It had taken visits to several doctors before syphilis was diagnosed. Matthew had pulled a face.

'That'll teach me to have a girl in every port,' he'd said.

Had he forgotten that his doctors had been unable to say if he would ever father a child? Clearly, he hadn't discussed the matter with Emmy.

Chapter 49

October 1947

Alice's teacher, Mr Goodwin, was a large, elderly man who always wore the same thick tweed suit; it smelt of tobacco and sweat. He spent a lot of time out of the classroom once he had set work for this class. To ensure there was no noise in his absence, he had appointed the largest boy in the class to be his second-in-command. That boy, Eric, sat next to Alice. She thought he was horrible to bully the rest of the class; he scared her.

Mr Goodwin struggled to his feet and trundled towards the door.

'Right Eric, you're in charge, no talking from anyone.'

As soon as the door closed Alice heard a whisper. She looked down at her exercise book and kept as far away from Eric as possible. He nudged her.

'Who was that?' he asked.

'I don't know,' she said.

Eric picked up his pencil and wrote her name, 'You just spoke.' He watched her and grinned. She turned away and carried on with her work; it was pointless to say anything.

'Good, nice and quiet, any problems, Eric?' Mr Goodwin said on his return.

'Alice Warren spoke.'

Without a word, Alice got to her feet and walked to teacher's desk. She held out her hand for the customary three whacks of the ruler. Bit her lip and walked back to her desk, determined a smirking Eric would not see her cry. She carried on with her work, but moved her throbbing hand from desk to lap and finally tucked it under her thigh to curb the pain.

'Stop fidgeting will you,' Eric whispered, 'you're jogging my arm.'

Alice turned to glare at him, she watched as his face flushed then he looked away; she would never speak to him again.

At play-time several of her class-mates spoke to her, some for the first time, she'd even been asked to join in a skipping game. Eric, had permission to stay in the classroom. Perhaps he'd done her a favour; perhaps she was one of them now instead of the odd one out.

As she walked home, she decided she wouldn't tell grandma about Eric. Her hand had stopped hurting and the mark across her palm had faded. As she skipped along the road, she decided she'd call at the sweet shop. With rationing still on, it was difficult to buy sweets, but the man in the shop was kind and for three pennies, she could buy a bit of her favourite, coconut ice; it came in lumps with little crumbly bits. She knew Grandma didn't like her eating sweets before her evening meal so she licked her fingers and dipped them in the paper bag; it wasn't cheating to eat the crumbs, just a few delicious crumbs. She'd save the rest until later.

Once home, Alice wandered into her bedroom. She had some homework, but didn't feel like doing it. She could read her book, but Dr Dolittle didn't seem so exciting since she'd been to see Henry Vth with Grandma. That visit to the cinema reminded her of the time Grandpop and Grandma had taken her to see 'A Matter of Life and Death'. She had sat between them, in the dark, and Grandpop had held her hand. There had been a teardrop offered as evidence in a court scene; she couldn't quite remember why.

It was the stairway that she remembered most, moving steps carrying souls to heaven. She sat on her bed and tried to hold back her tears; was that where Grandpop had gone, and what about Nana? She would draw a picture for her after dinner; homework could wait.

'Wash your hands, please, Alice, your meal is ready,' Mary called.

'Coming,' she sat up and dried her eyes; she didn't want anyone to know she felt sad.

After the meal, Patricia disappeared into her room while Alice helped with the washing-up, it was her turn.

'I'm going to do a picture for Nana; I can give it to her now Daddy's home on leave.'

'Come and show me your picture when you've finished it, but don't forget your homework.'

Alice collected paper and her coloured pencils from her school satchel. Daddy had bought them for her. She opened the pretty blue box with drawings of animals all over it; as she tipped the box, bits of coloured pencil fell out. Every pencil point had been broken. It must have been when Mr Goodwin sent her on an errand; Eric was getting his own back because she refused to speak to him. Why were people so mean? She hunted for her pencil sharpener; it was missing. She'd see if she could borrow one.

She knocked on Patricia's door but there was no reply, she opened the door and there on the bed was a pencil case; there was bound to be a pencil sharpener in there. She carefully picked her way across the bedroom floor, littered with home-made model houses. At that moment Patricia walked in.

'What are you doing in my room?'

'Some pig at school has broken all my pencils so can I borrow your sharpener? '

'No, you can't, I need it.'

'Just for a little while, please.'

'You don't even go to a proper school like me.'

'At least I learn things; I don't play all the time.'

Patricia stepped forward, hand outstretched, 'Give me that.'

As Alice moved forward, she heard a crunching sound. Looking down both girls saw the wreckage of a small house made of card and matchsticks.

'I'm sorry... I didn't...'

Nails scraped down Alice's face and neck as Patricia tried to wrestle her out of the room.

'I hate you everyone hates you nobody wants you, why don't you just go away.'

Alice crouched down to avoid the blows and fell against Patricia who lost her balance and banged her head against the wall. With a shriek of pain, she scrambled to her feet and rushed into Phillip's sitting room. Alice stood up; she was weary of it all. Perhaps Patricia was right, perhaps nobody did want her. She touched her face and found blood on her fingers. She walked back to her room and closed the door behind her.

She slipped off her shoes and stood on the bed, she stared at the cloudless evening sky, watched as the blue turned to crimson and gold. Above the setting sun the sky was the same colour as the walls in her room, her sanctuary. She opened the window and leaned out. The air felt soft and soothing to her sore cheek. Pigeons and starlings were flying home to roost and she envied them. She opened the window wider and swung her legs round until they hung over the ledge. She found a ridge on which to rest her feet. The sounds from below her were faint, unobtrusive, an amiable fuss and flutter like a swarm of friendly bees, going about their business.

She took a deep breath and wished she were a bird then she could step off the ledge and soar through the air, leave all her troubles behind. She was still holding tightly to the window sill with one hand while she watched the trees move their branches in the evening breeze. She loosened her grip and looked down; it was a long, long way. She had turned her back on everything, now she felt free. She only had to step out, lift her arms and fly to Grandpop; that would be the best thing, wouldn't it?

She noticed movement from one of the houses opposite, someone was waving. She waved back. It felt nice to wave to someone she didn't know, what a pity she couldn't say 'Hello', but she was too far away. Alice shivered, it was getting chilly, perhaps she should go inside and find out what Patricia had said about her.

Suddenly someone grabbed her and yanked her backwards so she fell on her bed. Phillip, Grandma and a white-faced Patricia were staring at her.

'What in God's name are you doing?' Phillip shouted, 'You stupid girl you could have killed yourself.'

Alice was too stunned to speak.

'Answer me.' Phillip's face was scarlet and Alice wondered if it was fear as well as anger. But fear of what, of what she might do, and what had she been going to do? She wasn't sure.

'Look at her face,' Mary said. The words fell into the silence like a grenade. 'Did Patricia do this?' she asked.

Alice nodded and Patricia started to cry.

'I think you had better have a serious talk with your daughter, Phillip, while I do something about this child's face.'

Once Phillip had led a sobbing Patricia out of the room, Mary sat on the bed and rested her hand on Alice's.

'Tell me what's wrong.'

Then, half dragging and half lifting, Mary got Alice on her lap. Great, gulping sobs shook her body and Mary waited. Alice leaned against Mary; it felt nice, she could tell Mary everything; she trusted her.

'What a truly horrible day, you've had, you should have told me about all this before.'

'I didn't want you to send me away.'

'I shall go to your school and discuss the whole thing with the Head teacher. I will also have a serious talk with Patricia; I will not tolerate such behaviour in my house. Of course, you shouldn't have taken the sharpener without asking first.'

'I said I was sorry.'

'That girl has a lot to learn.'

Alice managed a smile and looked at the tear stains she had left down Mary's blouse.

She touched them with her finger.

'Sorry I've cried on you.'

'It really doesn't matter, my dear, and don't think I will ever send you away. Let's look forward to something nice. I've heard from your father; he will be coming to see you tomorrow. So, we must try to do something to hide your war wounds.' She paused. 'Promise me you will never sit on the window ledge again.'

'I wasn't going to do anything silly; I was watching the birds.'

'Of course, you were, but the poor woman who saw you nearly had a fit. She and her husband worked out which house it was and he came round to tell us where you were.'

'I didn't mean to be a nuisance, I just felt sad.'

'WelL, we can't have that. Promise you'll tell me next time you feel sad; you are very special to me.'

Alice kissed Mary on the cheek and smiled.

Chapter 50

October 1947

Helena stretched then rubbed her back, it ached all the time now and unseasonably high temperatures didn't help. She glanced at the kitchen clock, it was time to walk to Stephen's school and collect him. She sighed as she buckled on her sandals, it would be nice to walk barefoot but people were bound to stare. That was the problem; here everyone was so ordinary, so ready to pass judgment. The French had a much more relaxed attitude to individuality, perhaps she should have stayed in Paris. She felt restless, constrained, Cyril was always at work and Stephen was at school while she waited at home for something to happen.

The baby kicked hard and Helena rested a hand on her taut stomach. Would it be a boy or a girl? Of course, Stephen wanted a boy, he would. She thought about Alice, so quiet and thoughtful, too old for her years. She reminded Helena of Frances, the sensible older sister, they had not got on in childhood and still didn't. Who would this baby take after or would it be a law unto itself?

She walked downstairs and into bright sunlight, smiled and nodded at several mothers as they too walked to their children's school. Although they returned her smiles, contact never got further than that. Helena felt isolated and she suspected she was often the subject of their gossip. She was bored by the life of a housewife, hated housework and had no interest in talking about what she was going to give Cyril for his evening meal.

In the past, before it became obvious that she was pregnant, she enjoyed the wolf whistles she attracted from any nearby workman. She always pretended to ignore them, but she could not hide the twinkle in her eyes. It made her feel desirable and she didn't care what other mothers thought. The glorious exaltation, she had felt for months, had been slipping away, day by day, like blood oozing from a wound. The sparkle had been replaced by a dark cloak of depression. This was just the beginning; she knew worse was to come. Her only comfort was that doctors would not prescribe E.C.T. while she was pregnant.

Stephen raced out of school and, as usual, flung himself into her arms. If only she could absorb some of his vitality, if only his boundless energy could pass through her skin to push back the dark clouds. She took his hand which was hot, sweaty and caked with grime; how did he manage to get so dirty?

'I want to go to the park, Mummy, let's go to the park.' He was hopping from foot to foot. Helena knew she should take him, let him run about, tire himself out, so he would sleep better and not wake her up before it was light. Somehow it was all too, too much, let Cyril take him out after tea.

'I'm tired, Stephen, ask Daddy when he comes home.'

With a wail of frustration, Stephen pulled his hand away, stamped his feet and shouted.

Helena sat on a low wall in front of a neat house and garden. Her legs were throbbing and she suspected there was a varicose vein. She wondered if the owner of the house would come out, ask her to move. Stephen's shouts grew louder and he tugged at her hand.

'I want to go to the park,' he yelled. Finally, he threw himself down and drummed his heels on the pavement. Helena stood and let out a piercing scream; it startled Stephen into a tear-streaked silence. A group of young mothers hurried past, eyes averted; they only resuming their conversation when they were out of earshot. Helena grabbed Stephen's arm and hauled him to his feet, they walked home in a silence.

Helena checked her watch, a quarter past four; how long before Cyril got back. She hadn't had the energy to go shopping and had no idea what they would have to eat once he was home. She wondered if she dared call him at work and get him to get something in the Co-op. It all seemed too much. She leaned back in her chair; she wanted to go to bed, slide into sleep and never wake up. Stephen was tugging at her arm,

'Mummy I'm hungry.'

Helena heaved herself upright and looked in the cupboards while Stephen whined and grizzled.

'For heaven's sake, Stephen, will you be quiet.' She shook the biscuit tin; something was in there – a few broken bits, it would have to do. She poured a mug of water for him and sat down. She could do no more.

When Cyril got home, Helena was asleep and Stephen was sitting under the kitchen table chewing on a raw carrot.

Chapter 51

October 1947

Alice examined her face in the bathroom mirror; although the scratches were still there, they were faint. If asked about them, she would tell Dad everything. Grandma had promised it would never happen again. Alice smiled; Patricia deserved to be in trouble after being so horrible.

Alice wondered what to wear, not the red dress which was tight now. Dad wouldn't have liked it anyway. She chose the white dress with red spots which she had worn when she went to the Albert Hall. It must be two years ago and it was a bit short, but it reminded her of her special day with Grandpop and Nana.

She wondered what Dad would be wearing, he always had his uniform on, but surely, he must have other clothes. Where would they go? Dad always arranged something exciting. Was it best to have a dull dad who was there all the time or an exciting dad who rushed in, made a fuss of her then disappeared, in the blink of an eye? She decided she was the lucky one because when Dad left the army, as he must one day, he would still be exciting.

She wandered through the apartment, unable to settle at anything; all she could do was wait. The door to Patricia's room was always kept shut now. The two girls had been polite to each other after the fight, but kept apart as much as possible. Leaning on the window sill in Grandma's sitting room, Alice pressed her nose against the glass and looked down the street. Dad was bound to arrive soon; he was never late, not like Mum.

Alice had felt uneasy the last time she saw Helena, her mum had seemed sad. Grandma had explained that having a baby was strenuous business and probably Mum was just tired. Alice thought about when Stephen was born, it was a long time ago. That was the last time she saw

Mum and Dad together. She swallowed hard, took a deep breath and hurried to the kitchen to see what Grandma was doing.

Mary glanced at her watch, 'Your Dad will be here in ten minutes, but you can help me with these, if you like, until he arrives.'

Alice put on her apron and waited for instructions.

'You look very pretty in that dress, Alice, your dad will be proud of you.'

Alice felt herself blush, how lovely to make someone feel proud. She moved the used utensils to the sink and began washing-up. After a few minutes she glanced at the clock and then at Mary.

'Off you go, my dear, he's probably walking up the road now.'

Alice peered out of the sitting room window; she saw the flash of sunlight on gleaming buttons and the buckles of Robert's uniform jacket.

'He's coming,' she shouted and ran to the front door. She knew he would be walking up even though Grandma's apartment was on the fourth floor. He had told her it was lazy to use the lift so she clattered downstairs and met him on the second flight. She launched herself into his arms and hung like a limpet round his neck. The buttons of his jacket and Sam Browne belt dug into her chest, but she didn't care. She breathed in the aroma of St. Bruno tobacco that would always remind her of him. He kissed her on the cheek and hugged her.

'My goodness,' he said, 'you smell fishy. What have you been doing?'

'Helping Grandma to souse herrings, they're lovely.'

She grabbed his hand and half-dragged him up the stairs. 'Where are we going? Can I see Nana and how long is your leave? Did you know Mummy's having another baby?'

As soon as the words were out of her mouth, she knew she'd made a mistake. In all the excitement she'd forgotten Dad got cross if she mentioned Mum. It wasn't quite the same with Mum who always told her how awful Dad was. Alice hated that, it wasn't fair and anyway, Dad wasn't awful. She glanced at his face; it had the tight, hard look she'd come to dread. She crossed her fingers and hoped she hadn't spoiled the afternoon.

'I was moved into a new class at the beginning of term.

'Is that because you're very good or because you're very naughty?'

She giggled; he must be teasing her. 'I'm not naughty,' she protested, 'well, not often.'

'I should hope not or I would have to slap your backside.'

He tapped her lightly on the bottom as she ran ahead to announce his arrival. Mary met them in the hall; she shook Robert's hand.

'I expect you two will want to be off at once.' She turned to Alice, 'Do you know where you are going or is your father keeping it as a surprise?'

Alice shrugged her shoulders, 'Don't know,' she grinned.

'I thought we'd go to South Kensington to the science museum and then on to my mother, for tea. She's not well; I had a shock when I got home.'

'So, I can expect Alice later this evening.'

'It's difficult at the moment to have Alice staying overnight, but I'll see what I can arrange for next time.'

Mary bent down to kiss Alice, 'Have a good time.'

'Oh,' said Alice, 'I'd better get that picture I did for Nana.' She hurried to her bedroom.

'I think it would be a good idea to have a talk when you get back, once Alice is in bed.'

'No trouble, I hope... Alice tells me Helena's pregnant again.'

'It's not about that; I just want to bring you up to date with your daughter's progress.'

Robert had given Alice the key and when she let herself in, she realised she was now taller and altogether larger than Nana who seemed to have shrunk. Flesh had melted from her face and body; Alice could feel bones when she gave Gladys a kiss and a hug.

'Are you alright, Nana?'

Gladys smiled, 'It's lovely to see you, my darling, look what I've been knitting.' She held up a red, short-sleeved jumper with contrasting bands of yellow and blue.'

Alice grinned, 'It's beautiful, thank you.' She loved red and would be able to wear it without upsetting Dad.

'Right, you two, have a natter while I sort out food. We're having pilchards and tomatoes with brown bread and butter; you need building up, Mother. I won't give too much to Alice or she'll end up a real little porker.' He laughed and went into the kitchen.

'But Gran...'

Gladys put a finger to her lips.

'Yes, but Gran, you hate pilchards. What are you going to do?'

'Shush, don't let your father hear.'

'Gran let me tell him and you can have a boiled egg.'

'No, don't upset him.'

Alice was amazed. Gran was scared of Dad; how could she be scared of her own child? How strange, she felt more relaxed at Grandma's, now she'd got to know her. Perhaps the problem was because Dad was away so much; she didn't really know him.

211

Robert hurried in with their plates. Gladys picked at the fish and said how good it was. Surely, if she said things like that, Dad was bound to serve them up again. Grown-ups were odd. As soon as Robert had finished his, he bustled to the kitchen for teapot, milk jug and cakes. Without a word Alice passed her plate to Gladys who slid on the rest of her fish. When Robert sat down, he glanced at his mother, but said nothing. Alice broke the silence by talking about their visit to the Science Museum.

All too soon it was time to go home and Alice gave Nana a hug before going to get her coat. It was dark as they walked down deserted streets. Alice felt sad, when would she see Nana again. They stood at the bus stop and waited as cold winds tugged at their clothes.

Robert and Alice sat on the top deck of the bus, in the front seat, Alice's favourite. She leaned against his shoulder and gazed out of the window. She wondered if she should talk about pilchards and how much Nana hated them; something stopped her. Such moments as these were too precious to risk spoiling.

'I wish I could stay at Nana's flat sometimes.' She paused, 'It's quite difficult to get on with Patricia at times.'

'You must do your best; you are in someone else's house.'

'I know, but… it was difficult to get on at school; there's this horrid boy.'

Robert raised his eyebrows.

'Anyway, Grandma sorted it out.'

'Good.'

'Is Nana going to get better?'

Robert paused, 'Not completely, she's an old lady. Let's hope she gets stronger so we can take her out.'

'But who would take her; you'll be going away again soon.'

He turned to stare out of the window and didn't reply.

By the time they got back to Mary's apartment, Philip and Patricia were in their own rooms. Patricia must have heard the front door open; she stalked through the hallway to the bathroom without a word. Alice was stunned, but made no comment.

'Are you going now, Dad?'

'Grandma wants to talk to me so I think it best if you got ready for bed.'

'I'll come in to say goodnight, shall I?'

Robert sat straight-backed and attentive while Mary told him about the incident at school. Why did Mary always made him feel at a disadvantage; a discussion with her was like being interviewed by a prospective employer.

Alice soon raced back, washed and ready for bed.

She decided not to sit on Robert's knee; he looked disappointed so she sat on a stool at his feet.

'We had a lovely time at the museum, Grandma. I turned handles and pressed buttons and things. Then we had tea with Nana; she isn't very well is she Dad?'

Robert nodded.

'Would you like me to take Alice to see your mother? I'm happy to do it.'

Robert smiled; perhaps she wasn't such a battle axe. She seemed to have Alice's best interests at heart. He put his arm round his only child and drew her close.

'It's time you were in bed, young lady, you've got school tomorrow,' he kissed her.

'Give your grandmother a kiss.'

Chapter 52

December 1947

Mary was in her sitting-room playing patience, all was peaceful; everyone was out. She listened to the Third Programme which was presenting a Mozart concert. It was time she arranged a family reunion since all three of her children would soon be in London. It would be a good time to introduce Emma-Jane. She would have to include Cyril with Helena and the indomitable Stephen.

She jumped when the front door was banged open then slammed shut; she heard Patricia wailing and Philip shouting. Mary wondered how two people could create so much drama. She walked into the hall where Philip was incandescent with rage and Patricia was unrecognisable. Her once magnificent hair, her father's delight, was gone; it had been cropped. Mary struggled to supress a smile. She could imagine the delight with which the child's mother had marched her to the hairdresser. Mary could hear, in her head, the satisfaction with which the words 'Cut it all off,' would have been said.

'Have you ever seen anything like it, Mary? The bloody woman's insane, how could she do this to her own child?'

'I tried to stop it, Dad, truly I did.' Patricia wiped away tears.

'I'll take her to court over this, I won't have it; she had no right. She won't see Patricia again, that's it.'

'Be careful, Philip, I don't think you can stop Patricia seeing her mother.'

Philip stood, arms slack by his sides, head drooping. 'How could she?'

'Go and put the kettle on, Patricia, I think we could all do with a cup of tea.' Mary's expression ensured Patricia did as she was told.

'I can't cope with her.'

Mary wondered if he were referring to his daughter or his ex-wife.

'I've done it Aunt Mary.' Patricia rushed back from the kitchen; she clearly had no intention of missing anything.

'No, my dear, I want to talk to your father. I'm sure you are sensible enough to make a pot of tea. If you look in the cake tin, you can choose which cake we will have.'

Patricia pulled a face and turned to her father for support. He said nothing so, with bad grace, she left the room. Mary smiled, but hoped the child would not take her temper out on the crockery.

Philip had always been dramatic and Mary wondered if she would do more harm than good. She was not a good example of how to conduct a happy marriage. Someone had said 'Marriage was an institution and who wanted to live in one.' Perhaps it drives everyone mad in the end. She could hear the noise of drawers being opened and crockery clattered; Patricia would soon be back with the tea trolley.

'Do you know why Sophia had Patricia's hair cut?'

'How should I know; what does the poor child look like?'

'Who is going to be most upset by what she did?'

'Patricia of course.'

'No Philip, you are. Sophia set out to get at you and she has succeeded, beyond her wildest dreams. Have no doubt Patricia will tell her mother how much her actions have upset you.'

Philip opened his mouth and shut it again.

'Has the haircut done any permanent damage?'

Philip shook his head.

'It will grow again. I suspect Patricia has wanted to have her hair cut before this, but didn't dare ask.'

'But…'

'All Sophia has done is to take it further than Patricia wanted. The best thing you can do is play it down. Next time you wash her hair say how much easier it is now.'

Patricia pushed the tea trolley into the room. She glanced from her father to her great aunt; neither spoke.

Christmas was approaching and Mary was happy; all her children and grandchildren were coming for lunch tomorrow. Although both butcher and greengrocer were delivering her order, she still needed some extras. She had decided on a traditional menu starting with soup followed by roast beef and then Alice's favourite pudding, apple crumble. Mary hummed a tune under her breath as she walked home. She enjoyed cooking and Alice would be home from school soon to help with preparation.

She did not see the young man, with a duffle bag, running up the road she was trying to cross. She was looking the other way when he crashed into her. His shoulder knocked her off balance. With a shopping bag in each hand, she could do nothing to soften her fall. She hit the pavement awkwardly and heard a sickening crack. At first, she felt nothing.

'Sorry, luv, you alright?'

The young man bent down for a moment and was gone. The fall had winded her and all she could do was gasp as pain radiated from her hip; she couldn't move. People gathered round, someone put a coat under her head. She listened to voices debating what should be done. Someone was gathering the contents of her shopping bags, stuffing things back inside.

'Shall I help you up, dear?'

'I think I need an ambulance.'

Someone else tried to sit her up; she screamed.

'Please, ring for an ambulance; I think I've broken my hip.'

She heard the ambulance bell ringing, getting nearer through heavy traffic. She looked at her bulging carrier bags, full of ingredients she would never cook.

Chapter 53

December 1947

Stephen slammed out of the room, thumped his way up the hall before slamming his bedroom door behind him. Cyril sighed; heaven help the poor neighbours. He wondered if the boy's behaviour would get even worse once Alice arrived. He'd made it clear he didn't want his half-sister living with them. Instead of listening to Helena asking why Alice was not with her, now Cyril would have to cope with Stephen acting up because she was.

Helena had been slumped in an armchair all day, her despair made the air heavy. Cyril had hoped her spirits would lift once she got her way. Mary Carlton was in hospital so, once again, Alice needed a new home. Robert was allowed a short compassionate leave, but returned to Singapore. Cyril poured himself a drink.

The family conference at Mary's had been a revelation. Robert had not once spoken to him directly, referring to him only by surname. He didn't want Alice left with her mother, but unless he could sort something himself, there was no other choice. Frances had suggested Matthew and Emma-Jane, now they were settled in their new house, but Emma-Jane was not willing to take on the responsibility.

Knowing that the man who 'stole' his wife now had his daughter, must have been the final straw. Cyril wondered why the pompous bugger didn't leave the army and take an active part in his daughter's life, perhaps he liked bossing people about.

'Alice will be here soon, darling; I'll check her bedroom's ready.' He stroked Helena's hair and kissed her forehead; her unnatural stillness was chilling. He knelt at her feet and took her hands in his, 'It's going to be all right; why don't you lie down; you must be tired.'

He helped her to her feet, steadied her. Her abdomen was taut, like a drum; she rubbed her back and stretched. 'Not long now.'

Cyril was not sure if she was referring to the imminent arrival of Alice or the baby. He walked with her to their bedroom and got her settled.

'I'm going to have a word with Stephen.'

Helena didn't reply.

Stephen was sitting on the floor of his bedroom, playing with his bricks. He ignored Cyril who sat on the bed and waited. Once piled into towers, he knocked them down; the construction/demolition work continued until Cyril grabbed the boy and hugged him.

'I know you don't want Alice to live here, but you wouldn't want her to be on her own, would you?'

No reply.

'You know Mummy is Alice's Mummy too.'

'No, she isn't and you're not her Daddy.'

Cyril gazed out of the window; the view over London was breathtaking, it made him feel insignificant. There seemed little point in arguing with a three-year-old about the complications of a shared mother and different fathers. Stephen would have to get used to the idea of an older sister and a new baby too. Life was going to be stormy whichever way he looked at it.

Cyril knew he should have been more forthcoming about Helena's mental state. To have suggested Alice didn't live with them would have sent her into a downward spiral; she would have seen it as a betrayal. He remembered the gentle days he spent with Gwen, a lifetime ago. That was gone, but Alice seemed a sensible girl and was bound to be a help once Stephen got used to the idea.

Alice walked up four flights of stairs. There was a sharp, unpleasant smell, cat's pee most likely. The taxi driver was climbing the stairs behind her, muttering under his breath. When she found out about living with her mother, she felt guilty. She knew it wasn't what Dad wanted. It wasn't her fault she had to go to live with Mum and Cyril, it wasn't her fault Grandma broke her leg. She had seen so little of Mum and even less of Cyril and Steven. She stopped on the stairs and clung to the bannister rail; she was scared. Perhaps they wouldn't like her, then what. Dad had explained there was nowhere else for her to go.

'Come on girl,' the taxi driver said, 'this thing weighs a ton.'

She moved to one side so he could struggle past with her green, tin trunk. She wondered if this was the last time she'd be moved around;

she was tired of it all. She ran upstairs and banged on the front door of 25, Gainsborough Gardens. Footsteps sounded on what must be an uncarpeted hallway. The door was flung open and she was scooped into Helena's arms.

'Oh, my darling, I have waited so long for this day.'

Alice blushing with embarrassment, tried to disentangle herself. Cyril, Stephen and the taxi driver were all staring at her. The light in the hallway was too dim for her to gauge their reaction. She heard the taxi driver clear his throat.

'That'll be fifteen shillings and nine pence, Guv.'

Alice watched as Cyril handed over a pound note.

'I'll give you a hand to get this inside,' the driver said.

Helena led Alice into a warm, cluttered kitchen; a clothes dryer hung from the ceiling and the smell of wet fabric reminded her of washday at Nana's. Perhaps she'd be able to visit both her grandmothers soon, but who would take her? She was nearly seven, was that too young to go on her own? It was all so difficult.

'I'm making a cup of tea; will you have one, Alice?' Cyril smiled at her.

She wasn't supposed to like him; Daddy had said he couldn't be trusted and he had taken Mummy away with all the furniture. Daddy would be sad and think she didn't care about him. She gave a tight-lipped smile and nodded her head.

'Tea for three then; what about you, Stephen, would you like some milk?'

'I want tea too.'

'Just this once as it's a special day and your big sister is here at last.'

Stephen glowered at Alice then kicked his legs against his chair.

Helena was sitting in a worn arm chair squashed in between the wall and a huge kitchen dresser. She pulled Alice close. 'I'd put you on my knee, but there isn't room for you and the baby.' She smiled, 'Will you help me when our baby arrives?'

'Yes, please.'

'Only girls play with babies,' Stephen said and slurped at his tea. 'Don't like this,' he said and pushed it away.

Alice noticed some movement on a cushion beside a black-leaded stove. It was a ginger cat. She leaned down and stroked it; she loved cats. The animal opened one eye, raised its head and yawned to show needle thin teeth and a very pink tongue. It stretched, extending its claws into the fabric of the cushion, gave a dismissive glance at Alice, curled up and was immediately asleep. Alice smiled and looked at the others.

'He's my cat,' Stephen said.

Chapter 54

December 1947

A consultant with a retinue of students stood round her bed.

'Have you seen your x-rays?'

'No, my daughter has; I believe it is a bad break.'

'It won't be straight forward because you have osteoporosis; your bones are fragile.'

Mary felt her stomach knot; she was glad the consultant was talking to her as though she were an intelligent human being and not a lump of meat, but his prognosis was bad. She waited while he discussed procedures and outcomes with his students. She closed her eyes and she was back in her beautiful apartment. Would she ever see it again?

The consultant leaned over and took her hand, 'I promise I'll do my best, but it all depends on how your femur behaves. If all goes well, you will make a fine recovery, but I don't want to raise your hopes.' He smiled and moved on to the next bed.

The moment of relief, from doubts about the future, disappeared as quickly as it came. She picked up the book she'd been reading, but the words blurred into a tangled mass of squiggles. She lay back on her pillows and closed her eyes; she took a few deep breathes, she must not panic. The lift to her apartment was notoriously unreliable; much as she loved her new home, she could not risk being marooned. Therefore, she must think about moving to somewhere more suitable. Perhaps she could find a house near to Matthew and Emma-Jane.

If it were a large house, she would use the ground floor and take in a housekeeper to live upstairs. Choose a married housekeeper and her husband could act as odd-job man. She was not short of money; there was a solution to every problem. She would have live-in help, and by offering accommodation, the arrangement would not cost much. It would be like having servants again.

'Having a little snooze, are we?' Nurse Jones took Mary's wrist and checked her pulse.

Mary opened her eyes; she'd been making a mountain out of a mole hill; of course, she'd be fine. Being stuck in hospital was the problem and why she was losing her touch with reality.'

Frances arrived at the hospital with Matthew and Emma-Jane. Mary watched and tried to raise herself on her elbows as soon as she saw Matthew. She managed a wave before sinking back on the pillows. The three handsome, young people walked up the ward; she signalled to Matthew to sit beside her.

'How are you doing, Mother?'

'I feel like a trussed chicken.'

Frances examined the pulleys and ropes holding Mary's leg in traction 'It doesn't look very comfortable.'

'It isn't.' She grimaced with pain as she tried to move.'

'I'll have a word with Sister now, in her office.'

Emma Jane handed Mary some grapes, 'Poor you, I'm so sorry I couldn't help with Alice, but I'm hoping to get a job.'

Mary grabbed Matthew's hand.

'I'm scared. Nobody tells me anything, but from what I've overheard, it's a bad break.'

Frances returned, 'I've seen your x-ray, your bones are so thin, it may take time for them to knit together.'

No one spoke.

'I expect they'll get you up once the break is stabilised, I bet you'll be a whizz on crutches.'

Mary sighed and closed her eyes; the pain in her leg was wearing her down.

'What about a hip replacement?' Emma-Jane said, 'They've been doing them in the States for a while.'

'Yes, but Sister said it's not so easy with older people; I'm sure they'll sort it out.'

'Let's wait and see,' Matthew said, 'no point in gloom and doom yet.'

'What about Alice? I won't be able to care for her.' Mary paused, 'Will I even be able to stay in my apartment?'

Matthew patted Mary's hand, 'Don't forget, Mother, there is a lift.'

'A totally unreliable one.'

'As you know I wrote to Robert, told him about your accident,

Mother. His reply came yesterday; he's decided Alice will go to Helena and Cyril.'

Mary turned to Frances, 'Really, that does surprise me.'

'I don't think he had any other option.'

'Poor child, I'll miss her.'

'On a happier note, Emm and I have got our house; it's a large detached, in Hendon, overlooking a park.' Robert patted his mother's hand, 'and a large garden at the back.'

'Yes, it's lovely, the folks back home will be so jealous. We'll have a celebration once you come home.'

Frances stood up, 'You're looking tired, Mum; I think we ought to let you get some rest.'

Mary watched them walk away; there was so much to sort out. The prospect of permanent disability opened like a black chasm; life was unfair. She'd just got herself settled and now this; and what about Alice? She loved the child and would miss her dreadfully.

Chapter 55

December 1947

Alice and Stephen walked home from school; it was an uneasy truce. He knew he had to stay with her, but refused to hold her hand. Unlike Stephen, Alice liked school, but the cloud of end of term exams would soon engulf her. She had to do well; Dad would be so disappointed if she didn't. Mum was too busy being pregnant to say much.

'Hope Mum does a big tea, I'm starving.'

Alice smiled; Stephen was always starving. She supposed she'd better help Mum, but she had masses of homework and revision. Dad had told her he hoped she'd go in the army when she was older; he would get her a commission, whatever that meant. Alice wasn't sure what she wanted to do, but the army had never appealed; she didn't want to wear khaki knickers.

'I'm going to help Mum get tea, you can set the table.'

Stephen glared at her and ran off.

'Don't boss me about,' he shouted. 'I'll tell Mum you hit me then you'll be sent to your room.'

Alice sighed. She hoped the new baby would be a girl. She couldn't stand two younger brothers. She walked up the flights of stairs and handed Stephen the key; he liked to open the door himself. As they walked into the hallway, they could hear Helena shouting from the bathroom.

'Quick Alice, phone for an ambulance, I think the baby's coming.'

Stephen stood open-mouthed as Alice pushed him out of the way to make the call; she was frightened. Helena was gasping and crying between screams. If this was what having a baby was like, Alice didn't want any. Stephen clamped his hands over his ears and ran to his bedroom.

'The ambulance is on its way, Mum; can I get you anything? Should

I phone Cyril? Perhaps you should lie down.'

Helena grabbed Alice's hand; sweat stood in fat beads on her forehead and upper lip.

'Yes, call Cyril; his number's in the book.'

Alice fumbled through the phone book, her hands shaking so it was hard to turn the pages. As she found the number, a man shouted and banged on the front door; Alice rushed to let the ambulance men in.

Helena was put in a chair stretcher and covered in a blanket. Alice shouted, as Helena was carried downstairs, 'I'll call Cyril now.'

When she got through, he was out, visiting clients. She'd just have to get something for tea and wait for him to come home. She went to the larder, Mum had done little shopping recently, but there was a tin of spaghetti and some sliced bread. That would have to do. Feeling grown-up, she toasted bread and stirred the spaghetti and waited for the kettle to boil.

When Stephen didn't appear, she went to his bedroom. He was hunched up under the bedclothes. She shook his shoulder.

'Tea's ready.'

'Where's Mum?'

'Gone to hospital, to have the baby.'

'Who's cooked tea?'

'I have.'

'Don't want any.'

'I thought you said you were hungry. It's spaghetti, you like that.'

He wiped his nose on his sleeve and got out of bed. It was the first meal the children ate on their own. Stephen found some biscuits and they shared an apple.

Alice smiled, 'It's an indoor picnic. Now if you wash up, I'll dry and put away.'

'I'm going out to play.'

'After you've washed up.'

Stephen tried to push past Alice, but she got to the front door first. When she pulled the bolt across at the top, Stephen kicked her.

'Why are you such a pig?''

He threw himself on the floor and bellowed with rage. Alice cleared the table and got out her homework. It was nice being in charge.

Cyril phoned soon after.

'I'm at the hospital; Mum's had the baby, a little girl.'

'I'm so glad it's a girl.' She turned to Stephen, 'You've got another sister.'

He howled and ran to his bedroom slamming the door behind him.

'I'll stay with Mum a bit longer; can you manage?'

'Yes, we've had some tea. Do you want me to get Stephen to bed?'

'I'll do it when I get back.'

'Give Mum my love… and Stephen's'

'You're a good girl, Alice.'

Alice beamed at her reflection in the hall mirror. 'Bye Cyril,' she put the phone down, 'I'm a good girl, Cyril said so.'

Cyril looked down at a tiny bundle in the crib. A fragile head covered with damp black hair was all he could see. This baby girl looked like a porcelain doll, unmoving, silent, her grasp on life tenuous. He stroked her head and felt the fontanelle pulsate, the only proof of life.

He wondered if he would find characteristics similar to Stephen, as he remembered him. Stephen was a week old when he saw him for the first time; did babies alter much in a week? This child was a stranger; Cyril wondered if this was how Robert felt when he first saw Stephen, had it started as unease which grew until it could not be denied?

Cyril recalled Helena's sudden, unexpected return from Paris, before Christmas; it would soon be Christmas again. He was seeing problems that didn't exist, but Helena was capable of anything. He stopped; this would not do though Helena's sanity was often in doubt. He would have to be the sensible one and would not question the child's parentage. Of course, the baby was his. He would never know for sure, but one thing he did know, the child needed a father, she also needed a name.

Cyril tried to open the front door, but it was bolted. He knocked and heard the living room door being flung open.

'Alice wouldn't let me go out to play, it's not fair.' Stephen shouted through the letterbox.

Cyril smiled, where did his son get so much energy?

Alice unbolted the door, 'We've had some tea.'

'And I had to help'

'Quite right too, if Alice got the tea of course you should help.'

As he stood with Stephen clinging to him, Cyril realised he had never touched Alice. He had never given her a hug or kissed her; there was separateness about the girl. Was it her natural inclination or was it because he was her stepfather? Heaven knew what horror stories Robert would have told her about the man who stole his wife.

He patted Alice's shoulder, 'Thank you for looking after things. Let's have a cup of tea. Then you two must get to bed, there's school in the morning.'

'What's the baby like?' Alice said as she filled the kettle, 'What's her name?'

'When's Mum coming home?' Stephen asked.

'I'm not sure, but soon.'

'Can we help choose a name?'

'Well, I don't want to choose,' Stephen said and stomped off to bed.

'Is Mum going to be all right?'

'Give her time; I'm glad you're here to help.'

Alice nodded, 'I'll drink my tea in bed.'

Cyril nodded and once she'd left the room, he poured himself a large gin.

Alice sat propped up in bed and thought about events of the day. All her life people had told her what to do, but now she'd be able to do the same. She smiled at Stephen's reaction to her putting herself in charge. There would be a bit more of that and Stephen would have to get used to it. She was needed here, she wasn't a nuisance, she was a good girl; Cyril said so. Once Mum came home, she would have less time for Stephen; she'd be too busy with the baby and would need help from her older daughter as soon as she got back from school.

They'd have to give the baby a name soon; perhaps she'd make some suggestions. The baby was bound to be nicer than Stephen who was rough and noisy. He always wanted his own way, always tried to push her out of things; she wasn't going to put up with that any more. She would tell them about the baby when she went to school because, in all the excitement, she hadn't finished her homework and felt too tired to do it now.

She put the bedside lamp on; she'd read her library book for a while. The lamp shone on the wall opposite her bed. I HATE ALICE had been scrawled, in pencil, over and over. Stephen really was a pain.

Chapter 56

January 1948

Christmas had been a muted affair; the family visited, but until the surgery was over no progress would be made. The nurses did their best, but it was clear they would rather be with their loved ones. When Sister said the operation was scheduled for the following day, her feelings swung from joy to fear.

Mary felt sick; she opened her eyes and saw the rest of the ward going about its business. There was no pain, but everything was moving as though she were being rocked in a cradle. She closed her eyes again, but that made it worse.

'Are you awake, dear?' A woman in the next bed, Mrs Johnson, asked. Mary nodded.

'Nurse, nurse, Mrs Carlton is awake.'

The woman was only being kind, but her voice reverberated in Mary's ears, made the nausea worse. She felt a cool hand grasp her wrist; it was Sister taking her pulse.

'Well, my dear, that's the worse bit over; it won't be long before we have you on your feet.'

Mary smiled before drifting into sleep, deep and dreamless. Sister pulled the curtains round her bed.

'Thanks for keeping an eye on her.' Sister said.

'I'll let you know if she wants anything.'

'Mrs Johnson, it's people like you that make the world go round.'

It was only a matter of days before Mary was hoisted to her feet. The physiotherapist made her walk up the ward and back, with help. Now, sitting in a chair by her bed; she was exhausted. Breathless and shaking, her hip ached, but she was pleased; things could only get better. Matthew and Emma were coming to see her and she was determined to greet them from the chair.

She leaned back and sighed; Helena had given her another granddaughter to be called Ruth. As always, she felt unease in the pit of her stomach when there was anything to do with Helena. It was like waiting for a volcano to erupt. At least Cyril was a steadying influence, long may it last.

There was so much to sort out. Philip and Patricia had visited, but he had evaded any discussion on what would happen once she came out of hospital. Patricia was approaching adolescence and would become more precocious with every passing year. Mary did not want to live with that. She moved slightly in her chair, trying to ease the ache in her hip, but determined to stay where she was.

Her plan to buy a good-sized house and live on the ground floor must be the answer. In warm weather, she would have a garden to sit in. She let her mind drift; once again she was back in the countryside where she spent her childhood. Now all her brothers were dead. So much pain, but physical pain could be controlled; emotional pain had to be endured.

There was movement at the end of the ward; visitors were coming. She had dwelled on the past for too long; perhaps it was how old people spent their days. She must do more to keep her brain active and hopefully her body too. She watched as Matthew and Emma Jane walked towards her; her spirits lifted.

'How wonderful to see you up, Mother, how's the leg coping?'

He bent to kiss her cheek while Emma waited with the usual bunch of flowers and a polite smile.

'It's coping.' She smiled and took Matthew's hand. 'I walked to the table and back. I'm quite proud of myself, but it's amazing how quickly muscles weaken.' She patted the chair beside her. 'You sit here, my dear, Matthew can perch on the bed. Now tell me all about your new house; I'm longing to see it.'

'It overlooks a park and is set back a bit from the road; the garden is as wide as the house but longer. There is an enormous fig tree, but it's a bit near the house so it might have to come down.'

Mary nodded, 'What about inside, will it need decorating.'

'It certainly will, Mother, so once you're up and about we'll give you a paint brush.'

'What about the neighbours? If you have to live within shouting distance of other people, it's essential to have an understanding.' Mary smiled at Emma.

'Don't you agree?'

'I thought you English took pride in keeping away from your neighbours.'

'Well, yes, but while you don't want them in your house, you don't want antagonism either. Neighbours are like family; you can't choose them.'

Emma nodded, 'How true.'

'They seem pleasant enough,' Matthew said, 'young couple with two small children.'

'Most suitable, particularly when you start your own family.'

Neither Emma nor Matthew spoke.

'What about the other side?'

There was a pause.

'It's empty at the moment, but I believe there is a buyer.' Emma said.

Matthew cleared his throat, 'We have some news for you, about having a family.'

Mary looked at them both and felt her heart leap.

'You're pregnant, my dear, how wonderful.'

'No, Mother, you know I had some problems in the past.'

'But you told me it had been sorted out.'

'Apparently it was worse than the doctors said. Anyway, Emma and I have decided to adopt.'

Mary leaned back in her chair. The only true grandchildren she would have would be Helena's with, who knew what, potential for mental health problems. With every passing year it became less likely that Frances would marry. This was it, adopt or nothing. She tried to gauge Emma's feelings about the situation, but could not read the young woman's expression. Only time would tell if someone else's child could fulfil her desire for motherhood.

'How very sensible, under the circumstances, I'm sure it's the right thing to do. How long will it take to sort things out?'

'I don't know; we're making enquiries.'

When the bell for the end of visiting time clanged, visitors gathered their belongings and left. In five minutes, the ward was quiet. Patients chatted to each other, but Mary had too much to think about. For her, intelligence was all, but with unknown parentage it was impossible to assess a child's academic potential. She most definitely did not want Matthew to be saddled with a dullard.

The other piece of information was far more promising. There was an empty house next to Matthew's; she would ask him to make enquires. If, as she hoped, she made a full recovery, her life would continue as before and she would be no trouble to them. However, if things did not go well, it would be easier for Matthew to keep an eye on her. It felt as though fate were taking a hand and making the decision for her.

She rang the bell for a nurse.

'Will you help me get into bed; I'm tired now.'

The nurse linked one arm with Mary's and helped her to her feet. Without warning, Mary felt something give way. She whimpered as excruciating pain radiated from her hip and down her leg. She cried out as she struggled to keep her balance on one foot; she clung to the nurse.

'I can't stand this pain,' she whispered.

'Sister,' the nurse shouted.

The curtains were drawn round as Mary was lifted and eased into bed by several nurses. She bit her lip so hard she could taste the metallic saltiness of her own blood.

'Doctor is on his way,' Sister said. 'It may be nothing more than stiff muscles after your exercise.'

Sister smiled, but Mary could see the expression in her eyes. It told her all she needed to know.

PART FOUR 1950

I'm going to follow this invisible
Red thread until I find myself again…
Until I finally figure out
Who I'm meant to be.

—Jennifer Elizabeth
Author

Chapter 57

January 1950

After two years with Cyril and Mum, Alice felt confident she could cope with anything. Mum's mood swung wildly, but it didn't scare Alice any more. When Mum was high, it was best to say as little as possible to avoid arguments; when she was down, she needed conversation to stop her drifting into despair. Alice had an understanding with Cyril, they worked as a team. He took Ruth to the crèche each morning; and Stephen went to school with Alice.

Each Saturday Alice and Mrs Green, from downstairs, caught the tram to the Co-op in Kentish Town. She felt very grown up with her big shopping bag and list. Initially Mrs Green was to supervise the expedition, but soon Alice was confident enough to go on her own if Mrs Green was busy. She queued at each counter and eavesdropped on the conversations of the women around her; that was fun. As she went from counter to counter, she took pride in her efficiency, every item crossed off, the price written beside it. She checked her change and made sure she gave the dividend number after each transaction.

The hard part was carrying the heavy bag from the tram stop back home and up four flights of stairs. She felt it was worth it for the money Cyril gave after each trip. This had to be done secretly because on one occasion Stephen found out and threw a massive tantrum.

This Saturday was different. The weather after Christmas had been dull and mild, but by the middle of the month temperatures plummeted. Despite this, Helena had insisted she must go to Kentish Town to take advantage of some sale she'd heard about. She walked down the road, pushing a large second-hand pram. Alice and Stephen walked either side, holding on to the handle. Ruth wailed all the way. Alice hated going shopping with Mum; it was so embarrassing.

Ruth's birth had jolted Helena out of depression, but already Alice had picked up signs of Mum's mood becoming too extreme. This was the difficult phase which made Alice wary. Given the choice, that afternoon, she would have stayed at home, but Cyril had asked her to keep an eye on Mum.

The convoy reached Kentish Town without mishap; Ruth, with a heavy cold, had fallen into fitful sleep, Stephen had been bribed with sweets and Alice was relieved not to have seen anyone she knew. Helena's voice was powerful; it carried whether she was shouting at Stephen or singing as she walked down the road; now she was singing, an aria from 'Madam Butterfly.'

'Where are we going?' Stephen asked. 'Can we go to the toy shop?'

'No. Stop thinking of yourself all the time.'

'But, Mum…'

Helena stopped the pram and glared at him.

'You behave yourself; we're going to the furniture shop. I want to choose some chairs and a settee.'

Alice stared at her mother; from what Cyril told her, money was tight. What on earth would he say? How would Mum pay for it? Cyril didn't give Mum large sums, not after she was sent shopping for a winter coat and came back with a guitar she couldn't play. Alice opened her mouth to speak, but one look at Helena's face was enough; it was not her problem.

The pram was parked outside the store, but Helena took Ruth in with her. Had it not been such a miserable day, Alice would have volunteered to stay outside and mind both pram and baby. Although early afternoon, it was dank and the light was fading; lights in shop windows twinkled in the gloom and wisps of fog were gathering.

It was warm and bright inside and Stephen soon discovered it was fun to jump up and down on the furniture. A short dapper man, with a fixed smile, bustled over.

'Now then sonny, we don't want you to have an accident.'

'Oh, he's all right, he won't do any harm,' Helena said and handed Ruth to Alice.

'He will, if he has mud on his shoes; damage has to be paid for.'

Alice held her breath

Helena glared, but grabbed Stephen and pulled his shoes off.

'I'm looking for a settee and a couple of armchairs.'

'Oh, you mean a settee and two chairs, matched?'

'No, I know what I mean. I don't want everything matching… so twee.'

'We can't break up suites; the manufacturers would never stand for it.'

'So, they are more important than your customers.'

Instead of replying, the salesman went to a large settee in the back of the shop.

'We do have this.'

Helena sat on it and called Stephen over. Alice watched as she walked up and down trying to stop Ruth's howling. Her cheeks were scarlet; she was cutting her back teeth. Alice rocked from one foot to the other and hoped Helena would not ask her opinion on anything. She had learned it was not wise to become involved with Mother's wilder extravagances. If she approved Cyril would hit the roof, if she disapproved Mother would create a scene in the shop. She'd take Ruth out to the pram and walk her up and down, but when she looked out the fog was dense. She thought about Nana Warren and hoped she was all right. It was ages since she'd seen her; she'd write her a letter when she got home.

The salesman was writing in his pad. 'And where do you live, Mrs Davis?'

'It's Davies with an 'e'.

As Helena gave their address, Alice's heart sank; Mum was buying it.

'Now what about chairs, wing back or ordinary?'

'Let me see what you have, and its Davies with an 'e'

'Yes, Madam, follow me.'

Stephen was stretched full length on the settee Helena was buying. As the salesman walked past, he rolled his eyes at another salesman lurking in the back of the shop. Helena picked two chairs and watched as they were added to the invoice. Alice wanted to tell Mum about the fog, but didn't dare.

Helena raised her voice, 'How many times do I have to tell you, it's Davies with an e.'

'Yes, madam, I know.' He pushed the invoice towards her. 'Look, I've put Mrs E. Davis.'

'You fool,' she shouted. 'Come along children I will not do business with an idiot.

With that she swept out of the shop. Stephen was bundled off the settee by the salesman.

'If your lad's damaged this, you'll be liable,' he shouted as Helena and family disappeared into thick, yellow fog. 'Hope you get lost, you silly cow, wasting my time.'

Cyril glanced at his watch; time on his own was precious and with Helena and the children out of the way for a few hours, he would have some peace. The pattern was too familiar to ignore, he was going to need as much rest as possible before the going got rough. He unscrewed the bottle and searched in the fridge for tonic, the perfect before lunch drink except he didn't want food, it was alcohol he craved.

A drink in his hand, he sat in the comfortable chair in the corner of the kitchen. The cat yawned, stretched, jumped off his cushion and onto Cyril's lap. As cats will, it moved in a tight circle until assured it would be comfortable and then settled, asleep instantly. Cyril stroked the silky fur and sipped his gin. It was worthwhile to desperately want a drink, for as long as he could stand it, in order to experience the euphoric moment when alcohol started to work its magic.

The walk back from Camden Town had been hard work, but in a strange way exciting. The fog was so thick, trams had to move at walking pace, following a man with a flare.

'Would it be a good idea to keep up with the tram? At least then we can see where we're going.'

'My dear Alice, do you think I don't know my way home?'

'No, it's just that it's so thick.'

Helena tutted, but slowed down.

The light was eerie and fog stained everything the colour of sulphur. It clung to Alice's face and clothes like dank seaweed. Breathing was difficult as though fog was clogging her lungs making her body cry out for oxygen; it must be how Nana Warren felt. A dense ocean of moisture and smoke pressing in on her, wet her face left lank rats-tails clinging to her cheeks and neck. She wrapped her scarf over nose and mouth and hoped it would filter out the choking fumes.

Ruth wailed and coughed while Stephen kept up a steady and dispirited whining; nobody spoke. They followed the lights from the tram and listened to the muffled sounds of people nearby, people she couldn't see. Alice wondered how they would manage once they turned off the main road and had no lights to guide them.

Chapter 58

January 1950

Cyril woke with a start; the cat was scratching at the door. It must be late; he checked his watch; it was very late. The fog had formed a yellow wall outside the window. Where the hell were they? What possessed her to stay out so late, didn't she notice the fog coming down? He shook his head, of course she didn't. Helena was the most infuriating, exasperating, unpredictable woman he had ever met. Was he tied to her by love, or obsession? At times like these she was a leech sucking the life out of him. He was no more than a husk, incapable of breaking free.

He heard a commotion on the stairs, the familiar screaming from Stephen and wailing from Ruth. He gave a sigh of relief; at least they were all alive, he hurried to the door. Stephen, tear-streaked and dirty, was trying to hit Alice who had grabbed his arms to avoid injury. Ruth had ropes of green mucus streaming from her nose which she had smeared over her face. She appeared to have a particularly pernicious skin complaint.

Helena was dishevelled yet her skin had a silky sheen and her eyes sparkled; she was as high as a kite. Of course, she would not notice the fog; she wouldn't notice a bomb going off. Her duffel coat and beret sparkled with drops of silver. She rested icy fingers against Cyril's face and smiled; his body felt hot with lust.

'Get inside, for heaven's sake, the kids must be freezing.'

Helena put an arm round his neck and pulled him close. With her embrace came the sulphurous whiff of hell-fire and damnation.

'What an adventure we've had, haven't we children?'

Cyril watched them, poor little sods, freezing cold and hungry. He shepherded them through to the kitchen; the fun and games had begun.

'Were you worried about me?'

'Of course, I was, but there was no point in trying to find you in this.'

Stephen was sobbing, 'My legs hurt and Alice said if I didn't hurry, she'd leave me behind.'

'Hush, darling boy, she didn't mean it.' Helena turned, 'Did you?'

Alice said nothing.

Cyril glanced across the room to Alice standing in the doorway; he smiled at her. She did her best.

Helena settled in the corner chair with Ruth on her knee.

'I'll bath Stephen,' Alice said, 'and get in after him.'

'I don't want her to, I hate her.'

Alice grabbed him by the shoulder and marched him to the bathroom.

'Get in there and shut up, I'm sick of you trying to get me into trouble.' She turned on the taps and pulled off Stephen's clothes. She knew she wasn't being kind, but she didn't care. After checking the water, she manhandled him in.

'I can wash myself.'

'No, you can't, you dirty little tyke; I've seen the state of your neck. Come here.' She attacked him with flannel and soap. 'When Mum and Cyril aren't around, I'm in charge; you do as I say.'

Stephen glared at her. She dried him and took him to the kitchen for supper. Cyril nodded to Alice.

'Thanks,' he said. 'I'll do some toast for after your bath.'

She hurried back and smiled as she stretched out in the hot water, being the eldest had its advantages. She stayed up later, could read in bed as long as she liked and from now on Stephen was not going to have things his own way. Thank goodness he wasn't the eldest.

Once she'd had supper, she'd write her letter. It was difficult knowing what to tell Nana; she dared not talk about life with Mum and Cyril. She'd ask if Nana was well and mention the fog, but not the walk home. She could describe her new school uniform, but not that Mum took her to get it. Should she ask about Pauline, but did her Nana still see her? What about Dad? On his last leave he had said he hoped to leave the army and live with Nana, keep her company, go back to work at the Post Office. She could ask if Nana had heard from him. But what would happen then? Would Mum and Dad start fighting about her again? She sighed. Nobody asked her what she wanted to do.

She sat in the warm kitchen and sipped her cocoa and listened to Mum telling Cyril about the man in the furniture shop. She watched his face and smiled when he winked at her.

'I'm going to bed now.'

Helena hugged her. 'I'll be in to tuck you in in a minute.'

'I'm too old to be tucked in, Mum.'

'You'll always be a baby to me.'

Alice pulled a face; she'd have to leave the letter; Mum didn't like her writing to Nana. Why was life so complicated?

Chapter 59

January 1950

Alice snuggled down with her book; it was early to go to bed, but she was tired after the walk. She was reading 'Commodore Hornblower', C.S. Forester's latest. Her friends at school only read girly stuff; she preferred adventure and wished she were a boy, they had more fun. She had tucked a torch under her pillow because Mum was bound to come in to switch the light off. It was fun reading under the covers, like being in a tent and she could go on reading as long as she liked.

She didn't know how long she had been dozing, but her book was on the floor and Mum was sitting on the bed beside her.

'Sit up, Alice, it's time we had a talk.'

'Can't we talk tomorrow?'

'No, it's time I told you the facts of life.'

Alice blinked, what did that mean?

'You bathed Stephen tonight; why do you think his body is different from yours?'

'Because he's a boy.'

'Why does he need to be different?'

Alice had never thought about why he had a willy and she didn't. Sometimes girls, at school, had gone into giggly groups to talk about boys, but she'd never been interested.

'I don't know.'

'Where do babies come from?'

'Out of ladies tummies.'

'But how do they get in in the first place?'

Alice shrugged her shoulders. 'I'm really tired, Mum.'

'You'll be at secondary school in a couple of years; you need to know these things. I want you told properly, not hear some old wives' tales.'

Alice sighed and leaned back on her pillow. She would have to listen then Mum would let her sleep.

The phone rang and Cyril popped his head round the bedroom door. 'It's Robert for Alice.'

'What is he doing calling at this time of night?'

'His mother's very ill.'

Helena tried to grab the phone; Cyril turned away and handed it to Alice.'

'I'll come over tomorrow, Dad; I'll let them know at school.'

'As soon as you can, she longs to see you.'

'Yes Dad.' She handed the phone to Cyril. 'Can I go to sleep now, Mum?'

Helena pulled a face 'It's very sad about your grandmother, but she is an old lady. You are a young woman and you have much to learn.'

She grabbed a piece of paper and a pencil from Alice's desk and drew strange diagrams. Cyril put his hand on Helena's shoulder, 'Give the girl some rest; she's bound to be upset.'

Helena ignored him and after a pause he left

Alice watched and felt sweat trickle down her back, she couldn't get her breath. Uncle John was there, clutching at her, thrusting her face against the thing in his trousers. The drone of Mum's voice went on and on, she wanted to put her fingers in her ears, but some words penetrated the roaring in her head.

Seeds, men planted seeds inside women, how could Stephen do that? She recalled his body in the bath, pink and shining after she'd scrubbed him. His willy small, inoffensive like a little finger. How could that plant seeds? The hair on the back of her neck prickled, she wanted a wee, she felt sick, she had to get away. Why was Mum telling her all this? She scrambled backwards until she was pressed against the headboard and wall.

'Darling, what's the matter; there's nothing to be frightened of. When you're older and have a nice young man to love, you'll want him to put hipenis into your special place. It's lovely.'

'Where is the special place?'

'Between your legs.'

Alice felt again Uncle John's fetid breath on her cheek, heard again his grunts and moans. Why had she never associated noises coming from Mum's bedroom with what Uncle John had done? She had pushed the horror and pain to the back of her mind. Now, here it was, come to haunt her. Flesh, his flesh clammy with sweat, rough with coarse hair, felt but never seen; her hand made to grasp that great thrusting thing. What had she thought it was? What was that hard thing pushed into her face, suffocating her, hurting her, making her hurt.

She cried out and Helena stopped.

'For heaven's sake, what's the matter?'

Tears streamed unchecked, Alice rested her head and arms on her knees. Her shoulders shook; she could not speak, couldn't tell Mum of her past. She must never tell anyone; Uncle John had warned her. It was all her fault.

'Of course, you will start your periods in a few years; there's nothing to be frightened of, every woman has periods. It's nature's way of keeping the special place for babies clean and ready. You'll get used to it.'

'No, it's horrible. I won't do it, it's hateful.' She put her hands over her ears. 'I won't listen anymore.'

Helena put her arm round Alice, 'I thought you were a big, grown-up girl; it's no good getting upset. We all have to grow up. You'll feel different when you meet a boy you like.'

Alice slid under the bedcovers and pulled them over her head. 'I want to go to sleep.'

'When I was your age, my mother left a book for me in our library. 'Boy into Man, Girl into Woman', she told me to read it. It's the only instruction I got. I didn't want that for you.'

'Please, I want to go to sleep.'

Helena left the drawings by Alice's bed, put the light out and left the room. 'You're a strange child.'

Alice lay curled up. She could hear a buzz of conversation coming from the kitchen. They would be talking about her, laughing; she couldn't stand it. She was so tired; it had been a horrible day. Exhaustion helped her relax a little and finally she floated into sleep.

Everything was red, blood red and in the far corner of her eye, Alice could see a tiny worm wriggling closer. It grew and wriggled; great coils of segmented flesh wriggling round her. She could not see red now; everything was filled with the worm, swollen, pulsating, threatening to engulf her. She dared not scream in case it got into her mouth. She closed her eyes, but she could still see it, everything was a heaving, throbbing mass. She was going to die; the worm would eat her up. She whimpered; she couldn't bear to touch its slimy, sticky surface. It was pressing against her, leaving slime on her hands and face. She tried to wipe it off, but more appeared. It was squeezing her, its hot breath on her face. She lashed out and fell, with a thump, out of bed.

She lay in darkness; her heart pounding so hard she feared it would burst from her chest. She couldn't sit up; she was shaking too much. She listened to the night sounds and her own heart as it slowed down. After a few minutes, she struggled upright, leaned against her bed. In the light from the moon, she could see Mum's hateful diagrams. She didn't want them in her room.

She took them to the window and looked out. Moonlight had bleached away colour, it must be very late. No lights were on except for the pale gleam from street lamps stretching down the road to form a necklace of dingy pearls. She opened the French window and stood on the balcony.

She heard a throaty chuckle and the sound of bodies moving, in the bed next door. She shuddered and tore the paper into pieces. She held her hands to the sky as a breeze tugged at her nightgown. She watched the bits of paper flutter to the ground like confetti, brilliant white when they caught light from the moon. She heard her mother cry out, then silence.

Three days later Helena was admitted to Friern Barnet Psychiatric Hospital.

Chapter 60

January 1950

Alice sat bedsides Nana's hospital bed; Robert had left her to 'say her goodbyes' while he spoke to the consultant. The frail body reminded Alice of Egyptian mummies. She stretched out a hand to touch the gnarled, fleshless arm lying on the counterpane; the wedding ring so loose, only a swollen knuckle held it in place. The skin was dry, cold, unyielding; with so little flesh left it must be Nana's bones she could feel.

The face behind the oxygen mask was still and gave no indication she knew anyone was there. Alice didn't know what to do; she should feel sad, tearful, but there was nothing, just a void. She felt she was intruding; Nana had said she didn't want to live anymore, said she'd had enough. There seemed no point in holding Nana's hand; she wanted to go. It was for the best. She'd always wanted to be with Grandpop; soon she would be.

Alice sighed; why was everything so horrible? She'd often felt frightened and Nana had too, frightened of Dad. That didn't seem right; perhaps being in the army had made him like he was. She leaned towards the still figure, watched the angular chest give shallow but regular jerks so just enough oxygen maintained the old woman's slender hold on life.

It was then a wave of sorrow filled Alice's heart and tears gathered; she should have done more to help Nana, make Dad understand how she felt.

'I love Dad, but he is so difficult at times; I never meant to let you down.' She stroked the motionless hand which, for a moment, was once again the hand she used to hold, the hand that washed and dressed her and soothed her when she was ill. She wasn't frightened any more. She stood, leaned over the bed and pressed a kiss on her grandmother's forehead.

'Goodbye, Nana, God bless, give my love to Grandpop.'

She walked back to the waiting room where Dad was waiting; she didn't look back.

Robert stood as she walked in; he put an arm round her and wiped away her tears with his handkerchief.

'I'll go and sit with her,' he said, 'you'll be all right here. Keep an eye open for your aunt and Pauline. I told them your Nana was dying two days ago; I doubt they'll turn up now, if they leave it any longer it'll be too late.'

Alice opened her mouth to speak, but Robert was gone, hurrying down the ward, probably for the last time. She sat and took some deep breaths. It would be all right, she didn't have to speak to anyone, just sit quietly. She looked out of the window; light was fading although it was still afternoon. Everything was so uncertain; what had Dad got arranged for her. Once Nana died, he'd go off to Singapore. She'd liked it with Grandma Carlton, but she'd bought a house next to Uncle Matt and Aunt Emma; she didn't think she could go there. Aunt Emma didn't want her; that left Cyril and the kids. She wasn't sure she wanted to stay there now. Mum had been scary since the visit to the furniture shop.

What would Dad plan, he said he'd run out of people she could stay with. And how would Cyril manage with Mum the way she was? She stared out of the hospital window and it took her a moment to realise her dad was talking to her.

'It's over, child. You grandmother's dead, she just slipped away.'

Alice blinked back tears and stood. He held out his arms for her and she leaned against his chest; when he was like this, he made her feel safe.

'She had a hard life, Alice, but she's at peace now.'

He held her hand as they walked out of the hospital. It was the end of a special part of her life; Nana had been the last link. They walked in silence to the Underground. The train was hot and crowded; Alice felt herself sway as she clung to the hand strap and willed herself not to faint. They walked to Cyril's flat and Alice wondered if Dad would speak to him or leave her at the bottom of the stairs.

He kissed her. 'I'll ring once I've got the funeral arranged. Come over next weekend, there are things we need to discuss.' He hugged her and she watched him walk away. The stairs seemed steeper than usual and once she rang the doorbell, she leaned against the wall. When would something nice happen?

Stephen opened the door. 'We've got sausages for tea.'

He rushed away leaving her in the hall.

Cyril came out of the kitchen; he put his hand on her shoulder. 'Are you alright?'

Alice shook her head, 'Nana's dead.' She slumped against him and sobbed; he patted her back and made soothing noises.

'Gwen's here, do you remember her? She's been helping me with Ruth. Would you like her to make you a cup of tea?'

Alice nodded.

'Go in the sitting room, you'll get a bit of peace there until the meal's ready.'

Several days later, Robert phoned.

'It's about the funeral, Alice; I want you to remember your Nana as she was so I don't think you should go to the funeral. Funerals aren't for children, and besides you'd miss another day in school.'

Alice closed her eyes; she felt too tired to stand and let herself slide to the floor. Shouldn't she be there, what would Nana's friends think? Would they believe she didn't care?

'If you think that's best Dad.'

'I'll see you next weekend, child.'

Chapter 61

January 1950

Alice felt groggy and struggled to sit up. She looked at her watch, half past seven on a Saturday, she didn't usually get up so early. Stephen rushed into her room.

'Where's Mum, she's gone... I can't find her.'

'Don't worry; she's probably gone for a paper. Let's have some breakfast.' She knocked on Cyril's door. 'Is Mum there?' No reply.

Together she and Stephen went to the kitchen. Alice dished out corn flakes and left him to get on with them. She knocked on Cyril's bedroom door, again. He was dishevelled but clothed; he stared at Alice.

'Did you say your mother's gone somewhere?'

Alice nodded and pulled a face, 'What now?' 'Shall I get the other two sorted?'

'Please. I want them out of harm's way. Did you hear her last night, it's a wonder she didn't wake you all up; I can't cope with her.'

He picked up the telephone receiver; Alice felt sick. Suppose he was calling the police to say Mum was missing. She should be going over to Dad today, but she couldn't leave now. What should she do?

She took Stephen and Ruth to the swings on the Heath. After an hour, she could bear it no longer and hurried home; she must find out what was going on. The flat was empty, but Cyril had left a note.

Mum was picked up by the police, taken her to Friern Hospital. I'm meeting them there. Do your best until I get back.

Cyril

Yesterday was Nana's funeral and now this. Alice was sorting out some biscuits and squash for them when Cyril got back. He put his hands on Alice's shoulders, 'What would I do without you?'

Alice smiled, 'Want a cup of tea or...'

Cyril smiled and reached for the gin bottle, 'I can't interest you in some can I?'

Alice gasped, 'I'm not old enough.'

'I know love, just trying to keep my spirits up.'

'What are we going to do?'

'I was thinking on the way home: you already take Stephen school, could you take over with Ruth, get her to the nursery and bringing them both back? My boss is getting fed up with me getting into work late. I need to keep working otherwise we're up the creek and homeless as well.'

'Would I be allowed?'

'We're not going to ask.'

'Ruth's okay but Stephen's a pain.'

'If we don't make our own arrangements, all three of you could be taken into care.'

'But Stephen's so naughty.'

'Yes, I know, I'll talk to him, but you mustn't tell anyone what we're doing, especially not you dad. He slumped at the kitchen table head in hands.

'We have to make this work until Mum comes home.'

Alice rested her hand on his shoulder, 'Is it alright if I go over to Dad's, he's expecting me and I'm really late.'

'Okay, love.'

Robert opened the door and, by his expression, Alice knew she was in trouble.

'Why are you so late?'

'It's Mum.'

'What about her, what's she up to now?'

'She's in hospital; I had to stay with the little ones while Cyril tried to sort things out.'

'I'm sorry about your mum, but I don't want you to have to look after the others.'

'She won't be in long, we'll manage. I expect Cyril will be allowed some time off work.'

'I'll give him a call later and explain how I feel about this. Now come in and see what I've done.'

'Dad it looks lovely, Nana would be so pleased.' The room looked larger, less cluttered and smelled of lavender polish; everything shone.

Robert smiled, 'There's someone I'd like you to meet.'

A short, pretty woman stood and held out her hand. 'I'm Elizabeth, a friend of your father's.'

'I'm really sorry I'm so late and spoiled Dad's plans.'

'No matter, child, but it is courteous to inform people…'

'But you have no phone, Dad.'

Elizabeth laughed, 'Didn't you know your Dad is an old stick in the mud.' She turned to Robert, 'For heaven's sake man, get a phone.'

Alice watched his face flush and wasn't sure if he was angry or embarrassed.

Elizabeth picked up her coat, 'I for one suggest we go for a walk in Battersea Park. The fresh air will do us good and we are bound to find a café or snack bar, even if it's only fish and chips.'

Alice watched and decided Elizabeth knew exactly how to treat him. Perhaps they would get married; how would she feel about sharing him? She'd never really had him to herself because he'd hardly ever been there. How well did she know him? Perhaps some of the things Mum said were right, perhaps he was really difficult; Nana had been scared. She felt a lump in her throat and hurried to take her things upstairs.

She sat on the double bed where she slept many years ago. She'd lived there with Grandpop and Nana, felt safe then, but now they were both gone. She heard footsteps on the stairs.

'Are you ready or shall we go without you?'

'I'm so sorry I was late, Dad.

He ruffled her hair, 'Get your coat on.'

Chapter 62

April 1950

The arrangement with Stephen and Ruth had worked well, but it left little time for homework and no time to relax and play. She had too many responsibilities, but Cyril promised things would change once Mum was discharged from Friern Barnet. She was prescribed Largactil, a new drug, which helped to keep her calm.

Helena's cousins, Margaret and Bernard owned a farm in the Cotswolds and had invited the family down for Easter. It had been arranged by her Aunt Frances, to give Cyril a break. Grandma phoned to explain about the holiday.

Alice clutched the receiver in both hands and tried not to cry.

'It is so nice to speak to you, Grandma; I've not seen you for ages.'

There was a pause and grandma made a strange noise.

'We must make a definite arrangement for you to come as soon as you get home. I want to hear all about this holiday, it will do you all good.'

'I'll see if I'm allowed to come on the Undergound train, by myself.'

'Yes, do that; I really enjoyed our time together in my apartment.'

Alice gazed out of the train window. Wasn't it strange; for so long no-one seemed to want her and Dad said he'd run out of people, but now, suddenly there were lots of people who wanted her. Poor Grandma if she hadn't hurt her leg, she would have been able to stay in her lovely apartment. Still perhaps her house would be even better.

The train rumbled through green fields which had replaced the suburbs. Ruth was asleep in her carrycot and Helena was walking up and down the corridor with Stephen to keep him occupied. Cyril had been unable to get time off work except for the Easter weekend itself.

The sun was warm on Alice's face and the clackity-clack of the wheels on the track made her sleepy. Through half closed eyes, she watched cows and sheep grazing. She didn't think she would want to milk a cow; they were bigger than she expected. The carriage door slid open, but she didn't bother to look.

'Sssh, Stephen, Alice and Ruth are asleep.'

'When will we get there?'

'Soon.'

'How soon?'

Helena sighed, 'Sssh, have a little snooze, you must be tired.'

When was Stephen ever tired? As Alice drifted into sleep, she hoped they would all have a good time.

Cousin Bernard was at the station to meet them, a large, quiet man who stowed their collection of bags and cases in his ancient Morris van. Helena sat in the front with Ruth on her knee while Alice and Stephen joined the luggage in the back; there were no back seats. They sprawled on the floor, littered with hay, and giggled as they bounced down country lanes.

Cousin Margaret had the ruddy, raw-boned complexion of a country woman, out in all weathers. She welcomed them, and left them to unpack. Alice felt a bubble of excitement; this was going to be fun. They hurried downstairs for something to eat.

'Of course,' Margaret said, 'we're pleased to see you all, but this is a working farm. Even though you're on holiday, you will be expected to help out.'

The door opened and two boys came in. 'These are our sons, Richard and Andrew; now sit yourselves down, everything's ready.'

Alice sat between the two boys; they looked nice.

'Alice, I want you to feed the geese and help churn the butter. Stephen you will feed the hens and help Andrew muck out the cattle sheds.'

Stephen scowled.

'Isn't he a bit young for that?' Helena asked.

'No, it'll do him good.'

'And what are my duties?'

'You have Ruth to care for, but you can help me in the kitchen.'

'What do your boys do?'

'Richard milks the cows and Andrew works with his father preparing the fields for our spring crop.'

Alice stared at her plate and hoped Mum wouldn't make a scene.

Once the meal was over and the children had helped with the washing-up, they were told to go exploring. It was all so fresh and green, after the smog of London. Alice wanted to sing and dance. Fruit trees were dressed in puffballs of blossom which scattered petals like snow against the red sky of dusk. The air felt soft and she watched crows cloud the sky before settling in cackling clusters on every tree top. When she looked up she saw the faint hint of a crescent moon and wondered if her dad could see it too. Slowly the children walked back to the farmhouse; even Stephen was ready for bed.

Alice knew nothing of geese except what she'd read in nursery rhymes. Once kitted out with wellingtons and a large bucket of mush, she walked to the field where they lived. All she had to do was let them out of the wooden hut which protected them from marauding foxes. She hummed to herself and pretended she was a real country girl as she walked across the fields. She climbed the stile and lugged the heavy bucket towards the hut. She heard strange noises and much movement as though the geese were anxious to get out; poor things, fancy being shut in all night. She put the bucket down and lifted the sliding hatch.

In seconds she was surrounded; the birds mobbed her, pecked her legs, hissed in her face. She cried for help, but no-one came. She tried to tip the food out, but was scared they'd peck her eyes. In desperation she kicked out at the birds and then knocked the bucket over. She'd failed on her first job; what would Cousin Margaret say? Frightened of further attack, she ran like the wind back to the farmhouse kitchen, dishevelled, tear-streaked with filthy socks.

'You'll have to go back for the wellingtons and bucket,' Margaret said, 'you'll need them tomorrow.'

Helena was giving Ruth her breakfast, but made no comment.

Later Alice told Andrew and Richard what happened; after lunch they went with her, to rescue her belongings.

The rest of the day made up for the disastrous start. Margaret took her to the dairy where she learned to skim cream from the top of the milk. Better still was pouring cream into the wooden barrel and churning it into butter; it was like magic. Best of all, she used proper butter pats to make golden lumps into glistening curls to be spread on homemade bread.

That night, as Alice lay in bed, she decided how she'd deal with the geese. Tip the food into the feeding trough first then let the birds out. The hut wasn't tall; she could lie on the flat roof and pull the door up from above. Once the geese were eating, she'd creep away. Perfect. Satisfied with her plan, she listened to Stephen's steady breathing; he hadn't had a single tantrum today. Perhaps the country suited him too.

Alice soon decided wellingtons were best and with two pairs of socks, the soon became a permanent fixture. Once her chores were done, she rushed down to the stream with the others. They were looking for frogs' spawn. Alice wasn't sure what they'd do with it if they found some; she had a lot to learn.

Maunday Thursday was bright and sunny. 'Let's go to the bluebell woods after lunch.' Margaret said, 'I'll make some sandwiches.'

'You lot go, I'm putting my feet up.' With that, Bernard removed his boots.

Helena opened her mouth to speak.

'Of course, you must come too, Helena, what will Cyril say if you don't lose your city pallor?'

'What about Ruth?'

Bernard settled himself more comfortably. 'I'll keep an eye on her, just clear off, the lot of you and let the head of the house get some rest.'

Chapter 63

April 7th 1950

Richard and Andrew pointed out bird nests, rabbit holes and how to turn coarse grass into a reed and use it to make a piercing whistle. How would she leave this all behind? The days were moving too fast, perhaps she was a country girl; perhaps Mum was given the wrong baby. Perhaps her real mum was living on a farm somewhere with a girl who yearned for the city.

When they reached the wood, a blue haze of bluebells carpeted the whole area. Sunlight filtered through the trees, dappling the flowers and grass with molten gold. Alice remembered the magic of Kew Gardens when she'd played with Patricia and Stephen; this was even better. She knelt down among the tiny bells, so delicate, such a vibrant blue.

'Don't pick them, will you, they only wilt. They're best left where everyone can see them.' Alice looked up and smiled at Margaret. It was only then she realised her mum was crying.

'What's the matter, Mum?'

'Nothing, it's just so beautiful.'

Margaret patted Alice's shoulder, 'Off you go, dear, I'll look after your mum.'

Alice picked her way through the flowers. When she looked back, Margaret had taken Helena by the arm and was leading her back to the farmhouse. Alice shuddered; why did Mum have to feel so sad all the time? The new medicine was supposed to make her feel better.

She heard the shouts of the others and ran to join them.

Slowly the light faded; owls hooted and Alice watched as bats hunted for their supper.

'I'm starving,' Stephen said.

Richard glanced at his watch, 'Time to get back.'

They trooped down the track, but Alice stayed at the back, she was scared of how Mum would be.

Richard waited for her. 'Anything wrong?'

Alice shook her head. He was so nice and showed he cared, she wished Stephen were more like him. She'd been so happy here; would she ever have a holiday here again?

The kitchen was warm and welcoming; Margaret had made a huge pan of stewed lamb and vegetables. Alice looked round.

'Where's Mum?'

'She has a headache so I helped her put Ruth to bed; she decided to have a lie-down, she'll be fine in the morning.' Margaret smiled and handed Alice a full plate.

'Will Cyril be here tomorrow?'

'Yes, on the 2pm train.'

'Will Bernard be picking him up?'

'Yes.'

'Can I go too… to explain about Mum?'

'Don't worry, I'll call him tonight so he knows what to expect.'

Stuffed to bursting point, the older children decided to play a game of Monopoly while Margaret read Stephen a story. He was so sleepy, Bernard carried him to bed then he and the boys checked on the livestock.

Margaret and Alice sat in front of the range.

'I don't know what to do when Mum's so miserable.'

'I don't think there's much you can do, just see the little ones are okay.'

'But why is she like it?'

'Sometimes people's brains don't work as they should. We all feel happy sometimes and sad at others, but with Mum, she can't always cope.'

'Will I be like it when I grow up?'

'No, I'm sure you won't'

'Will she get better?'

'Doctors are working hard, I'm sure they'll find something to sort her out.'

Alice stood up, 'I'll go to bed now and read my book; thank you for a lovely day.'

She crept upstairs, careful to avoid the steps that creaked. At the top of the stairs, she paused then pushed the door to Helena and Ruth's room. If Mum were awake, she could say goodnight. Helena was sprawled on top of the bed; Ruth had kicked off her covers. She tucked her little sister in and placed a spare blanket over Helena who didn't stir. Alice bent to kiss her.

'Good night, Mum,' she whispered.

Once in bed, she picked up her book, the one Cyril had lent her 'The Cruel Sea'; she felt very grown up reading it, but he had warned her not to tell Dad. She soon found it impossible to read; her eyes kept closing. She took off her glasses and soon she was floating, it was the best bit about going to bed.

She was looking forward to tomorrow; Cyril would be down so he could keep an eye on Mum. Once she'd feed the geese and had breakfast, who knew what she and the boys would do, but it would be fun. She smiled as she drifted away. Slight murmurings from the kitchen combined with the sound of Stephen's breathing soothed her to sleep.

Chapter 64

April 7th Good Friday 1950

She woke with a start; it was light, but only just, Helena was sitting on her bed. Alice stared at her with sleep bleared eyes; Mum looked strange.

'What's the matter, it's very early.'

Helena bent to kiss first Alice then Stephen. 'I've come to say goodbye.'

'Where are you going; can I come?'

'No, I'm going for a walk.'

'Will you be long?'

'No.'

She kissed Alice again and left.

The sound of her footsteps on the stairs faded and Alice heard the click of the front door. She went to the window and watched as Helena crossed the yard. Her hair blew in the wind; she must be cold, but hadn't taken a coat. She was wearing her green polo-necked sweater and tartan skirt; they were her favourites. Alice wondered if she should go downstairs, call her back, make her take a coat. Helena was walking too quickly, Alice would have to shout and might wake everyone else. She was almost out of sight now, walking with great determination; perhaps she was feeling better.

Alice scuttled back to bed; her feet were freezing. It wasn't quite light enough to read and if she put the light on it would disturb Stephen; he was a pain if she woke him up. She snuggled under the covers and listened to the birds twittering in the eaves; there were sounds from the cowshed. In the distance, she heard the sharp whistle of the local steam train. She smiled; these were the sounds she would take back to London with her.

Margaret was in the kitchen, preparing breakfast, the boys were clumping around and Bernard was whistling in the yard. Alice was surprised to hear the sound of a car coming up the track. Margaret said they didn't have many visitors and the post van didn't come until later. The noise woke Stephen as Alice rushed to the window. It was a police van; a policeman was talking to Bernard. The word 'accident' spread its toxic message like a cloud of poisonous gas. Alice felt sick.

She hurried downstairs; Bernard and Margaret stared at her, but said nothing.

'It's Mum, isn't it.'

Bernard nodded and Margaret put her arm round Alice's shoulders.

'She came in to see us this morning, ever so early. She said goodbye.' Margaret hugged her but didn't speak.

'I watched her from the window, it was cold, but she didn't have her coat on. She was walking so quickly, I thought she was feeling better.' Alice choked on the words, 'She's dead, isn't she?'

'No sweetheart,' Margaret said and held her close, stroked her hair. 'But she has been hurt.'

'Can I see her? It's my fault, I should have stopped her.'

Bernard patted her back, 'Now that's silly talk, how could you have stopped her?'

'I knew something was wrong; she looked strange, but she was smiling.' She rubbed away her tears on her sleeve. 'What will Cyril think?'

'Now that's enough,' Margaret said, 'you're only a child, of course it isn't your fault. Wash your face and hands while I make you some breakfast.'

The brisk tone calmed her; she wouldn't have to make decisions; Margaret would do that.

'Go upstairs, but don't say a word to Stephen, not yet. I've phoned Cyril, he'll go straight to the hospital. You'll be able to see Mum when she's feeling better.'

Alice wiped her eyes again and went upstairs.

Stephen ate his breakfast then rushed out to do his jobs and play; he didn't question Helena's absence. Alice stared at the boiled egg and bread and butter in front of her. She tried to eat, but every mouthful felt like a boulder. Exhausted by the effort of swallowing, she sat, mute with shock. Without a word, Margaret removed the uneaten food.

'There's nothing we can do at the moment; it would be best if you kept busy. Cyril will give us more news when he arrives. Why don't you feed the geese; Richard will go with you. Then would you like to help me in the dairy?'

It was more than Alice could bear. Such kindness made it harder to cope with her sorrow; it was easier when no-one understood. Tears flowed in burning streams and dripped unchecked from her chin. What would happen to them all now, would she be sent away again?

Margaret sat beside her, gave her a handkerchief, but said nothing until Alice had calmed down.

'You'll have to be very grown-up now, your mum needs you and so does Cyril.'

Alice leaned against Margaret and sighed. 'I wish you were my mum,' she whispered.

Margaret stood up, 'Nonsense child; now then those geese must be starving.'

'Your wife is lucky to be alive. Thankfully the train driver sensed she was going to jump and slowed down, just in case. We treated him for shock; he thought he'd killed her.'

A nurse took him to the side ward where Helena was still unconscious, her head swathed in bandages, drips and tubes everywhere. Her face, in repose, reminded him of statues on the tombs of long dead nobility. So peaceful, so unlike how she really was.

'Your wife cannot be moved yet; we don't know the full extent of injury to her brain. She has multiple soft tissue injuries, but they are not life-threatening.'

'She was still breast feeding out youngest… morning and evening.'

'Unfortunately, she won't be able to carry on.'

Cyril's head ached, what on earth would they do?'

'I believe your family is on holiday with relatives.'

'Only until after Easter, then we must go back to London.'

'I suggest you take the children back and, once your wife is stabilised, we will get her transferred to a London hospital. I think it would be unwise for the children to see their mother until she is out of danger.'

'Of course.'

Cyril arrived in a taxi. Alice watched him walk up the path; he looked like an old man, his shoulders stooped, his face grey. He had arranged for them to go home that day. Stephen clung to Cyril as though scared his father would disappear too. Alice comforted Ruth who was fretful and had not taken well to being bottle-fed.

'Is Mum going to get better?'

Stephen wailed, 'I want my Mum.'

'Does my dad know what's happened?'

'Not yet, I'll send him a telegram.'

'Suppose he doesn't want me to stay with you.'

Cyril ran his fingers through his hair, 'For Christ's sake, don't even think about that.'

The parcel arrived several days later, an innocuous brown paper parcel. Alice undid it slowly; it was clothing. There lay the green polo necked sweater, stiff with blood and black with oil. She fingered the fabric, frayed where it had been cut from her mother's body. Perhaps it had been the brilliance of the colour that caught the driver's eye. Why had the hospital returned it? It was no good any more, it felt stiff, unyielding with a sickly smell. It was nothing like the garment Alice had liked. The fragments were defiled; they reminded Alice of what she wanted to forget. She pushed it away.

Underneath was the tartan skirt, that too was cut, but there was also a ragged tear down one side. Blood and oil had embossed the edges so they crackled when Alice touched them. She wrapped everything back in the brown paper.

'Let's throw these away,' Cyril said and took the parcel to the rubbish bin. When he sat down, Alice noticed his hands were shaking as he topped up his glass.

Cyril had warned Alice, but it was still a shock. Helena's head had been shaved and her skull was crisscrossed with wounds, all stitched. Her face and arms were a purplish-green with bruising and she lay on her side because part of her left buttock had been sliced away by the train's wheels. Alice took her mother's hand and watched as tears slid down her face.

'You'll be all right soon, Mum, once your hair grows…'

Helena nodded and pulled Alice close.

'I'm so sorry, my darling.'

Alice gulped back tears; she mustn't upset Mum by crying.

A tea trolley clanked and rattled its way down the ward.

'Would you like tea, dear?'

Helena nodded.

'And you, Sir? And I've got some juice for you, girly.'

'Thank you.'

Helena's drink came in an enamel mug with a spout.

'Do you want to help your Mum with that,' Cyril said. Alice nodded.

Helena said little, but clung to Alice who talked about Stephen and Ruth and about how well they were managing.

The journey home was subdued.

'Gwen's been coming over, so they can get used to her. She's agreed to move in for a while. She'll look after Stephen and Ruth for the time being.

'Won't Mum mind?'

'It's best we don't tell her. She's got to concentrate on getting better and we have no choice.'

What about me?

'I'm not sure; I expect your dad will sort things out.'

'Dad doesn't want me to stay with you, does he?'

Cyril didn't answer.

She gazed out of the bus window, when would she have a proper home? When would anyone ask what she wanted?

Chapter 65

May 1950

Mary soon settled into her new house in Hendon. The Booths had moved into the first floor with their baby son; they were happy to help with housework and gardening and other odd jobs. Mary was more confident with her crutches, and physiotherapy was helping. She smiled to herself; life was looking a lot brighter until Cyril's phone call. Helena had been severely injured. Gilbert's ghost, would she ever be free of it.

Robert knew about the accident; he didn't want Alice to stay where she was, but had no other ideas of where she should go. Mary sighed; if only it were possible for Alice to live with her. She'd suggest Matthew and Emm took her in for now. She glanced at her watch; Matthew would arrive soon.

He kissed her forehead, 'Can't stay long, Emm's upset, something to do with the Adoption Agency.'

'We have another problem.' She gave him Robert's letter.

'Poor kid.'

'Exactly. As Emm isn't working, could Alice come to you… just for a while?'

'It really isn't a good time, Mum, with the adoption business and everything.'

'She's no trouble.'

'If you can persuade Robert to leave things as they are, it would be best'

'I'll write, but I doubt he'll change his mind.'

They sat in silence and finished their tea.

'I'd better go, Mum. We will help if necessary.'

Mary didn't relish trying to get Robert to change his mind.

Alice was glad to be closer to Mary, but travelling to and from school was tiring. Sometimes Matthew gave her a lift, but she had to use bus and Underground to get home at night. Life with Uncle Matthew and Aunt Emm was uncomfortable; she knew she was in the way. So, she called next door after school for tea and biscuits with Grandma. They discussed what she'd been doing and Mary offered help with homework. They played patience, did crosswords together; it was like the time they lived together in Holland Park. Once Matthew arrived, Alice went next door to help Emm with the evening meal.

On several occasions, as Alice walked up the road from the Tube station, she saw a young man leave her uncle and aunt's house. Once he turned to blow a kiss before getting into his car; perhaps it was a friend, but why didn't he stay to see Uncle Matthew as well? Alice decided to say nothing.

Three months after Alice moved to Hendon, she found Uncle Matthew's house deserted. She decided to set the table and peel some potatoes. Matt must be with Grandma because his car was outside. There was a sealed envelope on the hall stand. She'd go to Grandma's and take the envelope with her.

'Aunt Emm isn't there, but this for you.'

Matthew ripped open the envelope.

'She's left me.'

Alice was stunned; was she supposed to stay with Uncle Matthew or go back to Cyril. She didn't think Dad would approve of either. Uncle Matthew went back to his empty house and Alice waited.

'Well, my dear, this is a fine state of affairs.'

'Where do I go?'

'I'll tell you what, you don't go anywhere; you stay with me.'

'What will Dad say?'

'Never mind your dad, how would you feel about it?'

'Oh, Gran, I love being here with you, it's quiet, peaceful, no shouting.'

'I'll write to him tonight and tell him what's happened. Shall I invite him over, next time he's on leave, for a chat?'

Alice smiled; she'd cope if Gran was there too.

'Perhaps we should tell him all this moving about is making it difficult for me to keep up with my schoolwork.'

'Of course, it is and it's very grownup of you to realise it.

Alice noticed a twinkle in Mary's eye.

Matthew drove Alice, with all her belongings, over to Kentish Town; Robert had said it was a temporary measure until something better could be arranged. Cyril and the kids seemed pleased to see her, but there was no news of when Mum would be home.

'Once Stephen and Ruth were in bed, we'll have a talk,' Cyril said, 'nothing to worry about.'

Alice felt her insides tighten, what now?

'Doctors have decided Mum's brain isn't working quite as it should.' Cyril paused.

Alice waited.

'They have decided to do something about it.'

'How?'

'There's a special operation that will help.'

'When will they do it?'

'Once she's strong enough.'

'How long will Mum be in hospital?'

'Not long and she won't have any stitches afterwards.'

'How will they do it?'

Cyril patted her hand. 'She won't feel anything, she'll be asleep and they'll carefully take her eyes out so…'

'She'll be blind.'

'No sweetheart, they separate the bits at the front that are causing the trouble then they can put her eyes back.'

Cyril put his arm round her, 'It's to stop her hurting herself; we all want that, don't we?'

Alice nodded.

Alice walked down Chelsea Manor Street; she wondered how much to tell Dad about Mum's surgery. To take a patient's eyes out was pretty drastic; Mum must be really ill. If she was really ill, she shouldn't be blamed, should she? It was all very confusing. If only he would stop talking about her the way he did, but Mum was no better. When she arrived, he seemed a bit odd, nervous almost. He was sitting in his armchair,

'Come and sit on my knee, dear.'

She felt uncomfortable, too large and too old for such things; it reminded her of Uncle John.

'I want to have a serious talk with you.'

She nodded.

'You probably realise by now, that years ago when you were very small, your mother behaved very badly.'

Alice stiffened and her mouth felt dry. She didn't want this; she was tired of the endless arguments. She looked away and said nothing.

'Because of that, I was forced to stay in the army, away from you.' He paused.

'But you said you loved being in the army, you wanted me to join up too. How could you be forced to stay away?'

She watched her father's face redden.

'You don't understand, the doctor's ordered it. I got the blame you see.'

Alice stared at him; surely that couldn't be right.

'Now your Nana's died, the time has come for me to come back for good. I'm seeing my old boss at the Post Office on Monday. If he gives me a job, I want you to live here with me.'

Alice was surprised. Dad had changed; he was angry all the time and sometimes he made her feel uneasy. She would be grown-up and sensible. He wanted her with him, but he would not want her to be irresponsible or selfish. There were still Mum and the little ones to think of.

'Of course, it would be nice to live with you, Dad. Mum's got Cyril, Stephen and Ruth, but now Nana's dead, you've only got me.'

She felt the atmosphere chill as she shifted on his lap. It had seemed a grownup thing to say; why did she always get it wrong?

'You'd better get down, you're very heavy.'

'Will I have to change schools?'

'Not if you don't want to; I'll discuss it with your Headmistress.'

In the silence that followed, Robert picked up the newspaper and Alice listened to the ticking of Grandfather's clock.

If she decided to live with Dad, she'd have a long journey to school again, right across London. But Mum and Cyril lived close to her school, she could pop in whenever she liked. Would she tell Dad it was what she would do? She was caught in a web of deceit and none of it was her fault. How would Cyril manage without her, who would take Stephen to school and Ruth to the nursery? Gwen helped but she still had to go to work. Mum wouldn't want Gwen there all the time.

She cleared her throat. 'Dad, would it be okay if I stayed with Cyril and the others until Mum comes home from hospital?'

Robert put down his paper. He looked annoyed, but what was she supposed to do? It would be wrong to walk away and leave Cyril in the lurch with the little ones. That wouldn't be fair.

'I will discuss the matter with your teachers; let them decide when it is best for you to move. I won't be responsible for disrupting your education.'

He walked through to the kitchen and she listened to him crashing about. Of course, he was cross, she knew he would be.

Chapter 66

November 1950

Alice hurried to the block of flats, glad to be out of the rain; it was a dismal day, and she would have to tell Cyril what Dad wanted her to do.

She opened the front door and Stephen rushed out of the kitchen.

'Guess what, Mum might be home for Christmas.'

'Hello Alice, he's told you then.' Cyril grinned.

'Has she had the operation?'

'Not yet, leaving it until after Christmas. So, we're going to have the best Christmas ever, all together.'

'What am I going to do?' She felt her eyes fill and turned away; she must not cry.

'Dad expects me to live with him all the time, now he's leaving the army.'

'Are you happy with that?'

'Yes, but…'

'It's difficult isn't it; you can't be in two places at once. When does he want you to go?'

'Before Christmas…'

'I see.'

Alice pulled a face, 'I think I'll have an early night.'

'Don't you want any supper?'

Alice shook her head.

'Tell you what, it's a month to Christmas, why don't we have a celebration in a fortnight then you can go to your dad for the real thing.'

'I'll have to tell him in good time; he was really cross the last time, when I was late.'

'It'd help if he had a phone.'

Alice laughed, 'His girlfriend told him that'

'Have you met her?'

'Yes, she's nice, but I think she's a bit young for him.'

'You mean you don't fancy a young woman bossing you about.'

'Nobody's going to boss me about.'

'Okay, an early Christmas here with Mum; I'd better leave the arrangements to you, you obviously like being in charge.'

Alice giggled.

'I'm going to miss you.'

Alice blinked hard.

'Do you have to stay at your mother's next weekend; I thought she was having a Christmas celebration on the day.'

'She doesn't come home every weekend.'

'What about me? I've spent years away; don't I deserve more?'

'But Dad, you decided to stay in the army, after the war: you didn't have to, did you? I've not been with either you or Mum most of the time. I've never had a proper home and it's not my fault.'

Robert turned away. 'I'm going for the paper.' He banged the door as he left.

Alice sighed; she was sick of it all.

I'm going home. I'll be over in two weeks.

She'd felt a bit shaky leaving such an abrupt note; why couldn't he understand? She picked up her stuff and went to the telephone box down the road. She dialled Mum's number.

Cyril answered. 'I thought it was the hospital.'

'Is Mum alright?'

'Yes, there's been some hitch with transport. I can't go to get her, not with Stephen and Ruth.'

'I'm coming back now.'

'That's early, anything wrong?'

'I want to see Grandma.'

'As soon as Mum arrives, you can.'

Alice ran up the road to catch the bus. Please, please let Mum be there when she arrived; she must speak to Grandma.

Stephen was out playing with his mates.

'Mum home yet?'

He shook his head and ran off.

Cyril opened the door. 'Dump your stuff and go over to Hendon. The hospital rang; one of the male nurses is driving her over at the end of his shift so you might as well go now.'

'Can you write down which way to go; I've not done it on my own before.'

She left her bags on the floor; she'd deal with them later.

'Make sure you let me know when you get there.' Cyril shouted as she hurried down stairs, two at a time.

Alice felt very grown-up as she strode along Queen's Road, Hendon towards Grandma's new house; there was so much to tell her about school. She hadn't seen Grandma since Emma Jane left. She knocked on the front door.

'You must be Alice.' Mrs Booth smiled. 'Mrs Carlton's told me all about you.'

A voice from the sitting room drew Alice in; her heart was thumping.

'My dear girl, I am so pleased to see you.'

And there she was, no different, just the same grandma. Alice knelt by her wheelchair and kissed her on the cheek.

'Are you hungry?

Alice nodded, 'Can I call Cyril to let him know I've arrived?'

'Yes, and tell him Mr. Booth will see you back to the station and I'll call to let Cyril know when you leave.'

Mrs Booth pushed a tea trolley into the sitting room; there were biscuits and cake. Alice leaned against the wall and listened to the phone ringing. She felt contented and, more importantly, safe. Why couldn't Mum and Dad manage that; in different ways, they both made her feel scared. She'd ask Grandma's advice. One thing was certain; she didn't want to go travelling any more.

'Grandma, I need your help.'

Mary sat back. 'I wonder if I can guess what the problem is.'

'It's Mum and Dad.'

'I'm not surprised. Two very obstinate people, your parents; I'd go so far to say they both need a good shaking.'

Alice gave a watery smile.

'It's been very hard for you; you are a great credit to them both. I think it's time you had a say in any arrangements made for you.'

Alice gulped and rubbed her eyes, 'Nobody asks me anything.'

'Well, I'm asking you.'

'I don't think they will ever agree who I live with; I hate that. I don't feel I belong anywhere.'

'Then we must do something about it.'

Although Mary's mother had died, she'd always known where her home was, known where she belonged. She glanced out of the window; it was dusk already and Alice must go home soon.

'We need to arrange a proper meeting. I'm happy to talk to your father and of course your mother and Cyril must be involved too. Will you leave it with me?'

'Yes, please.'

'And now I think you should go home before it gets really dark. Mr Booth will see you to the station and please call me when you get back.'

Alice leaned over and put her arms round Mary's shoulders.

'Could I stay with you, I wouldn't be any trouble.'

'How would your parents feel about that?'

'Mum would cry and carry on and Dad would slam doors and shout.'

Mary raised her eyebrows. 'Difficult to choose, I suppose.'

Alice stared at her and burst into tears.

'I don't want to travel so far to school every day, I don't want to look after Stephen and Ruth all the time 'specially Stephen. I've tried to be good and do my best, but…'

'It hasn't turned out as you hoped with your father?'

Alice shook her head. 'He's so angry all the time, but at least he doesn't talk about Mum so much.'

'But your mother does, talk about your dad?'

'Every time she says I'm sorry, Darling, but… I know she's going to say something horrid.'

'Mary squeezed Alice's hand. 'I'm going to have to do a bit of research here. When are you supposed to be moving to Dad's full-time?'

'Before Christmas.'

'That doesn't give me long. I'll wait until after the weekend and then phone Cyril and see how the land lies. Your father is a different kettle of fish; leave it with me. Now off you go, ask Mrs Booth to call her husband and he can walk you to the station. Take a piece of cake with you.'

Mary handed Alice a handkerchief, 'Wipe your eyes; I don't want your mother to think I've been beating you.'

Alice giggled. 'I'm so glad I came, Grandma.'

'So am I.'

Chapter 67

December 16th 1950

Alice fingered Grandma's letter; should she show it to Cyril? Would it upset Mum and spoil the early Christmas celebration? Alice didn't feel like celebrating anything; she was scared. A knock at the door made her jump. She listened to Stephen as he careered about and shouted with excitement, it made her head ache. Mum had arrived for her weekend visit. Alice folded the letter and put it back in her pocket. It was too late to say anything now.

Apparently, Grandma had spoken to Cyril about future arrangements and she'd written to Dad to suggest a meeting. It was a start, but had Cyril said anything to Mum? She could hear Mum's voice; she sounded okay.

'There you, darling, I thought you were hiding.' Helena clutched Alice to her, smothered her with kisses. 'I thought your father might have stopped you coming.'

'Why would he do that, Mum?' Alice glanced at Cyril.

'I'm sorry darling, but….'

'That's enough you two,' Cyril stood up, 'we've a surprise waiting, come on.'

Helena held Stephen and Alice's hands and was led into the sitting room where a large Christmas tree stood in the corner. Cyril lit the candles and switched off the lights.

'We did it, Mummy,' Stephen said.

'It's beautiful. I'm lucky to have such clever children.'

Stephen jumped up and down, 'Guess what, Alice's going to her proper Daddy for Christmas then you'll just have me and Ruth.'

Ruth's gurgles of delight as she pointed to the flickering candles made Alice want to cry; it was all so unfair. Everything was spoiled.

Cyril put his arm round Helena's shoulder. 'We'll talk about it later.'

'When was this planned, nobody asked me?'

Alice shivered, when her Mum was like this anything could happen.

'Now, come on, Helena, I need you to help me with this meal.'

'Shall we put the presents round the tree?' Alice asked.

Cyril patted Alice's shoulder as he guided Helena towards the kitchen.

Yes, you and Stephen do that while Mum and I sort the meal. Keep an eye on Ruth.'

'What shall we do?' Stephen asked.

'Help me get the presents.'

'Can we open some?'

'Yes, one each.'

The sound of raised voices, coming from the kitchen, reached a crescendo as they walked past the closed door. Ruth started to grizzle and Stephen grabbed Alice's hand. They picked up the parcels under Cyril's bed and could hear the sound of crying as they went back to the sitting room. No one spoke as Alice blew out each of the Christmas tree candles.

'Is Christmas over?' Stephen asked.

'No, it just candles are dangerous and I've got to go out.'

'Where are you going, can I come?'

'No, you must stay here. Keep an eye on Ruth.'

Alice clutched her pocket money; Cyril had given it to here as soon as she arrived. She had enough to get to Hendon, but would need Grandma to give her the return fare. She sat on the tube train and it felt as though everyone was watching her. It was better when they came out of the tunnel and she could look out of the window. What would Grandma say, supposing she was out? Alice felt sick, she shivered and the woman opposite leaned forward and asked if she were okay. Alice nodded.

She hurried out of the train at Hendon Central, up the stairs and along the high street. Lights were on in Grandma's sitting room and upstairs were the Booth's lived. Alice clung to the garden gate and gasped for breath; she had a stitch because she'd run as fast as she could. She waited until she got her breath back. She knocked on the door and heard the noise of wheels on the parquet floor in the hall.

'Who is it?'

'It's Alice, Grandma.'

The door opened and Alice stepped in.

Cyril shut the kitchen door and took Helena in his arms.

'He's won; he's got her at last, he doesn't want me to get better.'

'That's not fair; she's not a piece of property. How do you think she feels about all this?'

'If she cared she wouldn't go to him; he'll turn her against me.'

'Stop talking nonsense.'

Helena slumped against him and he patted her back as she cried.

'I want you home for Christmas. Okay Alice won't be here, but we will have a good time. Dry your eyes and give me a kiss.'

Stephen opened the kitchen door.

'What's the matter?'

'Alice has gone out.'

Helena gasped, 'Where's she gone?'

'She didn't say.'

'When?'

'A bit ago.'

'Why didn't you tell us?'

'Because I was opening my present... Alice said I could.'

'Christ almighty. Helena, crying won't help; let's think where she might go.'

'Back to her father, where else?'

'Helena, I know you're worried, but please give it a rest.'

'Alice blew all the candles out.'

'Just as well, Stephen, we don't want a fire do we. What about Ruth?'

'She's in the sitting room playing with some bricks. I stopped her from eating the wrapping paper.'

Cyril shook his head 'I'm phoning your mother; she might be there.'

Alice sat on a foot stool at Mary's feet and stared into the fire; she leaned against her grandma's legs.

'I've heard from your dad; he's difficult to pin down.'

'He hasn't said anything to me, but he didn't want me to stay at Mum's today.'

She felt Grandma stroked her hair, it comforted her.

'I shouldn't really have left Mum, should I?'

Grandma pulled a face, 'If I were you, I'd probably have done the same.'

'I think I ought to call Mum and Cyril and let them know where I am.'

'Yes, do that now, or would you like me to?'

'Please.'

Alice nodded.

'I'll make that call.'

Mary left the door open and Alice wondered if that was on purpose so she could hear. Under the circumstances she felt entitled to listen and marvel at how calm Grandma was.

'Alice is extremely upset and I do think we need to have a meeting as soon as possible.'

There was a long pause and Alice could hear Mum's voice getting louder.

'Have you considered it may not be a case of you or Robert?'

At this point, Grandma held the receiver away from her ear.

'Have you tried asking her what she wants?'

Alice walked to the wheelchair and put her arm on Grandma's shoulder, 'Sorry, Gran.'

'Helena let me speak to Cyril.' Mary raised her eyebrows, 'She's rung off!'

Alice wheeled Grandma back to the sitting room.

'Now then, Alice, I want you to write down exactly how you feel about all this. So, we silly grown-ups, can sort out what is best for you. Then you must go back because this is your mum's Christmas time with you.'

Alice nodded.

'Get paper and pen from the writing desk.'

'When you've finished, I'll call a taxi. Have you ever ridden in a taxi?'

Alice shook her head.

'It's never too early to start and you do have some presents to take back with you.'

Alice grinned and gave Grandma a hug.

Epilogue 1962

Sometimes you have to grow up
Before you appreciate how you grew up.

—Daniel Black
Author

All that is a long time ago now and the scars have healed. I will never know how Grandma managed it, but both Mum and Dad accepted my decision to stay with her. The first thing I did when I moved into Gran's house was to ask Mr. Booth to take the green tin trunk to the tip. I would never use it again.

After the lobotomy, Mum was different. Her ability to make decisions and remember anything had been affected, but there were no more suicide attempts. I often called in after school, but decided not to tell Dad. Usually, Stephen and Ruth were too busy playing when I arrived so Mum and I had a chance to chat on our own. We both enjoyed that.

As I got older, I realised why Dad had behaved as he did. Instead of coming home a hero, he returned to nothing. He was a proud man and my mother broke his heart. He never remarried, but I saw a photo of him, in uniform, with Mum; it stood beside his bed until he died. We did have a greater understanding which gave us both pleasure, but it wasn't a traditional father-daughter relationship. I think he was proud of me in the end.

Grandma was my inspiration; she had gone to university when few women did. I was determined to do the same. I lived with her until her health failed and she chose to go to a nursing home for her final years. She died when I was nineteen; I wish she'd seen me graduate, but as I collected my diploma, I felt her hand on my shoulder.

The most important lesson I learnt from my childhood was, never give up.

Author's Bio

Jo Howard taught English language and literature up to 'O' level for many years. She found great satisfaction in watching her pupils develop the necessary skills to achieve good exam results. Her love of language led to a desire to write novels in her retirement.

'Where Alice Belongs' explores the disruption caused by war. Alice was born, in London, during the Blitz. She also had to cope with the breakdown of her parent's marriage. After the war, her father remained in the army. Her mother had a severe mental breakdown and needed to be hospitalised. Alice seldom saw either of her parents.

Resilience enabled her to adjust as she was moved from one home to another. Finally, with the support of her maternal grandmother, she decided where and with whom she wanted to live.